# LOVE
# REVELATION

### BOOK ONE:
### *THE ROYAL LAW*

# BILL WALTHALL

*The Love Revelation* by Bill Walthall
Copyright © 2008 by Bill Walthall
All Rights Reserved.
ISBN: 1-59755-125-2

Published by:  ADVANTAGE BOOKS™
               **www.advbookstore.com**

All Scripture quotations, unless otherwise indicated, are taken from the NEW AMERICAN STANDARD BIBLE®, Copyright © 1960, 1962, 1963, 1968, 1971, 1972, 1973, 1975, 1977, 1995 by The Lockman Foundation. Used with permission.

Library of Congress Control Number: 2008937905


Cover design by Pat Theriault

Photo by Greg Schneider: www.gregschneider.com




First Printing: July 2008
09 10 11 12 13 14  10 9 8 7 6 5 4 3
Printed in the United States of America

# DEDICATION

This book is dedicated to my beloved wife, Nancy.

Through His word, God revealed to me that I should love.

My beloved Nancy has been showing me how.

Bill Walthall

*"If, however, you are fulfilling the royal law according to the Scripture,
'You shall love you neighbor as yourself,' you are doing well."
James 2:8 (NASB)*

# Table of Contents

# Introduction

## Love

Where does love come from? Did love evolve naturally as a part of human history, or does love have its origin from some outside source? Is love simply a part of human nature, part of our survival instinct, or is the source of love beyond human nature? Is love a result of natural selection, or is love a transcendent ideal to which human nature must always aspire? Is love a part of our "collective unconscious" as Carl Jung would say, or is love simply the product of complex chemical reactions only now being explored? Is love a product of genetic programming, or is love something beyond the capacity of discovery by human genome scientists?

Of course, to answer these questions, one must identify what exactly love is. So, how is love defined? Is love an absolute behavior with an infinite variety of expressions, or does love consist of a variety of human expressions each unique and requiring identification? Why are there varieties of love? Is one kind of love better than another kind? Does love mandate an adjective to be effectively communicated, such as romantic love or brotherly love or a mother's love? If there are varieties of love, how many varieties are there? What does it mean to love as opposed merely to like? When is love terribly selfish or legitimately selfish? Is there such a thing as pure love, or is love just a transient feeling or altruistic behavior?

If love requires definition, who should define it, or who best defines it? Is love real and tangible, or is love an intangible, abstract concept? Is love merely a convenient descriptor used to acknowledge the good part of interpersonal relations, or is it an ideal that many acknowledge but few experience?

Is love just an emotion or feeling that will eventually be relegated to the laboratories of human physiology? Can love be broken down scientifically into its chemical and physiological components, or is love beyond the realm of science to observe or explain? If love is an observable behavior, what is the motive? How is that behavior explained in terms of survival of the fittest? How does survival of the fittest explain the action of the stronger soldier falling on the grenade to protect his weaker comrade? Is love a behavior that can be learned? If so, who or what would be the teacher?

In the animal kingdom, a mother bear is a dangerous animal if her cubs are threatened. Baby penguins are the recipients of grueling sacrifices on the part of both parents. The lioness vigilantly protects her male cubs even from her mate. Where did these behaviors come from? Are they simply the result of the instinct to survive?

For humans, the expressions of love are countless: a mother's love, brotherly love, romantic love, platonic love, love of God and country, even sacrificial love witnessed in parenting or in time of war. Humanity indeed expresses a broad spectrum of love extending all the way from God-given instincts to great personal sacrifice.

On a more controversial level, does a pedophile practice love? Can a serial killer love? When a terrorist drives an airliner loaded with passengers into a skyscraper shouting "God is great!" is his ultimate sacrifice an act of love? When a suicide bomber explodes her device in a crowded market place to make a statement for her oppressed people, is she demonstrating love?

Or, from a Christian perspective, does love for correct doctrine justify token recognition for the poor? Is a pro-life Christian a better representative of love than a pro-choice Christian? Does passion for the evangelical mandate excuse evangelicals from having just as great a passion for third-world poverty, or the AIDS epidemic, or illiteracy, or Christians undergoing persecution? Does the evangelical community teach how to love one another as much as it teaches theologies involving salvation or the end times? Does an evangelical church disciple its members in how to love and behave toward one another as much as it disciples them how to interpret Scripture and believe correctly? Does a Christian worldview maximize belief systems and minimize love behaviors?

I have titled this trilogy "The Love Revelation" to answer these questions. The premise of "The Love Revelation" is that the origin of love is God himself and that our knowledge of love is the result of God's revelation. I will demonstrate that a central theme of the Bible is a message about love and learning to love; that, indeed, Christianity itself can be described as a love message that is presented from Genesis to Revelation. I will show that the love message is the very foundation upon which all the truths of the Bible are based. I believe, therefore, that Christianity can be narrowed down to two basic elements: truth and love. The purpose of biblical truth is to enable mankind to experience—and eventually express—God's love. There can be no biblical love without biblical truth, and there can be no expression of biblical truth without biblical love.

In Book 1, "The Royal Law," I will present the relationship between love and truth, for they are inextricably interwoven. I will show that all biblical truth points to love, but all love must be defined in the context of biblical truth. The premise of Book 1, therefore, is that God is the true and sole source of love, and his word is its revelation. That truth alone will drastically affect how we read, understand and apply God's word.

We will discover in Book 1 that what we normally describe as the ability to give and receive love, both in the animal kingdom and as a part of the human experience, has been built into creation. It is a part of general revelation. God created the ability to care in the same manner he created the ability to procreate. Because men and women are created in the image of God, however, his supreme creation is capable of developing natural love far beyond the general revelation given to the animal kingdom. The image of God provides humanity with a greater capacity to reason, to learn, to be self-aware, to create, and most of all, to receive revelation.

This book assumes that there is a love greater than that witnessed in creation. Whereas natural love comes with creation, there is a higher love that requires *special revelation*. The animal kingdom cannot experience it and humanity must learn it. It is "unnatural" in the sense that it is beyond the love found naturally in creation. Nor is it the product of humanity's invention or inspiration. Humans may have the ability to observe it and abide by it, but it is not the product of human nature or creative abilities.

The love to which I am referring is revealed only in the Bible. There are no sources apart from the Bible where this love originates. Any similarities in other religions are dramatically inferior and most likely have biblical revelation as their source. It is impossible for the animal kingdom to learn this love, and it is beyond humanity to grasp or manifest it apart from biblical revelation. The love that is revealed in the Bible is unique, unnatural, transcendent and revelational. It defies human nature. This premise, of course, assumes that the Bible is true and the only source of truth about God.

It is also the premise of this book that all Christian theology can be summed up with two words: truth and love. The Bible is the only source of absolute truth and the only revelation of what love truly is. *Truth, therefore, must always trump love because love requires definition.* Only biblical truth can define biblical love. On the other hand, the goal of truth is to teach us love: to love God, to love others and to look forward to the day when biblical love will characterize all human behavior. Without truth, love cannot be accurately defined. Without love, however, truth is merely conceptual, for the purpose of truth is to teach us to love. It is the God of truth who reveals through Jesus Christ the essence of love, and it is through Jesus Christ that the God of love reveals absolute truth. Therefore, Jesus Christ, the Son of God, is the agent—the only agent—through whom God reveals to humanity his very nature; that is, absolute truth and perfect love.

Book 1 is about the source of truth and love. I have used but one reference point for the revelation of truth and love, and that is the Bible. I believe it is the word of God, inerrant in the original manuscripts. Because much has been written about the truth of Christian theology, I have placed the focus of *The Love Revelation* upon love as revealed in the Bible, and more specifically, its relation to the truth. Book 2 addresses the meaning the revelation of love has to the body, the church, and how the church responds to the world. Book 3 approaches God's love revelation on personal and practical levels. That is, it answers the question, "So what? What does the love revelation have to do with me, and how do I put the lessons of Books 1 and 2 to practical, everyday use?"

Although there is an apologetic side to *The Love Revelation*, the ultimate goal of the three books and their accompanying study guides is to address Christian living. The apostle Paul wrote to Timothy, "But the goal of our instruction is love from a pure heart and a good conscience and a sincere faith" (1 Tim. 1:5). Is love actually the goal of instruction in today's church? Do we truly appreciate the love we so often expound? Do we Christians really understand the love lessons the Bible is teaching us, and do our lives reflect those lessons unequivocally? Do we understand the true message of love beyond quoting a few verses from First Corinthians 13? For evangelicals, is John 3:16 a message of salvation or a message of love? How does the love message enter into our eschatology (the study of the end times)?

There will be some Christians, of course, who will be offended by *The Love Revelation*. They will be offended not only by some of the concepts presented in this book, but by the illustrations and examples provided both in the body of the book and in the vignettes that precede each chapter. Why? Because the principles of this book challenge some classic evangelical belief systems and the very way we conduct our Christian lives. It will challenge our values and our notions of what it means to live a righteous life. I can accept that some will become offended, if not downright antagonistic. Being a pastor did not necessarily create for me a tougher skin, but it did help me to realize that no matter what you say or how carefully you say it, someone will be offended. Stories on this point, however, will take another book.

If I myself knew naturally how to live in pure biblical love, I probably would not have felt the need to write this book. I have found that consistently expressing biblical love does not come naturally for me, and I suspect that describes most of us. That is not to say, of course, that I have finally learned to live and love biblically, but at least I *know* what I ought to do. I have discovered over the years that the love that does not come naturally can be learned by appropriating truth, for without biblical truth it is impossible to love biblically.

Lastly, the most difficult part of writing this book was knowing when to stop. The more I examined Scripture, the more I saw the message. Who knows? Maybe someday we'll see Books 4 and 5!

As I have stated above, prior to each chapter I have written a vignette. The vignettes are fictional, sometimes fanciful tongue-in-cheek stories that serve to illustrate concepts presented throughout the book. In some cases the vignettes relate directly to the chapter that follows; other times, they relate to the principles of the book in general. The vignettes also provide a launching point for discussion in the study guides that accompany the books. I hope you will enjoy them and perhaps even chuckle a little.

# *Vignette for Chapter One*

# *"Welcome to My World"*

Not an evening went by that Clifford and Suzanne did not have a falling out when she came home from work.

"Your dinner's in the oven," Clifford gestured, lying lengthwise on the couch with the remote in his hand.

"Is it cold like last night's? You *could* heat it up, you know. *I'm* the one who worked all day."

"Like I didn't? You could have called telling me you'd be late. You always demanded *I* call."

"I was busy trying to make a living. *One* of us has to make a living."

"'*One of us has to make a living.*' And did you really make a living or did you blow this account too?"

"I won't know till next week."

"Meanwhile, I'm buying groceries with a paper route and recycled aluminum cans. You're not doing any better than I did out there."

"At least I'm not coming home feeling sorry for myself. I suppose the kids are already asleep?"

"Of course. And don't wake them up this time. I had a hard enough time getting them down."

"Welcome to my world," Suzanne snapped.

Things had been tough since Clifford had been laid off. A slumping economy and a small recession brought a wave of layoffs that mercilessly swept across the region leaving new homeowners and struggling young parents mired in financial chaos. Most were selling their homes at a loss and moving away in search of work. Others, like Clifford and Suzanne, were gutting it out the best they could. They had too much invested in the house and they loved the schools. Neither set of parents were financially stable enough to help and Clifford's meager savings had been used up long ago. Because the hard times were so worrisome for Clifford, for which he was now taking generic antidepressants, they'd struck a deal that he would stay home with the kids and she would look for work in the only profession she was somewhat acquainted with—insurance. All the waitress jobs had been taken by other desperate wives, and even though few families in the region had discretionary funds to spend on insurance, she would give it a try. So far, she had been entirely unsuccessful. Things were looking bleak; they both knew it and they were both very afraid.

Clifford and Suzanne's marriage faced financial obstacles from the beginning. They got married because she got pregnant. They had really loved each other in the beginning, and in their idealistic eyes, marriage was just coming sooner than planned. He had wanted to finish college, find a well-paying job and become financially stable before he settled down. She had planned to go to college herself when Clifford graduated. Meanwhile, she had been content to work as an administrative assistant in an insurance firm, and had been doing so since high school. As a result, they had struggled from day one.

The struggle had been livable until children numbers two and three came along. She, of course, needed to stay home to raise the kids. Never able to fulfill his dream of finishing college, he had settled for a job that gave him the most satisfaction, a computer programmer for an upstart tech firm. Like so many others, the idea of a dot-com crash had never crossed his mind.

The exciting, youthful infatuation that had propelled them into a risky relationship had long grown dull. The romantic love that had brought them together in the first place had cooled significantly, an intimacy struggle complicated by children. Feelings of love which had come so naturally in the beginning seldom surfaced. Now those feelings were relegated to duty more than desire. With the layoff and the ensuing crisis management of their relationship, romance became a luxury they could not afford. Their lost love was something they sensed, something they missed, but something which they could never confess.

"Welcome to my world" was a dig both used frequently. It communicated very clearly, "You have no idea what I go through." It was a sarcastic way of communicating a lack of empathy and interest. It implied, "My world is tougher than yours." When Suzanne had come home one evening utterly frustrated with a client, Clifford immediately responded, "Welcome to my world." Little did they realize that every dig dug a deeper chasm between them.

Bleak day followed bleak day. Every day became a matter of survival. Accounts occasionally came in for Suzanne but they were small, infrequent and never large enough to celebrate by going out to dinner. They were stuck in a quagmire of misfortune and creeping apathy. Until, that is, Suzanne came home one evening with a smile on her face.

"You're late, as usual," Clifford said, quickly changing the cable channel.

"I know," she said. "I'm sorry. I should have called."

Clifford's eyes narrowed—an apology? "Your dinner's in the oven. It's probably cold by now."

"That's all right. Don't get up. I'll warm it up. Taking care of kids all day...you're probably exhausted."

Clifford searched for sarcasm in Suzanne's voice but honestly could not find any.

"Are you okay?" he asked, resting the remote control in his lap.

"I'm okay. Actually, I'm quite good," she grinned. To Clifford's utter surprise, she came over and gave him a big hug and a kiss on the cheek.

"Well, well, well. You must have landed a big one!"

"No, I'm afraid not. Actually, it's better than that."

"You won the lottery?"

"No," she chuckled, "I never bought a ticket this week."

Clifford was puzzled. Suzanne turned on the oven, washed her hands, poured herself a cup of coffee and pulled up a dining room chair across from him. "There's something I need to tell you."

"Let me guess," Clifford half joked. "You've finally had it with this marriage and you've found someone else."

Suzanne paused, warming her hands around the coffee cup. "In fact, I *have* found someone who loves me."

Clifford sat upright on the side of the sofa. His first thought was that he was right about her having an affair. The problem was that her demeanor was not consistent with someone who was confessing infidelity to her spouse. Besides, it would have been out of character. Suzanne was not an innately mean person.

Suzanne went on to explain. During a sales visit, she had broken down emotionally in front of a client. The client, a church deaconess, was not the least bit interested in buying insurance but became intensely interested in Suzanne. For reasons she could not explain, Suzanne shared with "the church lady" all her problems and fears: having to leave the kids to go back to work, his layoff and depression, their growing apart. The church lady listened to every word and began weeping with her.

"After I spilled my guts to her," Suzanne explained, a little bit embarrassed, "she did something no one's ever done for me before."

"She bought a huge policy?"

"No, she prayed for me."

Suzanne shared with Clifford that the harder she wept the harder the church lady prayed. Above all, she prayed that Suzanne would experience how much God loved her and cared for her, and that if she trusted in him through Christ, God would never abandon her. She encouraged Suzanne that no matter how bleak things looked, God loves his children and always looks after them.

"I can't explain it," Suzanne confessed. "Afterwards, I just felt really at peace, like this ugly shadow had been chased away. I feel warm now. I feel at peace. I just know everything's going to be all right."

Clifford sat still, not knowing what to say or if he should try to speak at all.

"But that's not all," Suzanne went on. "After she prayed, the church lady wrote us a check for a thousand dollars. She said, 'I don't need insurance. When you and your hubby get your feet on the ground again, you can pay me back. God has always provided for me, so I can help provide for you.'"

Clifford, partly in disbelief, sat stunned. There was a long silence between them as he examined the check. Finally, he had the courage to speak.

"Where did you say this lady goes to church?"

*Chapter One*

# "Monkey See, Monkey...Love?" (Love and Its Origins)

*Beloved, let us love one another, for love is from God...*
(1 John 4:7)

In the preface, questions were raised concerning the origin of love. Where does love come from? Did love evolve spontaneously as a part of human nature, or is love simply the word used to describe a variety of altruistic emotions that have developed through human evolution? Is there such a thing as an "altruism gene"? If so, can the presence of a gene explain the complexities of love, especially biblical love? The basic question is this: is love an innate part of human biology, or does love come into human experience from some outside source?

Historically, it appears impossible to track down when the concept of love first entered into human history. Hinduism, which claims to be the world's oldest organized religion, traces its origin back only to 1,500 years before Christ and, as we shall see next, would have no basis for claiming that it is the original source for love.

Paleography, the study of ancient writing, is self-limiting because we can only go back so far with written records. Ancient Sumerian literature, the oldest substantial body of written records in existence, represents the earliest written references to love. These records originated in what is now referred to as Mesopotamia, the region of the world known today as Iraq. The Sumerian records date back to over 3,000 years before Christ, some 5,000 years ago. (Though ancient writing has recently been unearthed in Egypt, Pakistan and possibly China, the oldest substantive body of ancient literature remains the Sumerian texts.) Paleography leads us down a dead end, unfortunately, for archeologists inform us that language itself has been around a lot longer than writing. We really have no way of knowing whether love was a part of early language or not.

Perhaps the most interesting aspect of the recognition of love in the Sumerian literature, however, is that the concept of love in its various forms appears to have been extremely well developed. In the Sumerian texts, references to love are as natural and contemporary as they would be today. The concept of love is not explained or qualified, as if love were something new. It is simply taken for granted that the reader is completely familiar with the meaning and use of the terms.

What is perhaps most interesting about the use of the word "love" throughout the Sumerian texts is that there was little difference in its usage then and now. When it comes to expressions of love, the Sumerian texts are very contemporary. A word search through the "Electronic Text Corpus of Sumerian Literature" turns up 277 paragraphs containing the word love in its various form.[1]

There are many references to sexual intimacy ("make love"), but there are equally as many if not more references to "my beloved," "loveliest one," "lover," "whom he loved," and "loves" (non-sexual). Every aspect of contemporary use of the word love can be found in literature that is over 5,000 years old!

The Sumerian texts confirm that the concept of love has been around a long time. To have been used so contemporarily in this oldest of ancient literature means that it must have been predated by centuries of language and oral tradition. There is, of course, no record of that.

This historical black hole concerning the origins of love once again raises the question, "Where did love come from?" Unfortunately, love cannot be traced back to its beginnings in human history, for our written records go back only so far. Although it would not be difficult to trace the development of the concepts of love forward through history—from the Egyptians to the Greeks even up until modern day—for science, factual investigations into the origin of love must come to a screeching halt. Beyond what is written, nothing is left to science but theory.

For paleoanthropologists (those who study human evolution) and evolutionary psychologists, what appears to modern man as love is nothing more than a very advanced expression of survival of the species. The evolutionary development of human intellect and language skills have taken something very basic and instinctive—the survival of the species—and developed it into a highly complex system of human behaviors we call love. To the evolutionists, love is really the product of millennia of natural selection whose origin can probably be located in the bonding between the female and her offspring, from which empathy evolved. With evolving intellect and empathy comes the capacity for self-awareness, and eventually the self-awareness of others from which love eventually evolves.[2] All of this is pure theory, of course. Biblical love, as we will learn, fits neither the theories of natural selection nor the survival of the fittest. The presence of love in human experience poses a serious contradiction for evolutionary biologists, and the problem of altruism, the term preferred by the scientific community, has been recognized since Darwin himself.

Frustrated by the antithetical persistence of altruism in the evolutionary hypothesis, science has taken a new tack—the search for an altruism gene. The theory is this: since the observable presence of altruism in both humans and the animal kingdom cannot be explained by basic evolutionary theory, altruism must be a part of genetic structure, thus the "altruism gene." There must be a gene present that is the source of altruism. While the theoretical presence of an "altruism gene" may satisfy the evolutionists, it does nothing to satisfy the question of origins. The creationist would simply ask, "Well, where did that gene come from?" Additionally, an "altruism gene" does nothing to explain why all creation fails to live altruistically, why the same animal species will eat each other, or why humans kill each other. The leap of faith required to believe that an "altruism gene" can even survive in an evolutionary world and eventually develop into the complexities of human love is greater than simply accepting creationism itself.

If one chooses not to accept an evolutionary or genetic hypothesis for the phenomenon we call love, then there is but one alternative left—love must have come into human history from an outside source. Love did not evolve in humans...love was revealed.

As a Bible-reliant Christian, I believe love—or altruism if you will—was an integral part of God's creation of the heavens and the earth. Why? Because love is a part of God's nature (1 John 4:8). As God creates, so his nature is reflected in all creation.

When God created the heavens and the earth, the earth was "...formless and void and darkness was over the surface of the deep..." (Genesis 1:2). The creation account continues on to reveal that God created light, the heavens, dry land and seas, vegetation, and living creatures (Genesis 1:20). His creation included all the living creatures in the seas, in the skies, and on the earth. When God completed his creation, he saw that "it was good."

The creation account, then, informs us that after the first five days of creation, before God created man and woman, everything was perfect and good. Regardless of whether a Christian believes that God's creation took millions of years or six days, the result is the same—God created everything. His imprint is upon everything. Nothing existed that did not come from the word of God.

That the three persons of the Godhead were present during creation is evident. He who moved over the surface of the deep was the Holy Spirit (Genesis 1:2). The apostle Paul informs us that Christ, the second person of the Godhead, was also present, if not the agent of creation:

> *"For by Him* (Christ) *all things were created, both in the heavens and on earth, visible and invisible, whether thrones or dominions or rulers or authorities—all things were created through Him and for Him."* (Colossians 1:16)

By deduction, if all living creatures were created good, then all living creatures were created with the ability to care for the young (the female-offspring relationship) and to demonstrate empathy, both of which have been identified by the evolutionists. All creatures, therefore, were created with an innate ability to care, beginning, of course, at the level of the species.

For the purpose of this book, we will call the "altruism" part of God's creation the *general revelation of love*. Without rudimentary love, peace and harmony throughout the animal kingdom could not have existed. When God created the earth, he created it in such a way that primitive love was present. We can call it empathy or sympathy or animal instinct for the survival of the species, or, if one chooses to assume a six-day creation, we can define the primitive love by what wasn't present: hostility, killing and death (although we do not know for certain what was taking place in the animal kingdom before the fall of Adam and Eve). Whether one chooses a lengthy creation process or a six-day creation, the outcome is essentially the same: God's creation included the ability to care and to empathize, even if that took place only on the level of the species. Caring for the young and empathy represent love in its most elemental form.

The effects of the general revelation of love, of course, remain with us today. I have included this recent news article, not only because it is fascinating, but also because it illustrates the point. It is only one of hundreds that could be cited. (The story has been edited and shortened due to its length.)

*NEW YORK—When Eve and Norman Fertig rescued a sick, two-week-old half wolf, half German shepherd puppy from a breeder almost seven years ago, they'd never dreamed that the animal one day would save their lives.*

*"God is watching; he's watching all the time," Eve Fertig told FOX News from her home at the Enchanted Forest Wildlife Sanctuary in Alden, N.Y.*

*He apparently was watching on Oct. 12, when the 81-year-old Fertigs were treating injured animals in the forest sanctuary on their property. One such animal is a near-18-year-old raven, while another is a crow who was shot, blind in one eye with two broken legs.*

*It was routine for the couple to feed and exercise the dozen or so animals there around 7 p.m. every night.*

*"While we're in there, the lights go out and I realized something's wrong," Eve Fertig said. "We go outside to see what's happening and down comes one massive tree ... the trees came down across us."*

*The massive storm that hit upstate New York that night felled trees, blocking the Fertig's path to the other sanctuary buildings — such as the school and storage building — and to their home, which was at least 200 feet away.*

*"We were in big trouble. ... I said to my husband, 'I think we could die out here,'" Eve said.*

*The Fertigs huddled in a narrow alley between the hospital building and the aviary, where they were sheltered from falling trees. They couldn't climb over the trees without injuring themselves. Neither had warm clothes on since it was a clear, crisp fall day just a few hours ago. They hugged each other for warmth, since by 9:30 p.m., temperatures had dropped.*

*"I wasn't prepared for this ... I thought, 'we're trapped, we're absolutely trapped,'" Eve said. "That's when Shana began to dig beneath the fallen trees."*

*The 160-pound dog that habitually follows her owners around — Eve likens it to "Mary had a little lamb," when the lamb went everywhere Mary went — eventually found the Fertigs and began digging a path in the snow with her teeth and claws underneath the fallen trees, similar to a mineshaft, and barking as if to tell them to follow.*

*A reluctant Norm said, "I had enough in Okinawa in a foxhole," referring to his service in World War II.*

*"'Norman, if you do not follow me, I will get a divorce,'" Eve said to her husband of 62 years. "That did it. He said, 'a divorce? That would scandal our family.' I said, 'all of our family is dead, Norman!'"*

*After Shana tunneled all the way to the house — a process that took until about 11:30 p.m. — she came back, grabbed the sleeve of Eve's jacket, and threw the 86-pound woman over her back and neck, which Eve described as "as wide as our kitchen shelf."*

*Norman grabbed Eve's legs, and the dog pulled them through the tunnel, under the trees and through an opening in a fence to the house, at which they arrived around 2 a.m.*

*"It was the most heroic thing I've ever seen in my life," Eve said. "We opened the door and we just fell in and she laid on top of us and just stayed there and kept us alive ... that's where we laid until the fireman found us."*

*There was no electricity and no heat in the house, so Shana acted as a living, breathing generator for the exhausted Fertigs until the local fire department arrived the next morning....*

*"She kept us alive. She really did," Eve said.[3]*

On the sixth day of creation, God said, "Let us make man in Our image, according to Our likeness.... God created man in His own image, in the image of God He created him; male and female He created them." (Genesis 1:26-27). In addition, "God saw all that He had made, and behold, it was very good. And there was evening and there was morning, the sixth day" (Genesis 1:31).

Scholars continue to debate exactly what it means that God created man and woman "in His own image." Although we may never know what the image of God means entirely, we can safely say that self-awareness was part of it, as evidenced by the interactions of Adam and Eve in the following chapters. Thus, with self-awareness came the capacity to recognize the self-awareness of others—in Adam and Eve's case, each other—laying the groundwork for the ability to give and receive love. Although there is no clear evidence from Scripture that a special revelation of love was introduced with the creation of man and woman, certainly the capacity for receiving and comprehending love did occur with their creation. The first use of the word "love" in Scripture does not occur until much later in time, during the period of the patriarchs.

So, once again we are faced with the question, "Where did love come from?" As a Christian, I do not believe that love, particularly that described in the New Testament, is a product or even could become a product of human evolution. To discover the source of love, we must look at love in its very beginning.

---

1.  Faculty of Oriental Studies, "The Electronic Text Corpus of Sumerian Literature." Last updated 2006-10-24 by JE. *The ETCSL Project: http://etcsl.orinst.ox.ac.uk* (Accessed July 13, 2007).

2.  Robin Allott, "Evolutionary Aspects of Love and Empathy," *Journal of Social and Evolutionary Systems* 15, no. 4 (1992): 353-370: *www.percepp.demon.co.uk/lovempat.htm* (Accessed July 13, 2006).

3.  Liza Porteus, "Half-Breed Wolf Dog Hero Rescues Elderly Owners From Snowstorm," *FOX News*:

    *www.foxnews.com/story/0,2933,234599,00.html* (December 6, 2006). Accessed July 13, 2007.

# *Vignette for Chapter Two*

# *"Forever Warm"*

His daughter touched his shoulder; "It's time to let go, Dad." For an hour, he had been leaning on the rail of the hospital bed holding the hand of his beloved. This precious hand, once so warm, was warm no more.

He had been thinking about the youthful thrill of first taking her hand in his. It was a simple walk after class. She had slipped accidentally on some wet grass and let out a shriek as her books spilled onto the ground. He reached out and grabbed her arm to help her right herself. Their hands met and he never let go.

He remembered how firmly she grasped his hands as they faced each other saying their vows. Her hands said what her words could not: "This is real. This is forever. I am putting all my trust in you. Do not let me down. Do not ever let me go. I'm counting on you...always."

He recalled how she would take his hands and rub lotion on them, coming home from the lumberyard with cracks and cuts and calluses. It was her hands that restored the strength of his own.

He remembered putting his hand over hers as they held their firstborn, and he remembered taking her hand in his when that same daughter stood at the altar to say her own vows.

But most of all he cherished the nights. The blending of his body next to hers, the warm caresses as she turned and rubbed his back and neck, the touch of her warm flesh, the beauty of the moment as they snuggled and cuddled and gave each other tender touch. Her hands brought him such pleasure, such comfort, such bliss. Words were never needed. It was her warm, caring hands that said everything important.

Now that hand was warm no more. His tears had dampened the back of her hand. He gave her hand one last kiss and reluctantly let go.

That night he was truly alone for the first time. He lay under the covers, disoriented and exhausted but unable to sleep. There was no longer her hand to caress his back, and there never would be again. He laid there in and out of sleep, anticipating her hand would reach over to him at any moment. It never came.

But he was not cold. All along, it was her love that had kept him warm, and it was her hands that spoke the intimacy. Her loving nature had changed him. The oneness he knew was theirs had guided him to become a loving, caring husband and father. It was her persevering love that taught him everything he knew about compassion, empathy and faithfulness. It was her loving touch that taught him how to lovingly touch and care for others.

He remembered how he lovingly wiped away the tears of his young son when his birthday balloon popped. He remembered hugging his daughter tightly and compassionately when she came home crying from school because her friends had been mean to her. He remembered the way he reached out to his beloved when her own father passed away. In the end, he realized that he himself had become as loving as she had.

Every memory made him warm. His beloved's love had taught him how to love. Her touch had taught him how to touch. Her warm hands had become his warm hands. The memories were there even if her hand was not.

He tossed throughout the night drifting in memories, but his heart was forever warm.

## Chapter Two

# "It Takes Three to Make One" (Love and Its Beginning)

*"The glory which You have given Me I have given to them,*
*that they may be one, just as We are one..."*
(John 17:22)

Have you ever imagined what heaven was like before the heavens and the earth were created?

I asked my home Bible study once, "Before anything existed, what was there?" Having been taught correctly on creation before, they all agreed there was nothing. God had created everything *ex nihilo*...out of nothing. They knew the answer by heart, as would many well-informed evangelical Christians.

Then I rephrased the question, "Okay, then before anything existed, who was there?"

"Well," said one, "God, of course."

"And Jesus," another added quickly.

Then another, "The Holy Spirit must have been there."

I asked them if they could prove it from the Bible. The first verse quoted to me was John 1:1-3:

*In the beginning was the Word, and the Word was with God,*
*and the Word was God. He was in the beginning with God.*
*All things came into being through Him, and apart from*
*Him nothing came into being that has come into being.*

Another read from Colossians 1:16-17:

*For by Him all things were created, both in the heavens and on the earth, visible and invisible, whether thrones or dominions or rulers or authorities—all things have been created through Him and for Him. He is before all things, and in Him all things hold together.*

Still another read right from Genesis 1, verse 2:

*The earth was formless and void, and darkness was over the surface of the deep, and the Spirit of God was moving over the surface of the waters.*

We all agreed the Bible teaches that, from the very beginning, just as the Nicene Creed states, there was one God, three persons: God the Father, God the Son and God the Holy Spirit; God the Son being Jesus, also called the Christ, the second person of the Trinity. These three make up the Godhead, exist eternally and existed before anything was created.

Validating the group for their knowledge of biblical truth, I then posed the first question again: "Before anything existed, what was there?"

This time they looked puzzled. "What do you mean what was there? There was nothing but God."

"Are you sure?" I probed. "Think about it some more." Again, they looked puzzled and there was a long, awkward silence. Each member carefully searched his or her theological knowledge bank for the correct answer, or at least an answer that didn't seem outrageous.

"Is this one of your trick questions?" joked Peggy. Peggy is a program manager at a local Christian camp. Everyone laughed at Peggy's question.

Finally, one of the members of the study named Sherry peered intensely at me, her face expressionless, her pupils going in an out of eye contact and deep thought. Sherry is a homemaker and on the side works as a professional clown. She was still puzzled but I could see ideas clicking in her eyes. She was having a hard time turning the sudden insight into words.

"Well," she thought aloud, "there was God, there was Jesus and there was the Holy Spirit. The only thing I can think of that must have existed before creation was..." again, hesitating and rather sheepishly, forming a question more than an answer, "a relationship?"

"Bingo!" I declared, and applauded her.

"Why didn't I think of that?" Peggy's husband Lou reflected.

"That *was* a trick question," Peggy chided. We all laughed again.

Somehow, in the years of learning as evangelical Christians, we were all slow to reach a rather obvious conclusion. If there are three persons in the Godhead, then there must be a relationship. That relationship is eternal and must have always existed. Therefore, my next question was to ask them to describe the relationship. Again, they paused and looked puzzled. The whole subject seemed foreign and distant from the many truths they had learned in church over the years. There were no immediate, automatic theological answers that emerged from their mental resources of Bible studies, sermons and discipleship.

"I doubt they ever argued" Lou said while nudging Peggy, attempting—and succeeding—at raising an eyebrow. Unwittingly, he could not have been more correct.

"I'll give you a hint," I said. "Remember what God said when John baptized Jesus in the Jordan River?"

Quickly, Peggy quoted the verse word for word from Matthew's gospel: "This is My beloved Son, in whom I am well-pleased."

"So this prompts another question," I quickly inserted. "When God created the heavens and the earth, did he also create love?"

"No way!" Lou responded without hesitation. "Love must always have existed because God has always existed."

"So if love wasn't created, how do we know about it?"

"From the Bible," a young man named Troy asserted. "Love must be a part of God's revelation."

With that statement, the floodgates of insight opened and the rest of the evening was spent reflecting on the nature of the relationship that exists and has always existed among the members of the Godhead.

"Perfect harmony."

"Unity."

"Pleasing the Father."

"Doing the will of the Father."

"Perfect communication."

"Trust."

"Obedience."

"Never correcting."

"Willing to sacrifice."

"Agreement."

"No conflict."

"Peace."

"Friendship."

"Entirely comfortable with each other."

"Beautiful."

"Oneness."

"...But individuals."

"Intimacy."

And of course, "Love."

"It seems strange," Sherry's husband Peter mused, "that we're trying to describe something divine in human terms. It seems that their relationship would be so much more superior to anything we could describe."

He was right. The relationship among the persons of the Godhead is transcendent, more than anything humans can describe. Therefore, we must rely on the Bible and the theological terms that emerge from it.

"Holy." The relationship is free from any blemish or imperfection, and is transcendent, beyond human attainment.

"Eternal." The relationship lasts forever. It has always been, now exists and will exist throughout all eternity.

"Blameless." Guilt of any kind does not exist in the relationship because there is no trespass or sin.

"Immutable." The nature of the relationship never changes. As it was in the beginning, it is now and will forever be.

"Omnipresent." The nature of the relationship pervades all of creation.

"Intimate." There is perfect intimacy because there is perfect oneness, and that oneness is characterized by love.

So went the evening. Our group recognized that everything describing a perfect relationship among individuals could be said about the Godhead, and much more. We concluded that what existed before the creation of the heavens and the earth was a perfect, loving, holy and intimate relationship among the Father, the Son and the Holy Spirit. If any one word could be used to describe the relationship, we all agreed, it would have to be "love."

In the beginning, there was love. Love was the defining relationship among the members of the Trinity: the Father, the Son, the Holy Spirit (first, second and third persons of the Trinity, respectively). There existed among the persons of the Trinity perfect harmony. There was no fear, no envy or jealousy, no hatred. There was no posturing for position. There was one will for the three, though each possessed his own will. There was one substance and essence for the three, though each possessed his own person. They existed in a state of perfect holiness, perfect purity and perfect unity. That unity was characterized by love.

The apostle John, superintended by the Holy Spirit, wrote often of the nature of the relationship among the persons of the Godhead. First, between the Father and the Son:

*Jesus said to them, "My food is to do the will of Him who sent Me and to accomplish His work."* (John 4:34)

*"I can do nothing of My own initiative. As I hear, I judge; and My judgment is just, because I do not seek My own will, but the will of Him who sent me."* (John 5:30)

*"For I have come down from heaven, not to do My own will, but the will of Him who sent Me. This is the will of Him who sent Me, that of all that He has given Me I lose nothing...."* (John 6:38-39)

*"...Keep them in Your name, the name which You have given Me, that they may be one even as We are."* (John 17:11)

*"Father, I desire that they also, whom You have given Me, be with Me where I am, so that they may see My glory which You have given Me, for You loved Me before the foundation of the world."* (John 17:24)

*"...And I have made Your name known to them, and will make it known, so that the love with which You loved Me may be in them, and I in them."* (John 17:26)

The relationship between the Spirit and the Father is also addressed:

*"I will ask the Father, and He will give you another Helper, that He may be with you forever; that is the Spirit of truth, whom the world cannot receive, because it does not see Him or know Him, but you know Him because He abides with you and will be in you."* (John 14:16-17)

The apostle Paul also addresses the intimate relationship between the Spirit with the Father.

*For to us God revealed them through the Spirit; for the Spirit searches all things, even the depths of God. For who among men knows the thoughts of a man except the spirit of the man which is in him? Even so the thoughts of God no one knows except the Spirit of God.* (1 Corinthians 2:10-11)

Finally, John writes of the relationship between the Spirit and the Son.

*"But when He, the Spirit of truth, comes, He will guide you into all the truth; for He will not speak on His own initiative, but whatever He hears, He will speak; and He will disclose to you what is to come. He will glorify Me, for He will take of Mine and will disclose it to you. All things that the Father*

*has are Mine; therefore I said He takes of Mine and will disclose it to you.*" (John 16:13-15)

It can be surmised without difficulty, then, that the relationship among the members of the Godhead is perfect in every way. It is perfect because it is characterized by perfect love. Perfect love is manifested in perfect harmony, perfect unity, perfect peace. The relationship represents the ultimate form of intimacy. When the apostle John writes in his first letter, *"God is love"* (1 John 4:8), he is describing the essential nature of the Godhead. There is perfect harmony and unity among the members of the Godhead because perfect love is the Godhead's nature.

There was another important point that needed clarification, however. We all agreed that love seen in creation was a part of God's general revelation because all creation had God's imprint on it. But what about all that we had learned about the relationship among the members of the Godhead?

"Well," Lou quickly responded, "we only know that through the Bible."

"Exactly," I answered. "And there's a term for that. It's called 'special revelation.' The love we see in creation is a part of God's general revelation to man. But the love that we see in the Godhead, and all the love that we read about in the Bible is special. It's over and above anything revealed in nature. To 'love your neighbor as yourself,' to 'love one another' and 'to love your enemies' isn't a part of general revelation. It's special revelation, and it's revealed only through God's word."

When our study group began to grasp the nature of God's special love revelation and the unique relationship that exists among the members of the Godhead, Peggy's daughter Nicki wondered, "Maybe that special relationship is what God wanted for Adam and Eve when he created them."

Bingo! More lights were going on.

Genesis 1:26-27 reads, *"Then God said, 'Let Us make man in Our image, according to Our likeness...' God created man in His own image, in the image of God He created him; male and female He created them."*

If God created human beings in his image, it is reasonable to assume that he created Adam and Eve with the capacity to give and receive love; to experience the same kind of love that exists among the members of the Godhead.

"But don't we have to choose to love?" Sherry asked astutely.

"Which means?"

"We also had to be created with free will."

"Why?"

"Because love isn't love unless you choose to love."

We all concluded that was the principle reason God created humankind with free will, for without free will, it would be impossible to choose to love as God loves. Had God created man and woman without free will, they would never have experienced the true nature of God's love. They would have been merely robots acting according to the laws of creation. However, love requires free will, for without free will there is no such thing as love that is established, defined and manifested by God. Nevertheless, with free will came the freedom not to love.

Troy, Nicki's husband, spoke up. "Don't you think that's what God wanted for Adam and Eve, to experience his love and to choose to love him back?"

It was a great question. Troy went on. "Maybe one of the reasons God created man was so man could share in God's love, just like the members of the Trinity share in one another's love."

I gently corrected Troy on one small point. "Say that again, but this time make it personal."

He thought for moment. "Oh," he said. "Maybe one of the reasons God created us was so that we could share in God's love and choose to love him back."

"Try it again. Make it even more personal."

"Okay, I see your point. So that *I* can share in God's love and *I* choose to love him back."

I asked Troy if any Bible verse came to mind that would indicate this. He paused for a second, and then turned back to John 15: "'This is My commandment, that you love one another, just as I have loved you.

Greater love has no one than this, that one lay down his life for his friends.' I see nothing there but choices, choices to love."

"I can't think of anything better than experiencing the love of God," Peggy observed quickly. "But you really can't appreciate God's love until you realize that love is a choice. And I can't think of anything more satisfying than to realize you've chosen to love God."

Sherry reflected a moment longer. "Doesn't perfect love result in perfect oneness?" Directing us to John 17, Sherry pointed out that love has to be present for us to experience oneness with God: "'…That they may all be one; even as You, Father, are in Me and I in You, that they also may be in Us, so that the world may believe that You sent Me. The glory which You have given Me I have given to them, that they may be one, just as We are one….'"

Everyone agreed: without love, there can be no oneness. Oneness is possible only through the medium of love. Furthermore, to be one with God through love would be the ultimate joy, the ultimate peace, ultimate intimacy.

"Isn't intimacy with God and with one another what we all long for?"

It was all coming together now. God wants us to experience the perfect love that exists in the Godhead, and he desires for that perfect love to exist among all men and women with one another.

Peggy confirmed this by reading again John 15:12: "'This is My commandment, that you love one another, just as I have loved you,'" emphasizing the words "just as."

And Lou was quickly reminded of what Jesus also said in John 15: "'Just as the Father has loved Me, I have also loved you; abide in My love. If you keep My commandments, you will abide in My love; just as I have kept My Father's commandments and abide in His love. These things I have spoken to you so that My joy may be in you, and that your joy may be made full.'"

Nicki responded with John 13:34-35: "'A new commandment I give to you, that you love one another, even as I have loved you, that you also love one another. By this all men will know that you are My disciples, if you have love for one another.'"

"What would the world be like," Lou wondered, "if everyone experienced God's love, and everyone truly loved one another?"

"It would be paradise," Peggy responded. "Maybe like the Garden of Eden."

"We'd all be one," Lou spoke up. "No more wars, no more suffering, no more crime or greed…none of that."

"Maybe like the world was supposed to be," Troy added.

"Maybe like the world will someday be," Nicki reflected.

We closed our Bible study with prayer and left Peggy and Lou's home that evening wondering what could have been. If only Paradise had not been lost.

# *Vignette for Chapter Three*

# *"Matchmaker"*

The matchmaker knew instantly they were perfect for each other.

He needed companionship; she longed to be a companion. He was insecure; she knew how to make a man feel important. He was feeling stress from the 24/7 pressures of his job; she desired to melt those burdens away. The matchmaker knew they would be good for one another. He would fulfill her emotional bank; she dreamed of meeting this man's fantasies.

He was not particularly handsome, as tall and handsome go, but he was very bright and witty. Charismatic, entrepreneurial, appearing confident almost to the point of arrogance, he prided himself on being a workaholic and, by all appearances, successful. He had begun with a handful of people and built the organization into a thriving, growing community of hard workers. Nothing had been handed to him on a silver platter. He had fought his way for everything. When board members balked at his decisions, he could pull the right strings either to have them voted off the board or neutered in their influence and effectiveness. It was their job to buy into his vision, not play the role of spoilers. Unity was paramount. He had worked hard to build a successful organization and he wasn't about to let a board or staff member undermine the process.

But the matchmaker's access to him revealed something about him others didn't know—there was a void in the relationship wing. For all his friendly demeanor, outgoing personality, incessant smile, self-confidence and poise under pressure, there was a longing for something more that was complexly interwoven with a longing for many things less. Privately, he longed for an escape. He craved a deeply intimate relationship that would carry him away from the stresses of his job and routine obligations of life. He frankly admitted that he was an ideal candidate to be a drug addict, but he was too smart to fall into that trap. He would also admit confidentially that he fantasized a lot. He was too embarrassed to do much about it. After all, he had a reputation and career at stake.

She, on the other hand, was attracted to the confident type. Being stunningly beautiful and demure by any standard, she would be the perfect match for a man of his stature. Other men had difficulty looking her in the eye, but not he. He could meet her eyes on the level of an equal. That greatly attracted her to him. She liked that about him, that he didn't seem intimidated by her as most men were. She alone could bring him comfort. She alone could heal the emotional wounds inflicted by his job. She and no other could give him the intimacy he longed for and smother him with her love. Really, there was no one else on earth worthy of him. She felt she had an insight into him that not even his wife had. Beneath that self-confident and proud spirit, she spotted a little boy who needed someone to take care of him. She would take care of him.

The matchmaker, ever the observer, spotted their attraction to each other the instant they met. The matchmaker could see his eyes dilate when he gazed upon that perfect face, and the matchmaker could see how she trembled inside at the touch of his gentle handshake. The matchmaker knew what a perfect match this would be!

And so it became the matchmaker's intent to bring the two together for good. It would have to be, of course, the right circumstance. Something of this magnitude, with gossips about, would have to be arranged in private. But who should make the first move?

A chance meeting was arranged; that is, by chance to them, cleverly arranged by the matchmaker. Neither of them had a clue the matchmaker was working so quietly behind the scenes. In the end, the chance meeting led to a private appointment about which no one else was told, of course. Lingering telephone calls throughout the day were carefully disguised as counseling. Then they met in a hotel lobby, then in a hotel restaurant and, eventually, in a hotel room.

"I've never felt this way about anyone," she whispered softly in his ear. "I know it's love, and I know in my heart that it's God's will we're together." He was too infatuated and too tired to disagree. Besides, no one this beautiful had ever desired him before. He was addicted to her love.

When the gossips discovered the liaison, all hell broke loose—literally. The result was two families devastated, children emotionally crippled for life, a church split, and two people without jobs or a home to call their own.

The matchmaker had done his job perfectly.

*Chapter Three*

# "A Falling Out of Sorts" (Love and Paradise Lost)

*The serpent said to the woman, "You surely shall not die! For God knows that in the day you eat from it your eyes will be opened, and you will be like God, knowing good and evil."* (Genesis 3:4, 5)

Adam and Eve were the original "perfect couple." When God created them, they were spotless in every way, just as all that God created.

The Bible tells us that God created a perfect world. One would expect nothing less from a perfect God. The creation of the man and the woman was no less perfect. They were created without tarnish or blemish. Not only were they created perfect, they were created with a special gift:

> *"Let Us make man in Our image, according to Our likeness."* (Gen. 1:26)

Being created in the image of God meant the man and the woman were provided with self-awareness, something unique in creation. The man and woman could reason, could feel and could create. They were given free will to make choices. Being created perfect, they were without flaws, without sin, without shame, without guilt and without any encumbrances to receive or to give love. Being created by the Godhead meant that the man and the woman were not created outside of relationship. The very Godhead was present, and the eyes of the man and the woman were awakened to the perfect relationship that exists among the persons of the Godhead. Being created flawless, they were without any of the weaknesses that taint or hinder relationships, either between themselves or between them and God. Nothing existed within themselves that interfered with their ability to receive or return the pure love of God. No past memories, no failed relationships, no baggage. There was perfect harmony, unconditional unity and flawless intimacy. They were created in such a state of existence that they would experience the presence of the holy Godhead without fear. The relationship between the man and the woman, and between the three persons of the Trinity, was perfect. It can only be described as a love relationship that was in the likeness of the relationship among the Godhead himself. It was Paradise.

There was oneness between God and his human creation.

That the three persons of the Godhead participated in creation is evident. In the Hebrew language, the original language of the Old Testament, the use of the plural form *Elohim* for "God" (sing. *El*) is the first hint of the presence of the Triune God. It was "the Spirit of God" who "was hovering over the face of the waters" (Gen. 1:2). In the creation of the man and the woman, "God said, 'Let Us make man in Our image…'" (Gen. 1:26). Theologians differ as to whether or not these verses provide proof of the Trinity, as referring to God in the plural was not uncommon in ancient literature. When observed in the context of the New Testament, however, the use of the plural forms in the creation account cannot be ignored. Relationship in creation, if not proven beyond doubt, is at the very least strongly implied. Indeed, the woman was created because, "It is not good for the man to be alone; I will make him a helper suitable for him" (Gen. 2:18). Although the man and the woman were blessed purely by the presence of perfect earthly companions suitable for each other, the importance of relationship is again immediately addressed. Could it be that the reason it is not good for man to be alone is because, without an earthly companion, the relationship and intimacy enjoyed with God through love can never be fully experienced or appreciated? *God wanted the man and the woman to experience with each other what they experienced with God.* Oneness between the man and the woman as a part of God's plan is evident:

*"For this reason a man shall leave his father and his mother, and be joined to his wife; and they shall become one flesh."* (Gen. 2:24)

There was oneness between the man and the woman.

The garden in which the man and the woman lived was called the Garden of Eden. It is described as Paradise. They lacked nothing. They feared nothing. They were safe, secure and satisfied. They had only to enjoy the presence of each other and the company of "…the Lord God walking in the garden in the cool of the day." More so than a place, Paradise was position, for the man and the woman were perfectly positioned to enjoy the love of God and experience perfect love with one another. God, being the creator of man, placed the man and the woman in the garden with only one measure for maintaining the love relationship:

*"The Lord God commanded the man, saying, 'From any tree of the garden you may eat freely; but from the tree of the knowledge of good and evil you shall not eat, for in the day that you eat from it you will surely die.'"* (Gen. 2:16-17)

It is reasonable to ask, "Why would God place something in the garden that might jeopardize the unity, the harmony and the wondrous love relationship between God and man, and between the man and the woman?" The answer returns us to the manner in which God created them. To create them in his own image, God had to give man and woman free will; that is, freedom to choose. Free will is necessary for love because love is not really love without the freedom to choose it or reject it. Without free will, there can be no true love. To give, recognize and receive love, one must have free will and the ability to choose. It is, in fact, why God created man with free will. Without free will, love of God cannot be recognized, received or offered in return. Had God made the man and woman without free will, love would have remained only within the Godhead. With freedom to choose, the man and the woman could not only enjoy God's love, but they could express that pure love to one another. Biblical love requires freedom to choose. Without free will, there is no such thing as biblical love.

Here is an illustration that might help. A person can make a digital recording that endlessly repeats, "I love you." The truth is, however, that the recorder does not really love the listener because it does not have personhood, and therefore, no free will or ability to choose to love. The words might be expressed but love does not exist. Had God made man and woman without free will, they might have obeyed him perfectly and endlessly recited their love for him but they would have been completely incapable of experiencing or giving love.

God did not make men and women like digital recorders. God made us with free will and the ability to choose. He gave us the ability to choose so that we might recognize, experience and offer true love. It is the love that is of God. It is the love that is higher than the love found in creation— it is the love that exists within the Godhead himself. That is why men and women have free choice, not so that we would choose just to obey, but that we would choose to give and receive God's love. Biblical love always results in obedience, but obedience does not necessarily result in love.

However, with free will also comes the ability to choose poorly. Free will gives us the opportunity to reject love, to violate another's love, or to choose not to love. One can choose to love the creation or the creature more than the creator. A man or a woman can choose to love themselves more than the one who made them. Adam and Eve had the opportunity to return God's love by choosing correctly, or to reject God's love by choosing poorly. God's command not to eat of the tree of the knowledge of good and evil was an opportunity to choose to love God.

Unfortunately, the Bible makes it clear that, given the right circumstances, Adam and Eve chose poorly. They chose not to maintain the love relationship they experienced with their creator.

> *Now the serpent was more crafty than any beast of the field which the LORD God had made, and he said to the woman, "Indeed, has God said, 'You shall not eat from any tree of the garden'?"*

*The woman said to the serpent, "From the fruit of the trees of the garden we may eat; but from the fruit of the tree which is in the middle of the garden, God has said, 'You shall not eat from it or touch it, or you will die.'"*

*The serpent said to the woman, "You surely will not die! For God knows that in the day you eat from it your eyes will be opened, and you will be like God, knowing good and evil."*

*When the woman saw that the tree was good for food, and that it was a delight to the eyes, and that the tree was desirable to make one wise, she took from its fruit and ate; and she gave also to her husband with her, and he ate.*

*Then the eyes of both of them were opened, and they knew that they were naked; and they sewed fig leaves together and made themselves loin coverings.* (Genesis 3:1-7)

Something did indeed die that day. Physically, the dying process began for both Adam and Eve. Spiritually, the perfect love relationship they had with God was now tarnished beyond what they themselves could repair. Emotionally, they experienced fear and shame. As we discover later in the chapter, they even attempted the blame game, which was the beginning of a broken love relationship that would plague them and their offspring, Cain and Abel. Relationally, they had chosen to reject their most precious possession: flawless love, seamless unity and perfect harmony with God and with one another. More than anything, what died that day was a relationship characterized by love.

Paradise was lost when the man and the woman chose not to love God. It was not a failure on God's part, but on man's. At no time did God cease loving the man and the woman. Sin entered the world when man chose not to love God. Sin, therefore, can be defined as falling short of loving God in the manner he designed. Sin is nothing less than missing the mark of God's design for love. The failure to obey was the failure to love, for to love God is to love him according to his design, not man's.

This point bears repeating in another way. God's "design" is expressed through God's truth. Sin is failing to love according to God's design, that is, according to truth. One may say, "I love God," but if his or her concept or expression of love is not in accordance with God's design, it may be love according to man, but it is not biblical love. It is not love according to his design and it is not love according to the truth. The love that God requires can only be defined by the truth; that is, the Bible, for the Bible is the only expression of God's truth. All other expressions of love fall short of God's design. The only love that is not distorted is love that is defined by the truth, and the only source of absolute truth we have today is the word of God. All other definitions of love, all other expressions of love, and all other pretenses for loving God are the result of man's design rather than God's. Because they come from a source other than the truth, all other expressions of love are blemished, incomplete, rationalized, expedience-based, ultimately self-serving, deceptive, mere imitations of the genuine, and created from man's fallen nature.

What was lost in the fall was the ability to enjoy the pure love of God; the pure love that existed between the man and woman, the love that should have existed between Adam and Eve's offspring, and the love that God originally designed for all the peoples of the earth. Paradise lost was love lost.

As it was for Adam and Eve, so it is for us today. God has a wondrous love he wants to share. His love not only results in the healing of our souls, it is the springboard for the healing of all relationships. The free will with which we are created determines the direction for accepting or rejecting God's love.

The good news, the Gospel, is that God is in the business of restoring love to our relationships, both with himself and with others. The restoration, however, must be done strictly according to his design and his definitions; that is, his truth. Love that is not consistent with truth is aberrant, arbitrary love gleaned more from creation and imagination than from the Bible. Therefore, in order to restore love, God must first reveal truth.

The first, most prominent revelation of the truth came in the form of the Ten Commandments. Before we look at the Ten Commandments, however, it is important to define love. Without a clear understanding of the biblical revelation of love, it will be impossible to understand its proper application.

*Bill Walthall*

# *Vignette for Chapter Four*

# *"God Is the Answer"*

Pastor Jenkins returned from the church growth seminar full of energy and ideas. "We need goals," he shared with his elders. "We need a new vision. It's time for a change. Image is everything!" he enthused, having thoroughly convinced even his most hesitant elder that the status quo would have to go. "Society is rapidly changing," he declared, borrowing statistics from *Newsweek* to make his point. "If we don't keep up with the culture, the culture will leave us in the dust." He presented a comprehensive plan for "bringing the church up to speed." He could no longer be satisfied "just to sit and grow fat." The church had to reach out to the unchurched and those disillusioned with the traditional church. The time was ripe to impact the population bulge called the "baby boomers." "We have to learn to speak their language. We need to communicate to them effectively." But he also warned them. "Just getting them through the doors is our first major task. Studies have shown that 'seekers' may attend the church for six months before they finally make a decision for Christ."

Receiving a majority approval from the elders by a vote of 5 to 2, Pastor Jenkins set out to change the way things were done. His "restructuring the church," brought about over a nine-month period, was not without a fiscal impact, causing the church to dip significantly into its building fund. The platform was rebuilt into a stage and the pulpit was removed. Lighting was completely revamped, eventually resembling a studio, complete with colors, effects and wireless dimming. He quickly switched from a microphone on a stand to a wireless mic on a headset. All the pews were removed and plush theater seating was installed. Stained-glass windows were removed, carpet torn up, walls painted with contemporary colors versus Navajo white, and a complete multimedia system installed which included a control center, cameras, remote TVs, state-of-the-art sound system, and screens and projectors for the pastor's PowerPoint™ messages. The choir was dismantled and the organ and hymnbooks removed. In their place was a worship team which included drums, bass and electric guitars, a keyboard, and "young people who really can sing." Drama teams were initiated. Sermons were limited to twenty minutes and related to real-life issues rather than exposition from the Bible. Greeting teams were formed, handpicked by the pastor and comprised of couples "good-looking enough to go on the cover of Charisma Magazine." Their training was intense: "Every visitor should be greeted seven times before they leave this church."

The grand opening was scheduled for Easter Sunday, to be preceded by three separate mailings advertising their church, which, by that time, had changed its name from Gramdale Bible Church to "The Answer." The new name for the church came to Pastor Jenkins in a moment of inspiration. He had just landed on his new slogan, "God Is the Answer." The slogan would be placed on billboards about the city, advertised on the local cable network, seen on bumper stickers and license plate holders, inscribed on pens sent with every mass mailing, and available on tee-shirts, coffee mugs, label pins, and on sports gear bags, all available at *www.theanswerchurch.org/shop*.

Easter Sunday came and the church was full of life. The results of months of hard work exceeded even Pastor Jenkins' expectations. Over 300 visitors crowded into the now-too-small-sanctuary to witness the new beginning of "The Answer."

"This is *wonderful*...an answer to prayer," Pastor Jenkins shared with his elders that day. "It's far better for the sanctuary to seem crowded than to seem empty," a principle he had learned at the church growth seminar. "It's the image of growth, and image is everything!"

Morale in the church could not have been higher. Of course, when only about 200 of the Easter visitors showed up the following Sunday, "That's to be expected," defended Pastor Jenkins. "After all, it *is* the Sunday after Easter."

However, the gradual decline in the Easter crowd continued throughout the next few months in spite of the continued mass mailings. "That's to be expected," defended Pastor Jenkins. "After all, it *is* the summer. People are on vacation." The few new spectators who showed up turned out to be mostly disgruntled worshippers from other churches.

Perhaps the most disturbing thing for the elders and their wives was the news that some of their good friends were leaving the church, members who had been there for years. It was always the main topic of discussion at elder meetings and men's breakfasts.

"Well, Pastor," said one of the elders when asked to share why the Barkers were leaving, "they said it's our slogan."

"Our slogan? You mean, 'God is the answer'? What's wrong with that?"

"Nothing's actually *wrong* with it. The Barkers think the name of Jesus Christ should be in it. After all, we are a Christian church."

"I see," responded Pastor Jenkins thoughtfully. "Well, if that's all it is, we'll just modify our slogan."

From then on, The Answer's slogan became, "God is the answer...through Jesus Christ." Unfortunately, in spite of the change, the Barkers and the two families they took with them did not return.

News of other families leaving with specific complaints resulted in other changes to the church's slogan. Complaints came in the form of "too many praise choruses and never any hymns," introducing messages with video clips from R-rated movies, failure to acknowledge "Sanctity of Human Life Sunday," unwillingness to allow voting fliers in the lobby when national elections rolled around, and the generic "It's just not the same church I signed up for."

The following Easter, The Answer's membership had actually grown smaller than before the last. Most of the faithful tithers had left. The few new folks who had come and stayed felt that "My personal finances are none of the church's business." Actually, the elders who called on the new attendees heard this phrase a lot; only the words "My personal finances" were replaced with words like "My sexual orientation," "My political views" and "Who I live with...."

Come October, Pastor Jenkins announced to his half-filled sanctuary that he was leaving. "The Lord is calling me to another church," he declared. "I've prayed a lot about this. I said to the Lord, 'Lord, you've called me to *this* church. This is my home. This is my family. Do I really have to leave?' The Lord answered my heart just as clear as if I'd heard a audible voice: 'I'm sending you to another church. Just as I sent Jonah to Nineveh, a prophet who kicked against the pricks, so send I you.'" And off he went.

After the pastor's announcement, the two remaining elders and their wives met for dinner. They spent the evening discussing how they were going to "pick up the pieces."

"I'll tell you the first thing I'm going to do," the head elder shared.

"What's that?"

The next morning the head elder went over to the church and took down the sign that advertised the church's slogan. It read, "God is the answer...through Jesus

Christ. A friendly, Spirit-filled, semi-contemporary non-legalistic but fundamentally based conservative evangelical immersion baptizing family church that is pro-life, supportive of traditional marriage, zealously patriotic and open to everyone. (Singles and gays welcomed too!)"

He put up the new sign. It read simply, "*God* is the answer."

## Chapter Four

# "Ice Weasels and Their Kin" (Love and Its Biblical Revelation)

**But now faith, hope, love, abide these three; but the greatest of these is love.** (1 Corinthians 13:13)

Look for a definition of love and the list will exhaust you. Here are a few of my favorites.[1]

*"And remember, my sentimental friend, that a heart is not judged by how much you love, but by how much you are loved by others."* (Professor Marvel, Wizard of Oz)

*"Love your neighbor as yourself, but don't take down the fence."* (Carl Sandburg)

*"I've made the most important discovery of my life. It's only in the mysterious equation of love that any logical reasons can be found."* (John Nash in "A Beautiful Mind")

*"Love is a word, what matters is the connection that word implies."* (Matrix Revolutions)

*"Love is when you tell a guy you like his shirt, then he wears it everyday."* (Noelle, age 7, participant in a survey of 4-8 year olds asked to define love)

*"Love is much like a wild rose; beautiful and calm, but willing to draw blood in its defense."* (Mark A. Overby)

*"Love is a snowmobile racing across the tundra and then suddenly it flips over, pinning you underneath. At night, the ice weasels come."* (Matt Groening, creator of "The Simpsons")

Also of interest are those on a more serious note.

*"Only through love can we obtain communion with God."* (Albert Schweitzer)

*"The success of love is in the loving—it is not in the result of loving. Of course it is natural in love to want the best for the other person, but whether it turns out that way or not does not determine the value of what we have done."* (Mother Teresa)

*"An ounce of love is worth a pound of knowledge."* (John Wesley)

Then there are those that are inspiring and seem valid, but in reality are questionable.

*"The laws of love are written in the heart of every human being by the hand of God."* (Anonymous)

Really? If that is the case, why is there so much hate in the world?

*"Raising a child is the highest form of love a human being can experience."* (Marsha Rock)

Is that true? Higher even than forgiveness?

## Biblical Revelation and Definition

In 1966, Joseph Fletcher, an Episcopal theologian, published a controversial book titled, "Situation Ethics: The New Morality."[2] Fletcher attempted to show that every moral choice had to be made according to the situation. That is, prescriptive principles such as rules or laws, regardless of their source, supernatural or natural, are insufficient to meet every situation in life and to address every contingency. Fletcher's solution to the problems of moral choice was what he called "situation ethics"; every moral situation in life needed some sort of guiding absolute that could be applied to any given situation. Fletcher declared the absolute to be love, specifically, *agape* love as found in the New Testament. When facing any ethical or moral decision, we should first ask, "What is the most loving thing to do?" Fletcher was only partly right.

It is beyond the purpose of this book to enter into an extensive debate over situation ethics or its cousin, ethical relativism. The point is that Fletcher attempted to establish the importance of love in making moral and ethical decisions. The weakness of Fletcher's theology, however, was his failure to define love. The *agape* love which he placed in preeminence was left hanging without absolute truth and definition to anchor it. Failure to define love meant failure to address biblical truth. According to Fletcher, everyone seems to already know what true love—or *agape* love—is. There is a problem, however, with a failure to define love. Love itself can be relative, for love means different things to different people. It is, in fact, a supposed sacrificial love that moves an Islamic suicide bomber to blow up himself (or herself) and take innocent lives in the process. It is often out of love and compassion that a family member will want to end a member's suffering through euthanasia. It is sometimes through genuine love and compassion for the disadvantaged and poor that a person is supportive of a woman's right to an abortion.

At the heart of the problem, then, is the definition of love. Do not look for a simple one- or two-word definition, however. Love can only be defined in context, and the context must be imbedded in absolute truth. *Without absolute truth, love cannot be absolutely defined.* If love is not correctly defined, it cannot be correctly applied. If it is not correctly applied, it becomes something other than absolute love. Love therefore requires truth to establish its limits and boundaries, to know when and under what circumstances it must be applied. Therefore, in the end, *truth must always trump love because love requires accurate and biblical definition.* The only absolute source for that truth is the word of God.

This, then, brings us to the uniqueness of biblical love. Only within the Scriptures can we truly understand what love is and how it is to be applied.

There is an odd problem, however. In the Bible, love is never defined. It is only described. In contrast, my paperback dictionary provides a clear definition.

> Love (luv), n., v., loved, lov-ing. –n. 1. A profoundly tender, passionate affection for another person. 2. An intense personal attachment or affection. 3. A person toward whom love is felt. 4. A strong enthusiasm or liking. 5. A score of zero in tennis. – v.t., v.i. 6. To have love or affection (for). –Idiom. 7. In love (with), feeling love (for). 8. Make love, a. to have sexual relations. b. to embrace and kiss. –lov'-a-ble, love'a-ble, adj. – love'less, adj.[3]

Although all the above definitions contain elements of truth, they are biblically incomplete and fall far short of the way love is described in God's word. In order to determine a biblical definition of love, logically one must look at the Bible itself.

## Love in the Old Testament—To Love Is to Obey

In the Old Testament, the Hebrew word translated "love" is not found until the 22nd chapter of Genesis. It states nothing about God's love for man or man's love for God. It is a familial love between Abraham and his son Isaac:

> *"'Take now your son, your only son, whom you love, Isaac, and go to the land of Moriah, and offer him there as a burnt offering on one of the mountains of which I will tell you.'"*
> (Gen. 22:2)

For the Christian, it is significant that the first use of the word 'love' in the Bible is associated with Isaac and not Ishmael.

Though it may be assumed a necessary part of submission and obedience, the stated need for man to love God is not found until after the time of the patriarchs and is associated directly with the Mosaic Law. We find it in the second of the Ten Commandments: "…but showing lovingkindness to thousands, to those who love Me and keep My commandments" (Exod. 20:6). It is important to note that the first biblical reference of the need for man to love God is found in the context of the Law. This is reinforced in the second giving of the Law, Deuteronomy, where the second commandment is repeated (5:10). Man's love for God expressed through obedience and submission is best described in Deuteronomy 6:5: "You shall love the Lord your God with all your heart and with all your soul and with all your might." This equation, then, becomes the first and foremost commandment, but it is clear from the wording that loving God is a command.

The rewards for loving God are also stated explicitly:

> *He* (God) *will love you and bless you and multiply you; He will also bless the fruit of your womb and the fruit of your ground, your grain and your new wine and your oil, the increase of your herd and the young of your flock, in the land which he swore to your forefathers to give you.*
>
> *You shall be blessed above all peoples; there will be no male or female barren among you or among your cattle.*
>
> *The Lord will remove from you all sickness; and He will not put on you any of the harmful diseases of Egypt which you have known, but He will lay them on all who hate you.*
>
> *You shall consume all the peoples whom the Lord your God will deliver to you…"* (Deut. 7:13-17)

It is clear that the rewards for loving God are earthly and material in nature and encompass the promise of a prosperous life.

God's love for man, on the other hand, though obviously implied throughout the Old Testament, is not explicitly stated until Deuteronomy 4:37, and only in the context of "His people":

*Because He loved your fathers, therefore He chose their descendants after them. And He personally brought you from Egypt by His great power...."*

(See also Deut. 7:6-9, 13.)

The word used for love in all of the passages above is the common, generic Hebrew word *aheb*. Another word indirectly related to love, however, is "lovingkindness" (Heb. *hesed*). This word is used not only in the context of personal relationships, but also of God himself (Gen. 24:27; 32:10; Exod. 15:13) and describes his mercy, compassion and grace. *Hesed* is, in fact, the Old Testament equivalent of the Greek word *charis* translated "grace" in the New Testament.

As the revelation of Old Testament love progresses, so does the command to demonstrate love for others as well as God does. This is first seen in God's command "...you shall love your neighbor as yourself" (Lev. 19:18), including "the stranger who resides with you" (Lev. 19:34) and, implied, "the orphan and the widow" (Deut. 10:17-19).

Equally important in this discussion of love in the Law is the observation that the Mosaic Law—specifically, Deuteronomy—is actually composed as a formal *treaty*. Called a "suzerain treaty," each party agreed to a set of conditions and consequences. If the conditions were met, there would be rewards. If conditions were not met, there would be serious consequences. Biblical archeologists have discovered that such treaties were common in the ancient world. Deuteronomy comprises a covenant treaty between God and his people, that is, between a ruler and his subjects. Studying Deuteronomy with this background in mind helps to understand the structure of the book.

If there is any definition of love that can be gleaned from its introduction in the Old Testament, it is a definition rooted in the Law. Love for God and love for others is intricately interwoven throughout the

Law. To love God is to love His Law. To obey God's commandments is to love him. Love is not an option; it is an imperative. It is obedience to the commandments that is the measure of a person's heart. The definition of love is linked directly to obedience; it implies faithfulness, devotion, submission and no little degree of perfection. In fact, obedience to the treaty God established is the standard by which love is measured, and therefore, defined. Love through obedience is also the pendulum upon which blessings swing, according to the treaty. According to this lawful Old Testament context for love, one does not have to feel love for God to love God. To love "with all your heart" is a call to obey rather than a call for intimacy. Love for God, therefore, is impersonal and mechanical. One simply needs to obey the Law whether he or she feels like it or not. Love for God is based more on acknowledgment for what he has done rather than on individual intimate acquaintance. Love is intimately tied into fear of God, for to fear God is to love him and to love him is to fear him. Love for God is not based on a friendship level but on a servant (vassal) level involving servitude; that is, love that a slave has for his master. Love is also expressed more corporately than individually. Individuals express love through the nation of Israel. The primary motivation for loving God, then, is to receive his favor. Obeying the Law (treaty) will demonstrate enough love for God to warrant prosperity and earthly blessings. Love, then, is revealed in an orderly progression: first love God (no idolatry), then love your neighbor (other Israelites), then love "the stranger (alien) who resides with you." There is, in this progressive sequence, no room for loving your enemy or anyone, in fact, who is outside the body of Israel. It is quite the opposite, in fact. Destroying your enemy is a command from God and a sign of one's love and devotion.

God's love and God's desire for his people's love, therefore, is revealed throughout the Old Testament. It is not necessary for his people to seek more revelation, for all the truth they need has been revealed to them throughout the Scriptures. It is enough to obey the truth to demonstrate their love for him and, from their perspective, ensure his blessings to them. If Israel loves God and God alone and keeps his commandments, they will be prosperous, protected and preserved. If they turn away from God and seek other gods, or fail to obey his commandments, not only will their blessings be withheld, but they will actually come under a curse (Deut. 27:11-26; 28:15-68; Mal. 4:6).

Though love for God is expressed through obedience to the Law, God's love for his people must not be misinterpreted as conditional. God's love was extended to Abraham long before the Law was given (Deut. 4:37; 7:8; 10:15). Hidden in the prophets, however, is the truth that, even if God's blessings are conditional, his love is not. God's love for his people is unconditional and everlasting.

> **Thus says the LORD, "The people who survived the sword found grace in the wilderness—Israel, when it went to find its rest."**
>
> **The LORD appeared to him from afar, saying, "I have loved you with an everlasting love; therefore I have drawn you with lovingkindness."** (Jer. 31:2-3)

This assurance of God's everlasting and unconditional love was given during the time that Israel had forfeited its greatest blessing resulting in the destruction of the temple and in the fall of Jerusalem to Nebuchadnezzar, king of Babylon. God makes it clear through the prophet Jeremiah that the loss of Israel's blessings does not equate to the loss of God's everlasting love. God was simply fulfilling the consequences of the suzerain treaty.

The mechanical, servile love for God rooted in Law manifests itself throughout pre-monarchical Israel. Only in the person of David is there a hint of love that transcends the Law. Through David, love for and from God is personal, individual and intimate. In David there appears to be a love for God based solely upon who he is.

> **"I love You, O LORD, my strength." The LORD is my rock and my fortress and my deliverer, My God, my rock, in whom I take refuge; My shield and the horn of my salvation, my stronghold. I call upon the LORD, who is worthy to be praised, and I am saved from my enemies.** (Psalm 18:1-3)

Though not completely apart from the Law, David's love for God represents a progression of the revelation of love. There is a communion with God that makes his relationship to him intimate and personal. It is the first time in the Bible we see love for God on an individual, interpersonal level that stands on its own apart from the Law.

With the exception of David, however, the love revealed throughout the Old Testament is parochial. It is a lawful love designed more for adolescents than adults. This love requires little explaining but great adherence. It is the kind of love that a parent expects, indeed demands, from a child. A child does not know what love is or how to give love in return; it must be learned from the parents through obedience. A child does not naturally know how to love and therefore must be taught. Obedience is the first step in learning to love. The child is unable to make intelligent, willful, loving decisions of the heart, much less sacrifices, because a child has neither the knowledge base nor the experience to make loving decisions. Children require instruction in love, and this love is rooted in do's and don'ts. Therefore, children must first learn love in the context of obedience to rules. Children require a healthy fear of their parents grounded in respect. They must learn that there are rewards for obedience and unpleasant consequences for disobedience. "You shall not run out in the street while chasing a ball" and "You shall not get into a car with a stranger" is the same presentation as "You shall not make for yourself an idol" or "You shall not take the name of the Lord your God in vain." There is little need for reasoning because often the reasons go far beyond what a child can comprehend. There is no need to ask why: "Because you can get hurt" or even "Because I said so" is initially sufficient. Parents make rules for children to protect them from harm. God made rules for the Israelites to protect them from harm. He made the rules to protect them from contamination by a godless world and to protect the Messianic seed line embedded in the nation through the tribe of Judah.

There can be no question, then, that ultimately the relationship existing between God and his people was based on love but expressed through obedience. Though few could see it at the time, it was love, not mechanical obedience that was at the heart of the relationship. Obedience was intended to be an expression of love on the part of God's people. Material blessings, the only thing Israelites could relate to at the time, were intended to be the expression of God's love for his people. It is through the agency of love expressed through obedience, then, that man was able to maintain a healthy relationship with God. Even when God's people failed to obey him, however, God's love never ceased. Nor has it ever ceased.

What the Old Testament teaches us about love, then, is that it has been revealed progressively. Love has been revealed in accordance with what the world, specifically the Israelites, could understand and accept. The Old Testament revelation of love began with God's unconditional love for Abraham and his descendants. It progressed into a parochial command to love expressed through strict obedience to God's Law. Eventually, through David, love progressed to the potential for an individual, personal love that transcends the Law. It is a foreshadowing of things to come.

Finally, in the Old Testament, it appears that expressing love for God is far more emphasized than expressing love for others. Simply observing how and when the word "love" is used would seem to make that clear. In reality, however, that is not the case. Imbedded throughout the Law are commands on *how the Israelites are to treat each other*. There are laws concerning property, boundaries, caring for orphans and widows, how servants are treated, and the fair exercise of justice. Though the word "love" is used only sparingly, the principle of caring for one another is pervasive throughout the Law. This is an important point, for when the prophets will later pass God's judgment on the Israelites for their disobedience, often the preeminent judgments concern how they have treated one another.

Nevertheless, reading the Old Testament without the revelation of the New Testament would seem to indicate that the emphasis is clearly on loving God and being faithful to him; that is, loving God versus loving other gods or the things that are not of God. It is the Law, then, not love that provides the platform for "An eye for an eye and a tooth for a tooth" (Exod. 21:24). There is no indication in the Old Testament that enemies are to be loved and prayed for. In fact, for the most part, they are either completely destroyed or made subservient.

There is one final observation, however, that is relevant to Christians today. Those whose theology keep them under the Law, or those who willingly choose to remain under the Law, will always fall short in their ability to love God. That is because love is incompletely revealed in the Old Testament. Reliance on the Old Testament for moral and ethical behavior, as the basis for judging right and wrong, or as the determinant for how one relates to others, will inevitably keep them in a parochial relationship with God. Reliance upon the Old Testament means reliance upon the Law. Being under Law, they will always be limited in their understanding and practice of love because their definition of love remains defined by the Law.

In terms of progressive revelation, then, Old Testament love is underdeveloped, parochial and shrouded in fear of the consequences of failure to obey. Love awaits its greater revelation, and therefore definition, in the New Testament.

## Love in the New Testament—To Love Is to Imitate

There was a television advertisement that came out in 2005 with the phrase, "Numbers this big are hard to ignore" (Arcalex Stocks). The same could be said about the volume of verses in the New Testament concerning the theme of love. The emergence of love in the New Testament as opposed to the Old is so pronounced that if it were not for the Messianic theme, one might not clearly see the link between the two testaments.

The revelation of love in the New Testament takes on an entirely bolder dimension than in the Old. Whereas the emphasis in the Old Testament focuses on the Law, the emphasis in the New Testament is truth and grace. Love is so interwoven throughout the New Testament that there is not a single book in it that does not use the word *agape*, the only exception being the Acts of the Apostles. Even in Acts the concept of *agape* is highly suggested in the form of the breaking of bread and in "love feasts" (Jude 1:12; 2 Pet. 2:13). Not only is the prevalence of the love theme startling, but also the definition of love in the New Testament is intricately interwoven into the very meaning of the Greek word.

At the time the New Testament was written, there were three Greek words commonly used for love: *eros*, *phileo*, and *agape*. *Eros*, from which we get our word "erotic," was intended for sexual or sensual love. Today we would also call it romantic love. The Greek word *eros* is not found in the New Testament. *Phileo*, a very common word, was used primarily (though not exclusively) to describe love that emanates from natural feelings. Its context came in the form of brotherly love, friendship, camaraderie or casual relationships. It was tied in with friendliness and everyday charity. The word Philadelphia—"The City of Brotherly Love"—comes from this word.

*Agapoo* (noun, *agape*), on the other hand, represented an altogether distinct and loftier form of love. It was love based on the value of the person; therefore, *agape* is always used when referring to love for God. In this sense, it is often given the meaning "sacrificial love," the thought being that the object of the love is so valuable that the one offering the love is willing to sacrifice on his or her behalf, even to the point of death. The value of the one loved was intrinsic, not something earned, merited or deserved, and consequently worthy of "unconditional love." Therefore, the one offering the love was willing to sacrifice on behalf of the person loved due to his or her intrinsic value. The unique twist found in the New Testament—you might say, the progressed revelation—is that *all* men and women are worthy of this kind of love. Why? Because all humanity is seen as victims of an unseen enemy, the devil, who has blinded the eyes of the world and held the world captive to do his will (2 Tim. 2:24-26). And, after all, it was the devil who seduced Adam and Eve out of their love relationship with God in the first place. The clear teaching of the New Testament is that only God's truth coupled with this kind of love is powerful enough to break the hold the enemy has on the world. *Agape*, then, is the word for love found most often in the New Testament.

Here are just a few verses in the New Testament where the verb *agapoo* is used.

*But I say to you, love your enemies and pray for those who persecute you, so that you may be sons of your Father who is in heaven....* (Matt. 5:44, 45)

*God so loved the world that He gave His only begotten Son, that whoever believes in Him shall not perish but have eternal life.* (John 3:16)

*A new commandment I give to you, that you love one another, even as I have loved you, that you also love one another. By this all men will know that you are My disciples, if you have love for one another. (John 13:34, 35)*

*Now faith, hope, love, abide these three; but the greatest of these is love.* (1 Cor. 13:13)

*Beloved, let us love one another, for love is from God; and everyone who loves is born of God and knows God. The one who does not love does not know God, for God is love.* (1 John 4:7, 8)

Other than what we have just described pertaining to the word itself, there is no specific definition of biblical love found in the New Testament. The closest thing we have to a definition is not a definition at all, but a description. This is, of course, found in the apostle Paul's first letter to the Corinthians, chapter thirteen.

Love in the New Testament is based entirely on relationships. Love of material things is never encouraged. In fact, Christians are warned not to love the world or the things of the world; giving *agape* to the world is idolatry and therefore makes it impossible to offer that same love to God (1 John 2:15). Love, rather than pure obedience to the Law, is the determinant of the nature of our relationship to God. The closer that relationship resembles New Testament love, the closer that relationship resembles the truth.

One wonders why the theme of love plays such a prominent role in the New Testament. Here are just a few of the many, many reasons.

- Love is the central part of God's nature (1 John 4:8; Jude 1:21).
- The relationship between the Father and the Son is based on love (John 17:23-24).
- Christ is called God's "beloved" son (Matt. 3:17).
- The very act of God sending his Son into the world was motivated by love (John 3:16)
- The motivation by which the Son was willing to come into the world was an act of love; that is, fulfilling the will of the Father (John 5:30)
- Jesus' clear teaching that those who recognize him as the Christ are those who are able to love him (John 14:21).
- The willingness of Jesus to suffer and give his life on the cross was based on love of the Father and love for a lost world (Luke 22:42).
- The instruction of Jesus to his followers is to love one another in the same manner in which he loved them (John 13:34).
- The instruction of Jesus to his followers that love, even *agape* love, is to extend even to their enemies (Matt. 5:44).
- The instruction of the Son that love for the Father, for one another, for the lost world and even for enemies, precludes any form of violence by his followers (Luke 22:49-51; also, by the records of Acts and the history of the early church).
- We are able to give *agape* to God because he first gave *agape* to us (1 John 4:19).
- The instruction of the apostles to subsequent followers of Christ that they are to love one another in the same manner in which he loved them (John 17:20-21)
- The lifestyle of the follower of Jesus Christ is to be characterized by love (1 Cor. 13)
- The attitude of Christ's followers toward the world is to value the lost in the same manner as the Son values them; that is, to love them to the point of being willing to die for the sake of a lost world (Luke 19:10)
- A characteristic trend in the world toward the end times will be that people's love for one another will grow cold (Matt. 24:12; 2 Tim. 3:2-3)
- That one's love for Christ includes a willingness to die for his name's sake (Rev. 12.11)

- ➤ The only "feasts" established by the Christian community were called "love feasts" (*agape* feasts; Jude 1:12)
- ➤ Love is to characterize the relationship of husband to wife (Eph. 5:25)
- ➤ To "love your neighbor as yourself" is called the royal law (Jas. 2:8)
- ➤ To "love your neighbor as yourself" is declared to "fulfill the Law" (Gal. 5:14).
- ➤ The love of Christ is to control us, to characterize the walk of the believer in regard to one another and in the world (1 Cor. 13; 2 Cor. 5:14)
- ➤ The goal of all Christian instruction is to love (1 Tim. 1:5).
- ➤ Believers and the church are referred to as "beloved brethren" (e.g., 1 Cor. 15:18).

Of course, this exercise could fill a book in itself, but the point should be obvious: the revelation of love in the New Testament vastly exceeds the revelation of love in the Old. Love is exquisitely more developed. Part of that is due to the development of the Greek language providing an etymological base for using *agape* for love. Part is due to the dispersion of the Greek language initiated by Alexander the Great, creating a *lingua franca* throughout the Mediterranean world. Part is due to the emergence and breadth of the Roman Empire, in a sense unifying the entire Mediterranean world, and the offer of citizenship even to Jews. Part is due to the accessibility to Jewish synagogues scattered throughout the Roman world via the Roman highway system. All is due to the timing and will of God.

Perhaps the most astonishing revelation about love in the New Testament is that the followers of Jesus Christ are called to love even their enemies. There is no other religion in the world where instruction to love extends even to enemies. Extending *agape* to one's enemy, therefore, precludes violence and vengeance. One has to conclude that any use of violence by Christians, whether it is the Crusades, the bombing of abortion clinics, the murdering of abortion doctors or abortion itself is contrary to the teachings of New Testament love. This would include physical, verbal, emotional or psychological violence.

There is an important observation, however, that is worthy of note about the revelation of love in the New Testament. Like in the Old

Testament, *love is still a command and requires obedience.* That love of one another is a command from Jesus is irrefutable:

> *"A new commandment I give to you, that you love one another…."* (John 13:34)

> *"If anyone loves Me, he will keep My word…."* (John 14:23)

> *"If you keep my commandments, you will abide in My love; just as I have kept My Father's commandments and abide in His love…. This is My commandment, that you love one another, just as I have loved you…."* (John 15:10, 12)

> *"I was very glad to find some of your children walking in truth, just as we have received commandment to do from the Father. Now I ask you, lady, not as though I were writing to you a new commandment, but the one which we have had from the beginning, that we love one another. And this is love, that we walk according to his commandments. This is the commandment, just as you have heard from the beginning, that you should walk in it."* (2 John 1:4-6)

Finally, when it comes to biblical love, there is an important distinction between showing *agape* love and *feeling* loving. That is not to say the *agape* love is void of feelings. But biblical love is based more on action than feeling; you show love whether you feel like it or not. In fact, it can be said that the less the feeling when biblical love is expressed, the greater the love. It is nearly impossible, sometimes, to love your enemy, to love those who have hurt you, or to love the unlovable. Biblical love is based on action more than feeling because, if we waited until we felt love, we might never love at all. Why? There are two reasons. First, some people just do not evoke from us loving feelings (e.g., our enemies, someone who has hurt us in the past or, very commonly, parents who have neglected, criticized or even abused us). Second, every one of us is different in how we perceive what it means to love. Expressing love comes easily for some people but difficult for others. For example, an absentee husband may think he is acting in love by providing for his family and being away all the time. Therefore, the Christian does not wait until loving feelings are aroused to show biblical love. The very opposite is true. The Christian shows biblical love knowing that the feelings will follow. We learn to *feel agape* love once we have been obedient to *showing agape* love.

The need to obey God has not changed. What has changed is that the Law has been superseded and fulfilled by love. The Law cannot address all of life's contingencies. Love, applied with biblical truth, can. Love supersedes the Law because love, if biblically defined, is to become the universal principle for all Christian behavior. It is love, not the Ten Commandments nor any part of the Old Testament law, that is the Christian's guiding absolute for any moral, ethical or relational situation. Nevertheless, it must be stated again. Not any definition of love will do. It must be biblical love, and biblical love can only be defined by biblical truth. That truth comes only from the Bible.

The good news is this: Christians are under the banner of love, not the Law. Will it come about someday that *agape* will not have to be commanded but that it will occur naturally? The answer is yes, as we will discover in the chapter titled, "Will I Ever Love My Neighbor As Myself?"

---

1. Wikipedia, the Wikimedia Project. http://en.wikiquote.org/wiki/Love (from update 4 December 2006).

2. Fletcher, Joseph, *Situation Ethics — The New Morality* (London: Westminster Press, 1966).

3. *Random House Webster's Dictionary* (New York: Ballantine Books, 1993), 392.

*Bill Walthall*

# *Vignette for Chapter Five*

# *"Dagnabbit That Wabbit"*

It was cute the first time Pastor Harley Hoogan said, "Dagnabbit that wabbit!" from the pulpit. It elicited a huge roar from the congregation when he imitated a cartoon character. Since that Sunday in the summer of 1986, it had become an habitual euphemism for those who taught or believed error.

It went something like this. In one of his sermons, Pastor Hoogan inserted a story about a young Christian who was given a Bible by a pastor from another church, "One of those liberal churches, you know. Instead of giving that young man the only Bible he needed—a *King James Scofield Reference Bible*—he gave that boy the worst Bible man ever made; an RSV, the *Revised Standard Version*! Dagnabbit that wabbit!"

And, of course, everyone roared. After a while, members of his congregation began to call him "Pastor Dag."

Harley Hoogan had been a pastor for over twenty-five years in no less than seven different churches. Like many pastors, he began his career as a youth pastor, then an assistant pastor, then a senior pastor. In the smaller churches where he first served, he was the organist as well as the choir director, the custodian and the church secretary. But that was okay with Pastor Hoogan. He was there to serve the Lord with all his heart, and if the Lord did not send him enough help, he would just have to make do. Regardless of where he was a pastor, his congregants loved him.

Harley's wife was a model pastor's wife. She spoke very little, never opined on anything about the church, directed the women's ministry and the altar guild, sang in the choir, accompanied her husband to visit the sick, delivered cookies on a decorative plate to first-time visitors, and, above all, worked to keep her lanky husband healthy. She never told him everything she knew that was going on in the church. She made sure, however, that her husband ate right, slept well, and dressed appropriately. She even liked the dagnabbit joke, primarily because it was so uncharacteristic of him. Usually, he just got mad. It was difficult for him to talk about false teaching, false doctrine, liberal churches and "These newfangled blasphemous modern translations" without steaming. At least he had found a clever way to joke about it. Moreover, she knew better than to let the children or guests bring up controversial subjects at the dinner table.

There were rules in the pastor's house as well. No movies, no TV, no dancing, only Christian music and only that which was approved by Daddy. The children were home-schooled, and dating was not allowed unless it was a group date. The girls were allowed to wear only long dresses and never pants. The boys were expected to wear a white shirt and tie to church. There were family devotions every morning at 7:30. "We're sheltering our children," Pastor Hoogan told others. "Shouldn't you? It's a nasty world out there. And the world is creeping into the church. By George, this is one church the world will not infiltrate!" His philosophy of ministry called for sheltering his flock in the same manner that he sheltered his children.

Pastor Hoogan prided himself on his pure doctrine. The first thing he had done when called to the church was to join the IFCA; that is, the Independent Fundamental Churches of America. He had an American flag placed in the sanctuary, along with the flag of the Christian church. He had a banner made that hung directly over the pulpit. It had one word on it: TRUTH. Pastor Hoogan felt it was his responsibility from God to ensure that every member entrusted to him by God had a firm grasp of the truth. Therefore, his sermons were either straight from the Bible with deep expositional teaching, or occasionally, he would insert a doctrinal series. He also taught the adult Sunday school. One of the deacons had offered to teach it, but Pastor Hoogan wanted to ensure that the Bible was taught accurately.

Pastor Hoogan had a very homogeneous congregation, to say the least. In the beginning, there were those who didn't agree with his eschatology; they were quietly asked to leave the church. New members were carefully screened by Pastor Hoogan himself before joining: "You know, a little leaven leavens the whole lump."

In spite of his narrow views, Pastor Dag had a fine reputation, both in and outside the church. He was seen as a man of great integrity. He was caring toward his congregation, always there when they needed him, and faithful to the core. As almost everyone in his congregation agreed, "He is such a blessing, a gift from heaven."

Things were totally under control and running "as smooth as slime on a frog's belly" Pastor Hoogan confided to one of his deacons. The church was running smoothly, that is, until Ms. Moss came along. Ms. Moss was the daughter of one of the charter members of the church who happened also to be the largest donor. Ms. Moss' father had donated the land for the church. Divorced and in her forties, Ms. Moss had left years earlier to attend the state university's nursing program. She stayed near the university until after her divorce, then moved back home to be with her aging mother. She brought two children with her and enrolled them in the local high school. Still working full time, she chose to spend her Sunday mornings drinking coffee and reading the paper rather than accompanying her mother to church. You see, Ms. Moss had long since rejected her parents' Christian faith. Her experiences had helped her develop her own view of religion. "No religion can be privy to the truth because every religion claims to have the truth. They can't all be right. But one thing they all have in common is love. Therefore, my religion is love. 'Love one another.' Isn't that what Jesus taught? Therefore, the only true religion is to love one another." These were not empty words. Ms. Moss made the poor and disadvantaged a personal cause.

The trouble began when Ms. Moss invited some of her mother's friends from the church to volunteer with her at the new AIDS hospice which had been organized by an openly gay couple to help their dying friends. Eventually, some of the women from the church began donating a portion of their tithe to the hospice program. News was being circulated that some of the women from Pastor Hoogan's church were finding opportunities to share Christ with dying AIDS patients. As more women became involved, and now even their husbands, others were getting involved with the Salvation Army's local thrift store. They also began raising funds for housing for the homeless. Of course, Pastor Hoogan's wife knew all about this but never chose to inform her husband.

It all exploded when Ms. Moss began visiting local pastors with the hope of recruiting their financial support for the AIDS hospice. Pastor Hoogan, of course, was on her list. Because she had not been attending church herself, and because she and her mother never discussed religion—it had long been a taboo subject—she was completely unaware of Pastor Hoogan's theological views. Innocently, she scheduled an appointment, and was pleased with the warm greeting Pastor Hoogan gave her.

"It's very nice to meet you, Miss Moss. Your mother is a true saint, a pillar in this church. Now, how can I help you?"

Without hesitation, Ms. Moss naively and enthusiastically explained her involvement with the AIDS hospice. "I know that Jesus taught compassion for the sick and dying," she appealed. "So, Pastor, I'm wondering if the church would be willing to donate funds to help provide for the distribution of free condoms. With just a little bit of education, I believe we can help curb the AIDS epidemic."

Pastor Hoogan was stunned. In a matter of minutes, with just a few pointed questions, he was able to discover that Ms. Moss had involved almost half of his congregation with the AIDS hospice and other "social gospel activities" outside the church.

"Oh, my Lord, my Lord," he moaned, burying his head in his hands. "Haven't I preached enough about the pitfalls of the social gospel? Haven't my sheep learned anything over the years? What have you gotten them into? Why have you led these sheep away from the flock?"

Ms. Moss was equally stunned. Staring in disbelief, she sat silently in front of Pastor Hoogan's desk which was piled high with commentaries and theology books.

"My child, my child. What have you done? What *have* you done?"

There was an awkward moment of silence as Ms. Moss sat assessing the situation. Finally, she said, "Shall I take that as a no?"

"Ms. Moss," Pastor Hoogan said, looking up at her sternly, the bifocals slipping down to the edge of his nose, "here's a commandment the Lord just gave me. Thou shalt not use the Lord's money to buy condoms! Those people have chosen to reject God, and just like the first chapter of Romans says, God has given them over to their own perversions. AIDS is God's judgment against them, and the last thing a church should do is to interfere with the hand of God."

"I see," Ms. Moss said, looking down and noticing a small coffee spill on her pants suit. "Well, I can see you're not in favor of the idea. I'm sorry I bothered you. Thank you for listening to me, at least. I had no idea you were against the idea so much."

"That's all right, that's all right," Pastor Hoogan said, leaning back in his judge's chair. "I'm sure your intentions are sincere."

Ms. Moss headed for the door.

"Oh, there's one more thing," she said, stopping and turning around to face Pastor Hoogan. "My mom asked me to invite you down to the hospice when you get a chance. She's volunteering in the office. She said Saturday would be the best day to come to see what's going on."

"Thank you very much, Ms. Moss. I'll take that into consideration. Give my best to your precious mother. If you don't mind, would you please close the door behind you when you leave. I think I need to spend some time praying."

"Of course," Ms. Moss responded. "Goodbye now."

"Goodbye."

For thirty minutes, Pastor Hoogan never changed his position in his chair. He just sat there, staring, hardly breathing, leaning forward on his desk with hands folded as if to pray.

"There's a wabbit in our midst," he kept mumbling. "There's a very bad wabbit in our midst."

*Bill Walthall*

*Chapter Five*

# "Are We Fighting the *Wrong* Battles?" (Love and the Ten Commandments)

*"You shall therefore love the LORD your God, and always keep His charge, His statutes, His ordinances, and His commandments."* Deuteronomy 11:1

One of the most famous battles in the Pacific during World War II was the battle for the island of Iwo Jima. This tiny island would become an important safety net for US bombers returning from Japan. One of the more notorious incidents of the battle of Iwo Jima was the planned capture of Hill 362-C, of tactical importance to the Japanese, and therefore, to the Marines. Having received their assignment to capture the hill, the 3rd Battalion, 9th Marines battled bravely against a ferocious, well dug-in enemy. The surprise attack was not without significant US casualties. The Marines eventually captured the hill, only to discover *they had captured the wrong hill!* They found themselves "surrounded by a sea of wide-awake and furiously counterattacking Japanese infantry."[1] In spite of their bravery, it would cost even more casualties to advance to the right hill, some 250 yards away. Precious time, energy and ammunition were wasted by advancing on the wrong hill. They eventually reached the correct hill, but only after additional casualties.

I believe many well-meaning, evangelical Christians today are fighting battles for the wrong hill. Occasionally they are winning the hill but losing the cultural war. That is because the issues we are fighting for are wrong. The battle over the Ten Commandments in Alabama represents a perfect example of fighting for the wrong hill.

In November 2003, former Alabama Chief Justice Roy Moore, an evangelical Christian, stood determined and defiant in front of the Alabama Supreme Court building. Surrounded by supporters and a virtual army of praying evangelicals, Judge Moore refused an order from a federal judge to remove the monument of the Ten Commandments he had placed in the rotunda of the Alabama courthouse. Christians across America watched closely as to whether once again US courts would undermine America's Judeo-Christian heritage. Unfortunately, Judge Moore lost not only his battle—he also lost his job. Alabama's Court of the Judiciary unanimously found him guilty of ethics violations and stripped him of his chief justice position.

Christians in other states such as Tennessee and Kentucky have joined forces in similar battles over the presence of the Ten Commandments in public places such as courthouses, schools, parks and community centers. The courts' pretext for removal of references to the Ten Commandments is that their presence violates an interpretation of the principle of the separation of church and state. Arguably, there can be no doubt that there is a media and legal assault on anything Christian in American society. Reaction against the Ten Commandments is just another sign of the Christophobia and anti-Christian bias that characterizes United States courts and today's entertainment industry and educational system. Challenging the constitutionality of the presence of the Ten Commandments is just one symptom of a much broader problem: the removal of anything associated with religious values—and in particular, Christianity—in American society. Thus, the concern of Christians. The Ten Commandments, along with crosses on hillsides and nativity scenes at Christmas, are symbolic of our Christian values.

The situation cited above raises an important question, not with the ACLU or America's judicial rulings. The more important question is this: when it comes to the Ten Commandments, are Christians fighting the right battle?

Let's ask some pivotal questions that foreshadow the subject of this chapter. What is God's design for the role of the Ten Commandments in the life of the Christian? Is the Old Testament law, epitomized by the Ten Commandments, the true measure of biblical behavior? Better yet, is obedience to the Ten Commandments the best measure of whether or not we love God? Can you command someone to love you? (Of course you can, but will he?) If that person does agree to love you, is it from the heart? Does he love you simply because you promise to bless him if he does and curse him if he does not? Or, is the love offered simply for who you are and without regard to consequences? Is love measured purely by obedience? Do we love God and then obey, or do we obey and then learn to love God? Are love from the heart and the command to love mutually exclusive? In other words, is the "love commandment" an oxymoron?

For many evangelical Christians, there seems to be no little confusion about the role of the Old Testament law in their Christian walk. Some well-versed Christians say they are no longer under the Law, yet continue to hold fast to the Ten Commandments. (When "law" is capitalized, it is used to refer to the entire body of laws found throughout the Old Testament, with particular reference to the Torah.) Other Christians proclaim that the Old Testament laws are still binding but choose what Old Testament laws need to be kept. In the courts, some evangelical Christians fight valiantly on behalf of the Ten Commandments as if they were orthodox Jews.

There are two ways most Christians determine their day-by-day love for God. First, by how well they adhere to the Ten Commandments. Why? Because that is the only tangible biblical standard they know. There is a second way evangelical Christians measure their love for God, however. It is by means of other, church-originated lawful behaviors. These behaviors include such spiritual practices as daily prayer and "quiet time," Bible study, tithing, church attendance and service within the church. However, they also include an infinite variety of other behaviors: being pro-life versus pro-choice, standing against gay activism, voting Republican, remaining abstinent from alcohol or drugs or pornography or dirty dancing or R-rated movies. Though these latter behaviors are not Old Testament law, they take on the genre of determining right and wrong by lawful living. They serve as standards by which we measure our love for God.

Whether Christians recognize it or not, one of the great conflicts in Christian living is the conflict between love, Old Testament law, and lawful living. What is the relationship between love and lawful living, and how is it supposed to be lived out on a day-by-day basis? Where does Old Testament law leave off and New Testament love begin? If Christians deny they are under the Law, does that mean they can do anything they want? Is the Law, especially the Ten Commandments, maintained to keep us in check from living sinful lives?

## The Old Testament Law—Is It Still Binding on Christians?

The Book of Exodus, the second book of the Bible, introduces us to God's first major revelation of substantive truth. This truth is presented in the form of codified law.

Exodus and the three books that follow (Leviticus, Numbers and Deuteronomy) comprise the Mosaic Law; that is, the Old Testament laws given through the prophet Moses. Until that time, no laws from God had been codified; i.e., formally written and ratified by the Israelites. (Genesis, the first book of the Bible, is also considered part of the Law, but for our purposes, we are speaking of codified law specifically.) Truth from God and truth about God was most likely oral traditions handed down over the generations from Adam through Noah through Abraham, Isaac and Jacob, and eventually to the Israelites living in bondage in Egypt. Through Abraham, God had chosen one family to become a great nation. Through this nation, God intended to manifest his glory and holiness to the rest of the world. The nation was to be a holy nation that would "bring light to the Gentiles" (other nations). It would be within this nation that the seed line leading to the Messiah would be preserved, and it would be through this nation and this nation alone that the nature of God's truth and love would be revealed.

What is important here is that, at this time in history, God chose to reveal truth through the Law. Through the Law God identified himself: "I AM THAT I AM," meaning "The self-existent One." Through the Law, God revealed his holiness and righteousness, his sovereignty and power, his uniqueness and transcendent nature, his mercy, compassion and lovingkindness, and his intentions for the nation of Israel; indeed, he revealed his holiness for the whole world to see. We learn from the New Testament that the Law was never intended to make a person righteous; that is, free from sin. Its greater intent was to reveal humanity's unrighteousness, sinfulness and helplessness apart from God. Ultimately, the purpose of the Law was to lead us to Christ, the one who is fully divine and perfectly human, the Messiah who would save humanity from its unrighteousness.

The Mosaic Law is enormous. It includes dietary and health laws, moral laws, social laws, ceremonial laws and laws of sacrifice. The keystone of the Mosaic Law is the Ten Commandments. The Ten Commandments serve as building blocks for all the other laws. The Ten Commandments can be roughly divided into two parts. The first four laws, it is said, relate to obeying God. The remaining six laws relate to people. We will look at the Ten Commandments more closely in the next section.

Everything about the Law changes when it comes to the New Testament. God revealed himself not through more Law but through the person of Jesus Christ. Jesus made it clear that he did not come to abolish the Law or the Prophets, but to fulfill them; that is, to become the only human ever to obey them completely, both in letter and in spirit, and therefore complete their cause (Matthew 5:17). Jesus could do this because he was fully divine and perfect humanity. He was the God-man. It was from him that the Law was given and it was through him that the Law was fulfilled. When Jesus uttered the words, "It is finished," on the cross, he meant that not only was his mission completed but that all the points of the Law, including the ultimate Passover sacrifice, was completed. He was, as John the Baptist affirmed, the Lamb of God that takes away the sin of the world.

Jesus' first disciples did not fully understand the ramifications of Jesus' having fulfilled the Law and the Prophets. It was through special revelation given to the apostle Paul that God's plan regarding the Law began to unfold. Jesus himself opened Paul's mind to the truth that God's purpose for the Law was not to attain righteousness, but to show us our sin that would lead us to Christ. It would be by faith in Jesus Christ apart from the Law that man would be free of sin and become right before God. Paul writes about these truths in his letters to the churches, especially to Rome and the area known as Galatia.

The truths revealed to Paul concerning the Law are stunning.

*"...By the works of the Law no flesh will be justified in His sight; for through the Law comes the knowledge of sin. But now apart from the Law the righteousness of God has been manifested, being witnessed by the Law and the Prophets, even the righteousness of God through faith in Jesus Christ for all those who believe..."* (Romans 3:20-22)

*"Therefore, my brethren, you also were made to die to the Law through the body of Christ..."* (Romans 7:4)

*"But now we have been released from the Law, having died to that by which we were bound, so that we serve in newness of the Spirit and not in oldness of the letter." (Romans 7:6)*

*"To the Jews I became as a Jew, so that I might win Jews; to those who are under the Law, as under the Law, though not being myself under the Law..."* (1 Corinthians 9:20)

*"For through the Law I died to the Law, so that I might live to God."* (Galatians 2:19)

*"Christ redeemed us from the curse of the Law...in order that in Christ Jesus the blessing of Abraham might come to the Gentiles, so that we would receive the promise of the Spirit through faith."* (Galatians 3:13-14)

*"But before faith came, we were kept in custody under the Law, being shut up to the faith which was later to be revealed. Therefore the Law has become our tutor to lead us to Christ, so that we may be justified by faith. But now that faith has come, we are no longer under a tutor."* (Galatians 3:23-25)

Paul clearly reveals in his letters that Christians, by virtue of being in Christ, are *no longer under the Law*; that is, the Law—and no part of the Law, including the Ten Commandments—is binding. That is not to say, however, that the Old Testament Law was of no value. Paul validates the Law for the very purpose God gave it. The Law reveals to us our sin and points us to Christ.

*"What shall we say then? Is the Law sin? May it never be! On the contrary, I would not have come to know sin except through the Law; for I would not have known about coveting if the Law had not said, 'You shall not covet.'"* (Romans 7:7)

*"So then, the Law is holy, and the commandment is holy and righteous and good."* (Romans 7:12)

That the law of Moses was no longer binding on Christians was a difficult concept for early Jewish Christians to accept, including the apostles. False teachings began to emerge from some Jewish Christians. They began teaching new Gentile converts that the Law was still binding. This false teaching came in the form of circumcision; Gentiles must first become circumcised before they could become a true Christian. After all, wasn't Jesus himself circumcised? Their teachings also included Old Testament dietary laws and Sabbath observance (Colossians 2:16). These false teachings were addressed at the first church council in Jerusalem, recorded in Acts 15. Once the apostles began to grasp that the law of Moses, the Old Testament laws, were no longer binding on the Gentile converts, an official letter was sent out from the church informing of such.

So, let's answer our opening question. Is the Old Testament law still binding on Christians? The emphatic answer is "No!"

What about the Ten Commandments? Did the Jerusalem council also mean to imply that the Ten Commandments were no longer binding on Christians? Before we answer that question, we must look first at what Scripture calls the "royal law."

## What Is the "Royal Law"?

In Jesus' day, Jewish theology was awash in laws. A tradition had been formulated over the centuries that the Torah, the first five books of the Old Testament, was only a part of what God spoke to Moses during his lifetime. An oral tradition developed that God taught Moses many more things than what was recorded in Scripture. These instructions and laws became known simply as traditions, known better as "the traditions of the elders" (e.g., Matthew 15:2). These traditions were oral teachings passed down from generation to generation and not written down until a few centuries after Christ. (Today the entire body of teachings is called the Talmud.) The traditions took on a life of their own and, because they were intended to interpret and apply the law of Moses, they actually became regarded as equal to if not superior to Scripture. It is primarily these traditions that the Pharisees referred to in accusing Jesus of breaking the Sabbath.

In spite of the complex system of laws in the Old Testament, complicated even more by a burdensome list of traditions, a few Jewish scholars, known as scribes, were able to sort through the minutia to see the greater principle taught in the Law. One such scribe approached Jesus in Galilee.

*One of the scribes came and heard (the Jewish leaders) arguing, and recognizing that (Jesus) had answered them well, asked Him, "What commandment is the foremost of all?"*

*Jesus answered, "The foremost is, 'Hear, O Israel! The Lord our God is One Lord;*

*And you shall love the Lord your God with all your heart, and with all your soul, and with all your mind, and with all your strength.'*
*The second is this, 'You shall love your neighbor as yourself.'*
*There is no other commandment greater than these."*
*The scribe said to Him, "Right, Teacher; You have truly stated that 'He is One, and there is no one else besides Him;*

*And to love Him with all the heart and with all the understanding and with all the strength, and to love one's neighbor as himself,' is much more than burnt offerings and sacrifices."*

**When Jesus saw that he had answered intelligently, He said to him,
"You are not far from the kingdom of God."** (Mark 12:28-34)

What Jesus quoted as the foremost commandment was known to Jews as the *Shema*, which means, "hear." The first commandment comes from Deuteronomy 6:4-5, and the second from Leviticus 19:18.

It is interesting to note that the word "obey" occurs in neither of these verses. The word "love" occurs in each, the thought being, "If you really love God you will obey Him."

What this particular scribe seemed to understand was that truly loving God always leads to obedience. On the other hand, obeying God does not always result in loving him. That holds especially true when it comes to the Leviticus passage, which is not a suggestion but a command. How do you love others out of obedience? One might say that when it comes to the Ten Commandments, it is a lot easier to love God than it is to love others.

That is why, perhaps, that apart from the Gospels, *the first and great commandment is never again quoted in the New Testament...only the second!* There is a specific reason for that, which we will discover later in this book.

So, let's review and discover what the apostles began to understand. First, a person does not become right with God ("justified") by the Law but by grace through faith in Jesus Christ alone (Romans 3:21-30; 5:1; Gal. 3:10-14; Eph. 2:8-9).

Second, Christians are "no longer under the Law" (Rom. 6:14-15) but instead "released from the Law" (Rom. 7:4-6).

Third, the purpose of the Law was neither to make us righteous (become right with God; justified) nor to earn God's favor. The purpose of the Law was to reveal to us our sin, (Rom. 7:7) and serve as "our tutor to lead us to Christ, so that we may be justified by faith" (Gal. 3:24). In addition, "Now that faith has come, we are no longer under a tutor." (Gal. 3:25)

Fourth, because the Ten Commandments are the cornerstone of the Law, Christians are also dead to the Ten Commandments in their lawful and traditional sense. If, then, Christians are dead to the Ten Commandments, by what standard would they measure their love for God? If the Ten Commandments are no longer binding on Christians, what is?

Through revelation given to the New Testament apostles and prophets, a new standard for Christian behavior was being formed, a behavior derived from but not dependent upon the Old Testament law.

What replaced the Ten Commandments as a measure of loving God was what James called "the royal law." If, however, you are fulfilling the royal law according to the Scripture, *"You shall love your neighbor as yourself,"* you are doing well. (2:8)

The royal law is closely related to Jesus' command to his disciples the night before his crucifixion: "A new commandment I give to you, that you love one another, even as I have loved you, that you love one another. By this all men will know that you are My disciples, if you have love for one another" (John 13:34-35). This particular passage will be examined more closely in chapter 9.

The truth that the Ten Commandments in their lawful form are no longer binding on Christians has enormous implications in both the courts of America and in the evangelical community. However, more on that at the end of this chapter under "Fighting the Right Battles."

There is a critical point that needs to be made: all ten commandments embody the royal law! Let's look briefly at the Ten Commandments and discover the relationship.

## The Royal Law and the Ten Commandments

Based on Exodus 20, I have interpreted the Ten Commandments through the royal law, "You shall love your neighbor as yourself." I go to this detail only to help the evangelical Christian in particular realize that to base one's moral and ethical behavior on the Ten Commandments is failing to realize that there is a greater law at work—the royal law. Here is how we Christians should interpret and apply the Ten Commandments. We will start with commandments five through ten (the "second tablet"), for they will be the easiest to understand in terms of the royal law.

## Commandment #5: "Honor your father and your mother...."

You shall "honor your father and mother" because to show them honor is to love them. Therefore, concerning parents, the royal law is easily applied. To honor is to love, and to love is to honor. Whether one interprets honor in the form of respect, or honor by providing for parents financially, there is little difference when it comes to applying the royal law. The royal law applies whether our parents have been good parents or bad. Remember, showing biblical love is not based on feelings; it is based on the right thing to do.

Likewise with the remaining five commandments, all of which have love as their basis.

## Commandment #6: "You shall not murder."

"You shall not murder" because murder is not loving your neighbor as yourself. If you love someone, you will not murder him or her, even with your words. That is why Jesus said in the Sermon on the Mount, "...Everyone who is angry with his brother shall be guilty before the court; and whoever says to his brother, 'You good-for-nothing,' shall be guilty before the supreme court; and whoever says, 'You fool,' shall be guilty enough to go into the fiery hell" (Matt. 5:22). You will not murder even your enemy, but rather love him and pray for him (Matt. 5:43-44).

## Commandment #7: "You shall not commit adultery."

"You shall not commit adultery" because adultery is the result of lust, not love. If you love your spouse, you will not hurt him or her by infidelity. Indeed, you cannot show love to your spouse and at the same time commit adultery. To commit adultery is a failure to love your children as well, for adultery always results in destruction of the family unit and disorder in the house. Additionally, adultery hurts the other party and the other party's children. Adultery destroys intimacy, violates the principle of "one flesh," forever tarnishes trust, and completely interrupts God's design to experience and express his love toward our spouse. Everything that is wrong about adultery, therefore, whether it be an act or a thought, can be summed up under the biblical definition of "You shall love your neighbor as yourself."

## Commandment #8: "You shall not steal."

"You shall not steal" because to steal from another, be it an individual or an institution, is a failure to love. Stealing is, in fact, loving things more than people, and it is loving yourself more than loving one another.

## Commandment #9:
## 'You shall not bear false witness against your neighbor."

"You shall not bear false witness against your neighbor" because bearing false witness is lying rather than loving. To bear false witness against your neighbor, to gossip, to pass down rumors…all are a failure of the royal law.

## Commandment #10:
## "You shall not covet your neighbor's house…."

"You shall not covet your neighbor's" anything because to covet is to love their possessions rather than their person. Here again, to covet is to love things. Loving things gets in the way of loving others and leads to strife, jealousy, envy, bitterness, competition and rivalry.

Commandments five through ten are relatively easy, therefore, to relate to the royal law. Commandments one through four, however, are less obvious when it comes to applying the royal law. With a little effort, I believe, we can see the relationship is clear when we realize that truth must always trump love. What commandments one through four present is the truth behind the commandments we have just observed (five through ten).

## Commandment #1:
## "You shall have no other gods before Me."

"You shall have no other gods before Me" because to do so will obscure the revelation of truth that empowers us to experience and express biblical love. The message for the Christian is a simple truth: worship only the God and Father of our Lord Jesus Christ. There cannot be a mix of Christianity with New Age, eastern mysticism, Islam, Buddhism, Mormonism, Jehovah's Witness, ancestral worship, animism, spiritualism, or any of the myriads of other forms of religion or religious practice that do not have their basis in biblical truth. The truth of Christianity cannot be mixed with secularism, pragmatism, rationalism, syncretism (the attempt to harmonize opposing theologies) or eclecticism (the blending of selected theologies). Nothing else can be a part of Christian worship because *not anything else is a part of biblical truth. If another god is worshipped or has equal or superior standing to the Father of our Lord Jesus, we will never fully understand nor be able to appropriate biblical love. To dilute biblical truth is to dilute biblical love. To worship another god is to never fully succeed at appreciating nor applying biblical love.*

Nevertheless, how does having "no other gods before Me" relate to the royal law? Let's say it again in another way. Diluted or polluted worship is the result of diluted or polluted truth and therefore results in diluted or polluted love. The greatest love Christians can bring to others is to bring to them the truth about God and about his Son Jesus Christ. Christian love is only as biblical as the truth behind it. If the truth is polluted with impurities, so will be the love. That is why God wants Christians to have no other gods; it pollutes our love as well as our truth.

Additionally, to love things more than people is to place other gods before him. To ignore the needs of others while serving oneself is to make oneself out to be God. We Christians are to love others, not to earn God's favor, but because, as children of God, we *have* his favor. Loving others, therefore, is the purest form of loving God. The apostle John tells us, "We love, because He first loved us" (1 John 4:19). To love God means to love him more than yourself, and we do that by loving one another more than ourselves. That is why a Christian would not fly an airliner full of people into the World Trade Center shouting, "God is great!" Loving God means complete devotion, but not at the expense of failing to love others, *"For God so loved the world that He gave His only begotten Son..."* (John 3:16)

## Commandment #2:
## "You shall not make for yourself an idol...."

"You shall not make for yourself an idol" because to do so will distort the revelation of truth that empowers us to experience and express biblical love. The second commandment is applied in a number of ways. God is to be loved by faith and not by sight. That eliminates worship of the Virgin

Mary, praying to saints or praying to icons. It also eliminates paying homage to the purported image of Mary on a tree stump or high-rise windows or a chocolate-chip cookie. The key word is worship. It is one thing to make a painting of Jesus; it is quite another to worship the painting or the artist. But idolatry takes many forms. Paul states that greed amounts to idolatry (Col. 3:5). Idolatry means to give one's heart to something, whether it is a celebrity or rock star or sports hero or charismatic healer or TV evangelist or local pastor. It is anything that captures our heart, be it money, possessions, job security, ambition, retirement, our body through narcissistic preoccupation, or another person.

Here again, the royal law is applicable. Having an idol interferes with offering the love that comes from God. Idols detour our love and the wrong road always leads to a dead end. Idolatry emasculates our ability to offer God's pure love to those who need it the most. The truth demands that nothing must hinder God's desire to love others through us. It is his love that he wants to give a lost world, and it is his love and only his love through Jesus Christ that can save humanity from its sin.

Jesus summed up the Second Commandment this way: "...Where your treasure is, there your heart will be also" (Matt. 6:21).

## Commandment #3:
## "You shall not take the name of the Lord your God in vain...."

"You shall not take the name of the Lord your God in vain" because to do so undermines our ability to express biblical love to a world hungry for his love. Swearing in the name of God is absolutely inconsistent with worshipping him, and therefore loving him. At risk is the sincerity of the love expressed. Taking his name and using it inappropriately confuses the world about the worthiness of God in our lives. To confuse the world from experiencing God's love is a failure to love the world Christ died for. Accepting the benefits and blessings of the Lord God in one moment and dishonoring him by acting hypocritically the next is not only a failure to love him, but a failure to love others by presenting a warped picture.

How, then, is the third commandment interpreted in regard to the royal law? By now, the application should be obvious. It is absolutely inconsistent to offer the love of God to others and then turn around and use his name in vain. To do this signals that our love is less than pure. To be inconsistent between our public life and our private life sends mixed messages to a lost world, and the picture it receives of God is anything but love. *No Christian can consistently love others and be angry with God at the same time.* Therefore, to take the name of God in vain is to invalidate the love we say we offer.

The apostle John writes it clearly: "If we say we have fellowship with Him and yet walk in the darkness, we lie and do not practice the truth" (1 John 1:6). Not to practice biblical truth is not to practice biblical love.

It is true, then, that the first three commandments involve loving God. Yet, for the Christian, all are directly related to the royal law. Loving God cannot be separated from loving others. *We best love God by loving others, and we best love others by loving God.* Another way of saying it is this: *We show our love for God by loving our neighbor as ourselves. We love God by loving others.* That is why Paul writes, "For the whole Law is fulfilled in one word, in the statement, 'You shall love your neighbor as yourself'" (Gal. 5:14).

The first three commandments, then, focus on our relationship with God and are directly connected to the royal law. The fourth commandment, however, is less obvious, much to the delight of the Sabbath-keepers.

## Commandment #4:
## "Remember the Sabbath day, to keep it holy."

Much has been written refuting those who believe that keeping the Jewish Sabbath (that is, Saturday) remains binding on Christians today. [e.g. 2, 3] It is beyond the scope of this book to review all those refutations other than to say that maintaining Sabbath-keeping as a point of doctrine is totally inconsistent with the New Testament teaching that Christians are no longer under the Law, regardless of how well Sabbath-keepers attempt to explain it away. But where does the royal law fit in?

At first glance, the fourth commandment is the only commandment in which the royal law does not seem to apply. A closer look indicates otherwise; the fourth commandment mentions nothing about worship or attending church. The literal meaning of the word Sabbath is "rest." The

Sabbath is to be a day of "solemn rest" and "complete rest" in one's own dwelling (e.g., Lev. 16:31; 23:3, 32; 25:4). Of course, this begs the question, "Rest for whom?" Obviously, it is for God's people. That is why Jesus taught, "The Sabbath was made for man, and not man for the Sabbath. For the Son of Man is Lord, even of the Sabbath." (Mark 2:27, 28)

Herein lays the key to understanding how the fourth commandment is related to the royal law. *It is the only place in the Law where a person demonstrates biblical love by taking care of himself.* God wants us to be healthy so that we will be better able to love others. We love God by taking care of the bodies he gave us. The royal law, then, helps us understand the principle underlying *all* the dietary laws in the Torah. If we take care of ourselves, we are better able to demonstrate biblical love. Those who do not take care of themselves are often those who require biblical love from others in the form of health-care issues and care giving. If we really love others, we will not put ourselves in a position where we negligently require others to take care of us.

The purpose in going into detail on the Sabbath is not to berate sabbatarians. If Christians wish to worship on Saturday, that is their choice. The only problem arises when the day of worship becomes a point of doctrine. I am not trying to discourage Christians from worshipping on Saturdays, but rather to encourage them to come out from under the Law.

It is clear, then, that all ten commandments are based on principles of love; more specifically, the royal law. *Love is the underlying principle behind all the commandments.* The apostle John will go on to inform us that it is impossible for a believer to say that he loves God while at the same time hating his brother (1 John 1:4-11). Loving God and loving others are inextricably intertwined. If we really love God, we will love others as well. If we love others, we will be showing our love for God. The one cannot be separated from the other. Why? Because it is all about relationship. There is no such thing as biblical worship apart from relationship. The believer is in a relationship with God and in a relationship with others. God wants his love to flow through the believer in both directions.

Here is the key point about the Ten Commandments: If you love others in a manner defined by biblical truth, *you will fulfill all the Ten*

*Commandments.* That is why "…The whole Law is fulfilled in one word, in the statement, *'You shall love your neighbor as yourself'*" (Gal. 5:14). If you love God with all your heart and you love your neighbor as yourself, you will keep all the commandments because all the commandments have love as their basis. However, the reverse is not true. Just because one keeps all the commandments, there is no guarantee that love will be the primary motive. That is why the Ten Commandments as law fall short. The Ten Commandments are mere examples of how to love. They represent a prototype for love. They are mere snapshots of what a life of love might look like. That is also why the Law was only a tutor. Children need tutors, not adults. Once the child is grown, he or she is expected to apply the right choices in any given situation. The Law cannot do that. To cover every contingency in life would require a set of laws and rules that would encompass the globe. The Jews tried that concerning the Sabbath, ending up with approximately two thousand laws and, as Jesus clearly pointed out in Matthew 12, their laws could not account for all the contingencies. Therefore, it is far better to have a global, operating principle upon which to interpret all situations and circumstances, and that operating system is called the royal law. The Law cannot cover all contingencies, but biblical love, defined by biblical truth, can.

That the Law, or Ten Commandments, is only a tutor or "rough draft" of Christian morality should be obvious by now. Where does it say in the Ten Commandments that we are to love our enemies? Where in the commandments is homosexuality, or bestiality, or pedophilia, or sadomasochism mentioned or forbidden? Even in the rest of the Old Testament law, some of these issues are never addressed. Where does it state in the Ten Commandments that Christians should not go to court against each other, and where does it give direction as to the use of illicit drugs, or alcohol, or anabolic steroids? It doesn't. In fact, some things mentioned above, about which all Christians would consider sin, are not found even in the New Testament. However, those under the Law go looking into other areas of law in the Old Testament, which in itself opens Pandora's Box of picking which laws are relevant today and which are not.

What is needed, then, and what God has provided for Christians, is a global operating system for determining all correct biblical behavior, including the Ten Commandments. That operating system is called the royal law, and it is based on love that is defined by biblical truth.

Here is another typical example Christians regularly face. It points out the fallacy of Christians engaging in lawful living. The Ten Commandments speak nothing of tithing, yet those Christians who remain under the Law find Old Testament tithing a convenient method of financial giving. Referring to Old Testament laws of tithing, even some evangelical pastors, for motives that are always suspicious, teach that 10% is the principle God established for tithing. (Actually, I once heard a very fine Christian preacher and scholar defend a 40% tithe as being closer to OT principles. He was, of course, in a building program.) Yet, tithing is nowhere taught in the New Testament. What is taught in the New Testament is that everything belongs to God, that "...whoever has the world's goods, and sees his brother in need and closes his heart against him, how does the love of God abide in him?" (1 John 3:17). One would have to be in a severe state of denial not to recognize that there are brothers and sisters all around us—within the church and worldwide—who are in need. There are always brothers and sisters with needs around us, and therefore, there is always the choice of addressing those needs in love by giving as much as possible, or by not exercising love and closing our hearts against them. The problem with Christians maintaining lawful living when it comes to tithing was reflected by an evangelical acquaintance of mine who said, "I give 10% of my net income to the church. I consider the rest is mine to do with what I want." The operating principles of giving in the New Testament are clearly taught throughout. The motivation for giving all one can possibly give is based on the principle of showing love to one another to address the needs of brothers and sisters in Christ. Love does not measure percentages. Love does not put a limit on giving. Love gives regardless of the tax benefit. Love gives to the point of sacrifice, and gives as much as one can give without himself becoming needy (2 Cor. 8:7-12).

The point is this: Christians no longer need the Law to determine right and wrong or to establish rules of morality. The guiding principle for Christian behavior is no longer the Ten Commandments or any part of the law of Moses; it is the royal law of love. Of course, that love must be defined. It is biblical truth that defines, limits, shapes and qualifies the love that Jesus commands.

## Fighting the Right Battles

Having acknowledged that the Ten Commandments are no longer binding on Christians, and that all the commandments can be applied according to the royal law, the question must be asked, "Why are Christians fighting so hard for the Ten Commandments? Are the Ten Commandments the right hill to die on?" One answer may be as stated earlier, that removal of the Ten Commandments represents an erosion of Judeo-Christian ethics in American society, and therefore, Christians are inadvertently affected. In defense of Judge Roy Moore, he stated, "The issue is: Can the state acknowledge God? ...If this state can't acknowledge God, then other states can't....And eventually, the United States of America...will not be able to acknowledge the very source of our rights and liberties and the very source of our law...."[4]

However, Christians should be asking another question. Why were the Ten Commandments put in the Alabama Supreme Court rotunda in the first place? Is Alabama a Jewish state? Were they placed there to represent Christian morality as an absolute standard of moral law? Most likely Judge Moore, like many evangelicals, is fighting to preserve America's Judeo-Christian heritage. The problem is this: for Christians, the Ten Commandments are the wrong standard to be placing before society. Christians should not be looking to the Ten Commandments as the basis for their moral behavior. There is a greater revelation for determining morality, for establishing correct behavior, and that behavior centers around the royal law.

If battles are to be fought for Christian values, if monuments are to be erected that truly represent the moral tenets of Christianity, the Ten Commandments are the wrong hill to die on. There is a new commandment—the right hill to die on—and that commandment was clearly covered under the royal law.

In the Alabama case, would the plaintiffs have had the same grounds for argument had the monument simply read, "You shall love your neighbor as yourself," or "Love one another"? (Of course, I am not naïve here. The ACLU and other anti-Christian groups would find some reason to sue, regardless of beauty and relevance of the statement.)

The point is this: Christians are no longer under and no longer bound to the Ten Commandments. The only people group that is bound by the Ten Commandments is the nation of Israel and the Jewish community at large; they do not recognize Jesus as the Messiah, and do not consider the New Testament inspired scripture. It is Jews who are bound by Mosaic Law, not Christians. Therefore, the Ten Commandments as law are in effect only to Jews and not to Christians. Christians are under a new commandment, the commandment to love your neighbor as yourself.

Of course, the command to "love your neighbor as yourself" seems a lot more abstract, less tangible and more difficult to grasp than the clearly delineated laws of the Ten Commandments. That is perhaps the reason so many well-intentioned Christians are willing to resort to the Ten Commandments than the more difficult-to-grasp royal law. It is also why, using Paul's analogy in Galatians 3:23-26, the Law is intended for children, but love is intended for grown-ups. Therefore, the issue is one of spiritual maturity, not spiritual zeal.

Understanding what it means to "love your neighbor as yourself" is also precisely why truth must trump love. Along with Jesus' command to "love one another," biblical love requires biblical definition, and the only means for acquiring biblical definition is through acquiring biblical truth.

---

1. Col. Joseph H. Alexander, "Marines in World War II Commemorative Series: Closing In: Marines in the Seizure of Iwo Jima: The Bitter End," *Marine Corps History and Museums Division*: www.nps.gov/wapa/indepth/extContent/usmc/pcn-190-003131-00/sec6a.htm (Accessed July 13, 2007).

2. Dale Ratzlaff, *Sabbath in Crisis* (Sedona, AZ: Life Assurance Ministries, 1990 and 1995).

3. Walter R. Rea, *The White Lie* (Turlock, CA: M & R Publications, 1982).

4. David Mattingly, contributor. "Judge suspended over Ten Commandments," *CNN.com/Law Center*: www.cnn.com/2003/LAW/08/22/ten.commandments (August 23, 2003). Accessed July 13, 2007.

# *Vignette for Chapter Six*

# *"Doing Lunch"*

"Well," John said, standing and pulling out Pam's chair as she approached the table, "we're *finally* doing lunch. I didn't know if you'd received my text message."

"I did. I just closed the clinic doors for a change and ignored everybody."

As Pam seated herself, the two conspicuously abstained from further small talk or even eye contact, preferring instead to scrutinize the menu. Pam suspected that John had an agenda and this whole lunch thing was a set-up.

"I'm craving fish for some reason," John said overly pleasantly. "I think I'll go for the tilapia. I've had it before here. It's quite tasty."

"That looks good to me, too. Can they serve it blackened?"

A radio blaring mariachi music helped drown the noise of the motorbikes passing by. The outdoor café was a little-known treasure for the locals of Cuernavaca—it was too mama-and-papa-ish for the tourism lists. Though a favorite for Gringo retirees and a summer retreat for the elite of Mexico City, Cuernavaca attracted its fair share of poor and underprivileged, which is why Pam chose to open a free clinic for children in the poorest barrio. Having to learn Spanish on the fly, John had become her primary tutor.

John, you see, had come years earlier to study Spanish. After completing his immersion training, instead of returning to the States to teach Spanish, he was persuaded to stay a year and teach English in one of the private schools, being compensated, of course, at a rate of about one tenth what he would have received in the States. His problem was that he fell in love with the people, and one year turned to two, two to five, and now to fifteen.

The two had been trying to get together for lunch for weeks now. Pam's clinic was non-stop. If it wasn't examining kids, it was trying to get legitimate medications from the *farmacias*. Children with skin, gastrointestinal and orthopedic diseases she'd only read about during her training in the States required constant online study, instant messaging, and consulting with the local medical school. Of course, brown-outs occurred at the worst times, and twice she had replaced the expensive heavy-duty surge protector for her laptop. Though trained as a pediatrician, Pam found herself doing much more outside her "domain of practice" and often her clinic served as an emergency room, a one-day surgery center and even, at times, a hospice.

After ordering, Pam finally broke the silence, her fingers tapping nervously on the table. "So, John, what's this about?"

John drew his chair closer to the table and cleared his throat, leaning heavily on his elbows and trying to make eye contact. "I'm still having a hard time understanding," he began, searching at first for non-confrontational phrasing and then eventually giving up, "why you still won't support abortions."

On her list of items she thought John might bring up, abortion was actually pretty low. There were other issues that seemed more pressing.

"*That's* what's bothering you?"

"Today I had to take a little guy to the principal's office because he was miserable and scratching himself uncontrollably. Later we discovered he was covered with scabies. It turns out the kid has twelve—count that—twelve siblings. His father works as a waiter here in town, the mother stays home and herds kids all day, and they live in a makeshift house of cardboard and fiberglass they grabbed from the dump. The next time she gets pregnant, if she came to you and asked for an abortion, would you give her one?"

"So, you think the answer to this family's problem is abortion?"

"Let's face it. The rhythm method doesn't work and his religion won't let her take birth control pills. There's no 'welfare' system to speak of, they're stuck in this never-ending cycle of intercourse as his only means of pleasure, which is tantamount to rape if you look at it logically. It just baffles me...no, it makes me angry that you don't recommend abortion to your clients as a viable option for helping them get out of this...this quagmire of poverty."

"So, you're saying that besides it being illegal to do abortions in Mexico, and besides the fact that the only places to get abortions locally are filthy butcheries, I should somehow find a way to do abortions? Look, if the mother's life was in imminent physical danger, I would get them to Mexico City where there are women's clinics that offer safe abortions. But that's not what's bothering you, is it?"

"You know what bothers me, perhaps even more than this family's plight? What bugs me most is your inflexibility. You say, 'I don't support abortions' and that's it. No compromise, no 'consider the alternatives,' no possibility that you might be wrong. I'm having a hard time understanding how you, being the penultimate of compassion, can take such an insensitive, illogical, heartless stance when it comes to abortion. It just *baffles* me." He took a long drink of soda and threw his napkin on the table. "There, I've said what has been on my mind all morning. I'm sorry if I've offended you. It just *baffles* me why you think like you do." John paused, shaking his head. "Now I notice every itch," he said, scratching his head. "Happens every time."

Pam smiled. She knew the feeling.

Familiar with John's upbringing, Pam could understand why he disagreed so vehemently with her concerning abortion. John's parents, Pam learned, were some of the few evangelical Christians who had been involved in human rights issues since college. They had been in the original group of 600 in the Selma-to-Montgomery march in 1965. Pam's parents, on the other hand, had expressed their compassion in different ways, being Christian missionaries in Africa where Pam grew up.

"So, what is it you want to hear from me? That I've changed my interpretation of Scripture? That I've decided two wrongs *do* make a right? That I need to invite Planned Parenthood down for a seminar? That after careful study I've come to the conclusion that there's no such thing as the sanctity of human life, that life doesn't begin at conception, that a woman's right over her body justifies murdering a fetus? Is this what you want to hear from me?"

John, looking down at the table, shook his head. "I don't know what I want to hear. I'm just frustrated. I understand *where* you're coming from, but I can't agree at all where you've landed. I respect you for it, and I respect the fact that you're not willing to compromise your principles." He paused, twirling his fork in his hand. "It just seems that the most loving thing to do, once these poor people get in these pitiful situations, is to help them out of their mess. They just keep digging themselves deeper and deeper into a bottomless pit. I don't think abortion is the only answer...not by any means. I don't believe in late-term abortions and I don't agree with a woman who chooses to have an abortion simply because having a baby is going to inconvenience her. But no matter what you say," he continued, pointing his fork at Pam, "a woman ought to have the right to choose *not* to have a baby if she has no means to care for it. In that case, she has a moral and ethical responsibility *not* to bring another child into a world of utter misery. If she *really* loved that child, she *wouldn't* have it. No, abortion is not the panacea for solving the world's problems. I just think it's one piece of the pie to help these folks out of their poverty...," he paused, taking a deep breath, and, as an after-thought, inserting, "...not to mention girls like Maria Gomez, the thirteen-year-old mother who dropped out of school in shame because her uncle raped her."

"I know," Pam said, "I know." She wanted to make sure he'd finished his diatribe. "I understand that you read the Bible a little different than I do, and I know you feel just as strongly about your position as I do mine. What I love about you is that your interpretation of Scripture—though I might not agree—stems from compassion. You're a well of compassion, John, and you are the perfect example of Christ's instruction to love one another. That's why you're here in Mexico and not in Orange County driving an SUV and surfing every weekend. It's also why I have every respect in the world for you."

Tears swelled up in John's eyes. He was frustrated with Pam, but he needed to hear her words. She reached across and placed her hand on his. He reciprocated by squeezing hers. "I'm sorry," he said. "My dad used to cry when he watched the news!"

Nothing more was said until their meal came. By that time, John had composed himself and the discussion was over. No more talk about abortion, and nothing changed in their beliefs.

"Feel better?" Pam queried.

"Yeah, I feel better. Thanks for letting me get that off my chest. I'll pray."

John and Pam lowered their heads and said grace before they ate, still holding hands.

"So," Pam said after she had finished half her blackened tilapia, "are you picking up the kids after school or am I?"

*Chapter Six*

# "To Be Truthful with You..." (Love and Biblical Truth)

*"Sanctify them in the truth; Your word is truth."*
John 17:17

### Where Is Truth? The World Wonders...

The largest naval battle in history occurred in World War II. The Allies had just established a beachhead on the island of Leyte in the Philippines. The central Philippines were of strategic importance both to the Allies and to the Japanese. Due to some clever deception on the part of the Japanese and miscommunication on the part of the Allies, Admiral "Bull" Halsey, assigned to protect the landing force with his Task Force 34, left the scene in pursuit of a decoy fleet of Japanese aircraft carriers. A contingent of Japanese battleships and cruisers, thought to be already withdrawn from the battle, re-engaged the now vulnerable Allied landing force called Taffy 3. Frantic communications for help went out to Halsey who was slow to respond. Finally, a communication directly from Halsey's senior, Admiral Chester Nimitz, got his attention. It read, "Where is Task Force 34? The world wonders."[1]

In the Christian community, the same might be said these days about truth. Where is truth? The world wonders.

In an insightful article in *Foundations Magazine* titled "Truth Is Stranger Than It Used to Be," Michael McKinney states it this way.

*Beginning in the 1970's, it became evident that we had lost the language of truth. Yet, human beings seek stability. Consequently, this post-modern society has retreated to the only thing we really can know—our own feelings. A self-defeating position at best. Enamored by our own feelings, we want contradictory things. We are lost but we don't want anyone to show us the way. We want justice but we don't want judgments. We want results but we don't want discipline. We want love but we are turned inward. We want tolerance but we don't like differences. We want unity but we want to be left alone. We want solutions but nothing is absolute. We don't even know how to know what we know.[2]*

As stated in the preface, much has been written by superb authors about the historical accuracy and authenticity of the Bible, the truth of Christian theology and the veracity of a biblical worldview. A polemic of biblical truth is beyond the purpose of this book. Moreover, this book assumes that the Bible is the only source of spiritual truth, as offensive as that may be to the tyrants of tolerance or those enamored by ethical relativism. But this is certain: if a person's Christianity is not founded purely on the word of God, that person will become a different kind of Christian, and eventually, one hardly distinguishable from one who is not a Christian. The source of truth directly affects one's definition and perception of love.

Let's consider an illustration. Suppose you desire to bake a cake for yourself. You go to the store and pick out what appears to be the perfect cake mix. But as you're walking down the aisles, you notice many other interesting food items in brightly colored boxes. Based on what looks good to you rather than what the recipe calls for, you begin picking up one item after another to mix into your cake, simply based on what sounds good or what looks good. When you arrive home and begin mixing your cake, you start adding the other ingredients you thought would go with it: paprika, olives, onions, horseradish, flavored coffee, garlic salt, cloves, mushroom soup and canned tuna. You mix it all together, bake it, take it out of the oven and admire your beautiful cake. Now you have your cake, but it's highly unlikely you'll eat much of it. Why? Because you failed to follow the recipe and mixed into the cake items never intended to be part of the mix. It may look like a cake, but in reality, it's not something you'd want to offer others.

So it is with truth. Failure to follow the recipe of God's word directly affects what kind of Christian is produced.

The premise of this book, therefore, is that love must be rightly defined. Without the recipe of biblical truth, love will turn out to be something other than what God intended. Love must be rightly defined because its true meaning is narrowly defined by the same source from which comes the truth. The general revelation of love is incomplete. *Love, to be rightly defined by the truth, requires specific revelation, and that revelation, or recipe as it were, is the word of God alone.* Love, if not rightly defined, becomes anything anyone wants it to be. Apart from the special revelation of the biblical truth, love becomes distorted, an aberration of what God intended love to be. Love requires truth to establish its limits and boundaries, to know when and under what circumstances it must be practiced, and how relationships are developed. Therefore, in the end, truth trumps love. The only absolute source for that truth is the word of God, and therefore the only absolute source for knowing love.

## Truth and Love — They Are Not Mutually Exclusive

When it comes to the relationship between love and truth, one need look no further than Ephesians 4:11-16:

> *And (God) gave some as apostles, and some as prophets, and some as evangelists, and some as pastors and teachers, for the equipping of the saints for the work of service, to the building up of the body of Christ; until we all attain to the unity of the faith, and of the knowledge of the Son of God, to a mature man, to the measure of the stature which belongs to the fullness of Christ.*

*As a result, we are no longer to be children, tossed here and there by waves and carried about by every wind of doctrine, by the trickery of men, by craftiness and deceitful scheming; but speaking the truth in love, we are to grow up in all aspects into Him who is the head, even Christ, from whom the whole body, being fitted and held together by what every joint supplies, according to the proper working of each individual part, causes the growth of the body for the building up of itself in love.*

Of the many principles that can be gleaned from this passage, here are a few:

- ➢ Absolute truth comes only through the apostles and the prophets (cf. Eph. 2:20) and is handed down through evangelists and pastor-teachers. That means that the only reliable source for spiritual truth is the Bible.
- ➢ The absolutes of biblical truth open the door for experiencing the fullness of Christ (cf. John 14:6).
- ➢ Truth is the essential equipping tool for faith, unity and spiritual knowledge. Truth is essential to Christian maturity and protects the believer from being led astray into believing what is not true, or failing to believe what is true.
- ➢ Truth defines, limits and establishes the boundaries of love; that is, without truth, love is open to individual interpretation and expression, and most often resorts to personal feelings. Therefore, truth is essential to understanding the *agape* love that is communicated in the Bible.
- ➢ Without love, truth is sterile and its delivery ineffective. Therefore, truth must not be delivered without love, and combined with love is essential to spiritual growth and maturity.
- ➢ The primary manifestation of spiritual maturity and a healthy life is love, love that is biblically defined.
- ➢ Above all, truth trumps love, but love is what the truth is all about.

## When Truth Trumps Love

The New Testament is full of examples when an overlying truth trumps love. It is not that love was not present. In most cases, however, the love was poorly defined.

In the Gospel of Matthew, Jesus asks his disciples who the people think he is.

*And they said, "Some say John the Baptist; and others, Elijah; but still others, Jeremiah, or one of the prophets."*

*He said to them, "But who do you say that I am?"*

*Simon Peter answered, "You are the Christ, the Son of the living God."*

*And Jesus said to him, "Blessed are you, Simon Barjona, because flesh and blood did not reveal this to you, but My Father who is in heaven."* (Matthew 16:14-17)

So far so good. Peter has been blessed by God to have his eyes opened spiritually to see the truth that Jesus the teacher and miracle worker is the Messiah, the Christ, the Son of God. However, Peter falls into a love trap. Jesus continues by informing the disciples of his imminent suffering.

*...He (the Son of Man) must go to Jerusalem, and suffer many things from the elders and chief priests and scribes, and be killed, and be raised up on the third day.* (Matthew 16:21)

Peter, no doubt desiring to protect Jesus from such a fate, pulls him aside and rebukes him for making such a statement: "God forbid it, Lord! This shall never happen to You."

There can be no doubt that Peter is motivated by at least some degree of love and caring. He does not desire to see his master suffer. He has placed all his hopes in the One who will establish his glory on earth and bring peace to humanity. He knows there have been threats against Jesus' life, and he is worried about his well-being. There is no doubt that Peter loves his Lord, loves the Lord's ministry, and loves being around him. His rebuke seems like the loving thing to do.

However, Jesus did not see these as words of love; rather, as words of temptation.

> *But He turned and said to Peter, "Get behind Me, Satan! You are a stumbling block to Me; for you are not setting your mind on God's interests, but man's."* (Matthew 16:23)

This is a stunning statement to Peter and the rest of the disciples. "Satan"? According to situation ethics, Peter said and did the most loving thing. Most likely, if Joseph Fletcher, you or I had been there we would have said something similar. It seemed like the most loving thing to do. Peter was attempting to take his leader out of harm's way. There was one major problem that Peter could not see, however: the truth that Jesus had to suffer, be crucified and rise from the dead in order to save mankind from sin. The truth was that God had a bigger plan. The truth was that suffering goes hand-in-hand with being a follower of Jesus the Messiah. The truth was that man's sin must first be addressed before he can experience God's glory. In this case, a greater love was at work, a love that could be grasped only through special revelation. The truth involved God's love for the world. Had Peter been able to grasp the truth of God's love, God's plan and the need to save humanity from sin, he would not have said what he said. Therefore, in the end, what seemed like the most loving thing to do is trumped by truth. Peter's love needed definition, boundaries and limitations, and only truth revealed through Jesus Christ could provide that.

After Pentecost, Peter and the apostles eventually experienced the truth about suffering when they were jailed by the High Priest and the Council for preaching that Jesus was the Christ.

> *...After calling the apostles in, they flogged them and ordered them not to speak in the name of Jesus, and then released*

**them. So they went on their way from the presence of the Council, rejoicing that they had been considered worthy to suffer shame for His name.** (Acts 5:40-41)

Therefore, love, without being guided, directed and defined by truth, is incomplete and will be misapplied, as Peter did when he rebuked Jesus.

However, there is an odd twist to the principle that "truth trumps love," for truth without love is equally incomplete. That is because biblical truth always points to biblical love.

## Biblical Truth Is All about Biblical Love

Although Pharisees often receive a bad rap from Christian theologians and preachers, many were no doubt sincere, godly and well-intentioned men (e.g., Nicodemus, John 3:1-15). Some Pharisees became Christians after Pentecost (Acts 15:5).

Pharisaism began sometime after the return of the Jewish exiles from Babylon some five hundred years before Christ. Their role in Israel's society was to ensure that the idolatry which resulted in the destruction of Judah would never again destroy Israel. Because much of the idolatry was the result of intermingling and intermarriage with Gentiles, the Pharisees were raised up as guardians of the Hebrew culture. Pharisees were separatists; that is, their job was to keep the people separated from the Gentile world. Living in a theocracy, Pharisees, along with scribes, became experts on the Law. Pharisees were the people's priests, and it was their responsibility to see that the Israelites learned and kept the laws of Moses and the traditions of the elders. Enforcement of Mosaic Law and the traditions of the elders was crucial to maintaining the purity of Israel. In short, the Pharisees regarded themselves as truth specialists; that is, truth as they interpreted it through the laws of Moses and the traditions of the elders. That, of course, was the problem. The Law, as a source of truth, was incomplete, often resulting in disassociation from love. The Pharisees and the scribes were unable to see and unwilling to accept that underlying the entire Law was the principle of *agape* love.

Here is an example from Luke's Gospel.

*And He was teaching in one of the synagogues on the Sabbath. And there was a woman who for eighteen years had had a sickness caused by a spirit; and she was bent double, and could not straighten up at all. When Jesus saw her, He called her over and said to her, "Woman, you are freed from the sickness." And He laid hands on her; and immediately she was made erect again and began glorifying God.*

*But the synagogue official, indignant because Jesus had healed on the Sabbath, began saying to the crowd in response, "There are six days in which work should be done; so come during them and get healed, and not on the Sabbath day."*

*But the Lord answered him and said, "You hypocrites, does not each of you on the Sabbath untie his ox or his donkey from the stall and lead him away to water him? And this woman, a daughter of Abraham as she is, whom Satan has bound for eighteen long years, should she not have been released from this bond on the Sabbath day?"* (Luke 13:10-16)

It is interesting to note here that the synagogue official quotes directly from the Torah. He is quoting part of the fourth commandment concerning the Sabbath. He is literally quoting God's truth. Failing to understand that the purpose of the Law is to experience and express biblical love, he has chosen instead to interpret and apply the truth in a manner void of love. The official believes he is defending the principle of loving God. He fails to understand that showing love for God cannot be separated from loving "your neighbor as yourself." The official has failed to see the relationship between Law and love, and has fallen into the trap of honoring the first and foremost commandment at the expense of the second. Therefore, he makes the erroneous application that the love Jesus expresses toward this woman is of no value. This incident is a classic example of the misapplication of truth because God's truth was interpreted in the absence of God's love.

Truth, therefore, cannot be void of love. There is no such thing as biblical truth apart from biblical love. Truth without love as its foundation is incomplete truth. The scribes and Pharisees, who prided themselves on being experts of the truth, were not truth experts at all. They were terribly deceived. Why?

*To experience and express God's love is what biblical truth is all about. Biblical truth always points to love.*

Evangelicals, like the synagogue official above, can easily fall into this trap. Many conservative evangelicals are perceived by some as insensitive and uncaring. That is because their knowledge of the truth is incomplete. Whereas evangelicals may have truth when it comes to theology proper, Christology, salvation and justification, we evangelicals can be woefully ignorant when it comes to the truth about love. All biblical truth is designed to lead to God's love. We have missed the mark when it comes to understanding that love is what the truth is all about. Instead of "speaking the truth in love," we evangelicals often fall into the trap of speaking the truth in judgment. It is one thing to stand boldly for the truth. It is quite another to stand coldly for the truth.

## When Love and Biblical Truth Collide

In an ideal world, there would be no conflict between truth and love. Truth and love would exist in perfect harmony in the same manner the Godhead exists in perfect unity. Perfect truth and perfect love would co-exist without tension or conflict. But we do not live in an ideal world, nor shall we until the millennium. As the apostle Paul stated in 1 Corinthians 13:12, "For now we see in a mirror dimly...." Instead, we live in a fallen world where neither truth nor love is completely understood or appropriated. There are many times, therefore, when a stand for the truth collides with what others believe is a call for compassion. Regarding social issues, this tension often plays out in political positions generally described as conservative and liberal. Although evangelicals tend to have a conservative outlook, the liberal base tends to attract Christians from mainline denominations, minorities, and those who are Christians in name only. In the United States, evangelicals have typically aligned themselves politically with the Republican Party, which is perceived as more conservative than the Democratic Party. That is because the Republican political platform tends to favor a conservative agenda. Democrats, from an evangelical perspective, represent a liberal agenda. Because these respective platforms go far beyond some of the social issues addressed in Book 2 (e.g., the platforms include foreign policy, the economy, environmental issues), discussion will be generally limited to just a few issues that point out the differences.

I believe the tension between truth and love is often at the heart of such social battlegrounds as abortion, stem-cell research and euthanasia. Most liberal and conservative Christians alike are motivated by some degree of compassion, caring and empathy. Each side has a different starting point, however. Each has differing values. Each believes it holds the best interpretation of the truth, and each believes it is acting out of love. Few Christians consider the other's political stance truly evil; that is, justifying or acquiescing to the destruction of human life in a Third Reich or serial killer sort of way. From the perspective of Christian liberals, Christian conservatives appear to be more interested in truth issues than love issues. They see conservatives as caring more for themselves and their values than for their fellow man. From a conservative perspective, liberal Christians do not appear to be interested in truth issues. Conservative Christians are motivated by a genuine concern that society has lost its grasp on Judeo-Christian values, such as the sanctity of human life. Conservatives are motivated by caring about the truth, for once one has lost a grasp of absolute truth relativism sets in, as in the case in modern American society were the majority of people, including people who identify themselves as born-again Christians, believe there is no such thing as absolute moral truth.[3]

One example where truth and love collide is the issue of stem-cell research. Evangelicals believe that life begins at conception. Based on the principle of the sanctity of human life, any willful, purposeful destruction of the fertilized egg can be considered no different from murder; it is, in their eyes, akin to murdering a human being, regardless of purpose or good intention. From their perspective, it is the same as willfully killing someone to harvest his or her organs. The most loving thing to do is to protect the rights of the unborn. The end does not justify the means.

Political liberals and liberal Christians see the opposite as true. In this case, the end *does* justify the means. Some may argue truth issues; does, in fact, life really begin at conception if it is merely an egg without will, feeling or emotions? Others would argue love issues, that the most loving act is to do everything possible to help those suffering from diseases such as Parkinson's or diabetes. It is simply a matter of sacrificing some cells that have not begun to emerge into human form for the sake of helping a living and breathing human being. Those who actually have the disease or have been close enough to see someone such as a family member suffer from the disease, tend to fall on the side of doing what appears to be the most loving thing; that is, endorsing stem-cell research. The closer one comes to the problem, the greater the stakes.

Like many controversial social issues, it is a case where one side, believing it has a handle on the truth, looks at the other side and scratches its head. One side asks, "How can they not see that sacrificing a human being (i.e., human embryo) is wrong?" The other side scratches its head and wonders, "How can they not care about those dying from incurable diseases?" Both sides believe they own the truth, and both sides believe they are acting in the best interest of love.

In a culture increasingly leaning toward ethical relativism, conservative Christians are correct in their concern over truth issues. What concerns the truly born-again Christian is that the love promoted by liberal Christians is poorly defined. And that is true. Liberals tend to avoid absolutes—that is what makes them liberals. Avoiding absolutes includes avoiding biblical absolutes, which is the source of all truth. Therefore, without absolute truth, love is not absolutely defined. Love becomes whatever the individual wants it to be, and more often than not, that love turns out to be self-serving.

Nevertheless, liberal Christians and social progressives are also correct in their observation that conservative Christians and evangelicals in particular appear more concerned with truth and absolutes than with love. There exists an enormous credibility gap between the evangelical's message and the evangelical's actions. From a liberal's perspective, if evangelicals were as concerned about love issues as much as they are about truth issues, the greater bulk of their financial resources would be spent on humanitarian needs rather than megachurches, media empires and an affluent lifestyle that is indistinguishable from that of a non-Christian or secularist.

This credibility gap is often fueled by the conservative media. More so perhaps than from the liberal media or entertainment industry, the credibility gap is only widened by conservative broadcasters. Conservative talk-show hosts, authors or commentators oftentimes come across as angry, argumentative, arrogant, sarcastic, mean-spirited, conceited, out of touch with those in need, insensitive, and concerned more about power and control than about love and compassion. If the conservative commentator promotes Christian values, the liberal will logically link the two, which further cripples the Christian message and widens the credibility gap.

From the viewpoint of liberal Christians, conservative evangelicals have often appeared cold and heartless in their proclamation and defense of the Bible and its values. A case in point involves the actions of Westboro Baptist Church in Topeka, Kansas. Led by Pastor Fred Phelps, the church members, identifying themselves as evangelical Christians, have made it their cause to appear at the funerals of American soldiers who had been killed in Iraq. They do not come to mourn, but rather to celebrate. Within earshot of the grieving families, WBC members celebrate the death of the soldier. They proclaim it is a sign of God's judgment on the sins of America, specifically homosexuality. Their websites *godhatesamerica.com* and *godhatesfags.com* say it all. This aberrant love for biblical truth may be seen as an extremist group by most evangelicals, but Phelps and his followers remain quite visible to the non-discerning public eye.

Those representing the liberal arm of Christianity, on the other hand, appear to the evangelical to be ignoring biblical truth issues in their efforts at social reform. (Use of the word "appear" is important. Appearance does not necessarily equate to fact. "Appear" is chosen because of the way each is portrayed by their respective camps.) For example, evangelicals assert that it is a failure to acknowledge biblical truth that results in a liberal's stance, for example, on abortion; that is, that life begins at conception and to destroy that life is tantamount to murder. Liberals respond, however, by defending a woman's right to choose. To deny a woman that right, particularly in the case of rape, incest or poverty, is to demonstrate a profound lack of love, ignoring the biblical teaching that we are to love one another. In their narrow view of the Bible, the liberals say, evangelicals lack caring and compassion for the disadvantaged. Although evangelicals see themselves as the standard-bearers of biblical truth and family values, liberals view themselves as crusaders and advocates for social justice. What's wrong with this picture?

The source of the credibility gap between evangelicals and their message is one of love. With few exceptions, evangelicals have consistently built empires for themselves at the expense of equally building empires for addressing the needs of the poor. They have taken Jesus' statement, "The poor you have with you always" (Matt. 26:11) and used it to justify an affluent lifestyle that is indistinguishable from secular America or the lifestyle of liberals.

Another obvious example of the tension between the two views surfaces in the abortion issue. From a liberal or liberal Christian's perspective, evangelicals have made only token attempts to provide alternatives to abortion. For example, I recently heard of a church that built an enormous family life center, including gyms, lap pools, juice bars, game rooms for kids, spas and hot tubs. Not only did they completely deplete the building fund that was supposed to be sufficient, but they had to borrow $14 million to complete the job. Can you imagine a church using its building fund and then taking out a $14 million loan to fund an adoption agency, a women's shelter or a pregnancy counseling center for a large area, rather than funding just a telephone hotline? The concern here is that the church seems more concerned about keeping its members in than sending them out. The evangelical Christian may not consider that a fair analogy because what is important to the evangelical is evangelism; that is, proclaiming the message of salvation. However, the liberal will justifiably ask, "What's the real message you're sending?" The liberal's or non-Christian's point is this: "If you say you are a Christian and have the truth, why are you devoting so much of your energy and money on yourself and ignoring the needs of the poor and oppressed around you?"

Granted, there are a few Christian adoption agencies, women's shelters, pregnancy counseling centers and telephone hotlines, but the effort and money put forth for social concerns is paltry when compared to the money we evangelicals spend on our infrastructure and ourselves. Yet even that pales in comparison to the lifestyle and spending habits of those who call themselves born-again Christians. One need only compare the amount of money spent by Christians through tithing compared to that spent on personal entertainment.[4]

The recent evangelical phenomenon of the megachurch has done little to convince liberals that Christians back up their message with action. (A megachurch is defined as having more than 2,000 members.) Those behind the megachurch movement justify the phenomenon based on, once again, the message. The megachurch, and all that it represents, is one method of contextualizing with the culture. Megachurch methods, even employed at the small church level, are necessary to identify and communicate effectively with the culture. After all, it is the message that is important, not the manner in which it is presented. With this kind of centralized growth and huge impact on the Christian community, one would think it would translate into a greater impact on social concerns, such as discovering alternative ways to deal with abortion. It would include infiltrating every aspect of society where there is poverty, illiteracy, crime and gang warfare, AIDS, concern for the environment, drug dealers, prostitution and so on. Unfortunately, the most visible evangelicals lead or belong to megachurches that are known more for their cutting-edge media presentations than their community outreach. Whether evangelicals like it or not, or whether it is even true or not, the problem lies in perception. Although Christians may be identified by the stickers on their windshields, liberals are justified in holding evangelicals accountable for being known rather by their love.

That is not to say that all churches fail to have as a part of their ministry pregnancy counseling hotlines, feeding programs, prison ministries and so forth. More and more humanitarian ministry is taking place behind the scenes in evangelical America. In the last decade, a number of mission organizations have focused their efforts on humanitarian needs around the world.[5] However, in spite of recent efforts to refocus ministry to addressing human needs, the weight of ministry effort and financial underwriting in churches is a pittance compared to what they put into themselves, particularly among white, middle-class evangelicals. That includes pastoral staff overhead. The world, therefore, perceives Christians as hypocritical. In spite of our heart-felt worship songs, evangelical priorities often do little to convince the world that "They'll know we are Christians by our love...."[6]

An acquaintance of mine who is pro-choice was once discussing with me her view on the abortion issue. She shared that one time she got into a debate with an evangelical co-worker over abortion. My friend told her co-worker, "You go out and adopt a baby of parents who can't take care of it, and I'll listen to you." Later she was surprised to hear that her evangelical co-worker decided to "walk her talk and became a foster parent to children of drug addicts." No, it did not change my friend's view on abortion, but it did change her view about her friend and her belief system. "I was impressed. She put her money where her mouth was."

On the other side of the coin, liberal Christians have been forced to side more with the liberal political ranks than their brothers and sisters in Christ. Frankly speaking, liberal Christians and social progressives can hardly be differentiated. That is because liberal Christians have, in perhaps an ironic way, thrown out the baby with the bath water. Although under the impression they are acting in love to guarantee a woman's right to choose or to support gay rights, they have ignored biblical truths and inadvertently supported causes they may not even believe in. For example, a liberal Christian may feel that a woman should have the right to have an abortion in the case of rape or incest. However, she finds herself defending all pro-choice causes, inadvertently supporting those who feel a woman has the right to a late-term abortion, simply because to end one freedom of choice would be considered tantamount to ending all choice. The liberal Christian will therefore gravitate toward churches (usually mainline denominations) where abortion is rarely addressed from the pulpit in favor of an uninspiring homily. The liberal Christian has drawn conclusions and taken positions in the name of love, and ignored issues of truth. For those who continue to attend conservative evangelical churches, especially megachurches where personal accountability and belief systems are impossible to monitor, I suspect there are hundreds if not thousands of closet liberals when it comes to issues of abortion, homosexuality, stem-cell research and euthanasia. Moreover, of course, the number of Catholic women who quietly support pro-choice causes might give the Pope a seizure.

Here is the sum of the matter: Truth without love is perceived as uncaring and compassionless. Love without truth, however, is often distorted and misdirected. Although Jesus clearly states that it's truth, not love, that sets us free, he also clearly states, "love one another," not "truth one another" to death. In fact, love has never saved anyone; it's biblical truth that saves us from our sins. However, truth spoken without love is rarely listened to. And, although it is truth that sets us free and not love, the whole purpose of being set free is to love. Truth sets us free so that we may experience and express God's love. Love, therefore, is what the truth is all about, and it is to be the Christian's love that points the world to where lies the truth.

Is it possible, therefore, that evangelicals could learn from liberal Christians when it comes to social concerns, and is it possible that liberal Christians could learn from the evangelicals when it comes to accepting biblical truth? Though biblical truth and love will always collide in this age, at least there may be some civility toward one another in the name of Christ.

## Where Is Love? The World Wonders...

If the world is looking for love, it must look to those who claim to have the truth about it. If evangelical Christians claim to have the truth about love, the world must see absolute consistency between the truth evangelicals revere and the love they are expected to show. Christians are expected to live the love they proclaim. It is up to the Christian to help the world see the difference between biblical love and worldly, expedient love. Although liberal Christians wave the flag of compassion for the poor, it is up to the evangelical to lead the way in actually addressing the need.

---

1.  The phrase "The world wonders" was not actually sent from Nimitz. It was a security padding added by a Navy radioman to indicate the message was completed. For unknown reasons, the radioman receiving the message left the phrase in and Halsey assumed the words were Nimitz',

which he took as criticism. Barrett Hillman, "William Bull Halsey: Legendary World War II Admiral," *historynet.com: www.historynet.com/magazines/world_war_2/7890117.*

2.  Michael McKinney, "Truth Is Stranger Than It Used to Be," *Foundations Magazine*: *www.foundationsmag.com* (Fall, 2006). Accessed July 13, 2007.

3.  George Barna, "Most Adults Feel Accepted by God, But Lack a Biblical Worldview," The Barna Group: *www.barna.org/FlexPage.aspx?Page=BarnaUpdate&BarnaUpdateID=214* (August 9, 2005). Accessed July 9, 2007.

4.  Generous Giving, generousgiving.org:*www.generousgiving.org/page.asp?sec=4&page=311*

5.  E.g., the evangelical mission organization "Samaritan's Purse® International Relief." Its mission statement reads: "Samaritan's Purse is a nondenominational evangelical Christian organization providing spiritual and physical aid to hurting people around the world. Since 1970, Samaritan's Purse has helped meet needs of people who are victims of war, poverty, natural disasters, disease, and famine with the purpose of sharing God's love through His Son, Jesus Christ. The organization serves the Church worldwide to promote the Gospel of the Lord Jesus Christ." Its website can be found at http://samaritanspurse.org.

6.  Peter Scholtes, "They'll Know We Are Christians (by Our Love)." (Los Angeles, CA: F.E.L. Publications, 1966).

*Bill Walthall*

# Vignette for Chapter Seven

# *"Twenty Years and Counting"*

"Oh, yes," Pastor Brubaker responded to the strikingly pretty journalist sitting in his office. "Steven VanderVeer. I know him well. He's a member of our church, you know."

"That's what I understand. Does he ever come to church?"

"Well, that's an interesting question. It's more like the church goes to him."

"How long has it been like that?"

"Oh...I'd say...twenty years and counting."

Terri Jacobson—freelance journalist. Her friends called her "TJ the Grinder." She began grinding out magazine articles to help pay her way through college and, being a prolific writer, she had never stopped. "I move around too much to settle down," she told people. "I like working at my own pace on my own schedule, doing what I want when I want." On this occasion, she was working on a story for *Guidepost*. Most of the time she did her own photographic work; at other times she called on her friend Alex, a free-lance photographer.

"Because there *are* no good men," Terri responded when someone asked her why she hadn't married. Everyone thought she was joking, but the reality was that she meant every word of it. She had known many men, but things had never turned out well. They either wanted to kiss and run, control her life, make her submit to *their* professional ambitions, or tie her down to the mommy track. That was not her. Besides, she had never met a man that came close to measuring up. "I *have* met men I liked, and I've met men I admired," she countered, "but I've never met a man I truly respected." Other than Alex who was gay, men friends didn't last long in Terri's life. Therefore, the other meaning of "Grinder."

"Would he mind my visiting?" she asked Pastor Brubaker.

"That shouldn't be a problem. He welcomes everyone. Just call ahead and let him know you're coming."

The source for her story came by word of mouth from a friend of a friend of a friend. Apparently, this VanderVeer fellow had been the caretaker of his semicomatose wife for over twenty years. He had never considered placing her in an institution or nursing home. He took care of her himself, and with the help of neighbors, family members and members of the church, he occasionally took time off for a vacation. He had sustained himself by working out of his house. Ironically, he, too, was a writer, but more into the mystery genre.

"I'm Terri," she said, reaching to shake his hand. "Everyone calls me TJ."

"Come in, Terri. Please sit down and make yourself comfortable."

To say the least, TJ was shocked. She had expected to find a worn-out man in his seventies or eighties with gray hair and trifocals. Instead, she found herself sitting across from a trim, handsome man who could not have been more than a couple of years older than herself. He was obviously physically fit, almost buff. He didn't at all have the haggard look she expected. She almost asked, "Are you Steven VanderVeer or are you his son?" She decided to keep her mouth shut and let things play out.

The house had a comfortable early American décor. The furniture was dusted, clean, and she picked up a hint of lemon Old English polish. The wood-finish floor was original. Against the wall was a hutch filled with china and crystal glasses of all shapes and sizes.

"You have a very comfortable place here," she said, looking around and noticing that there wasn't a hint of typical nursing home odors. "Do you mind if I tape our interview?"

"Of course not. Coffee?" Steven asked, holding up two mugs.

"Yes, please."

"Caf or decaf?"

"Either is fine."

"I'll give you the real stuff. Cream? Sugar?"

"Sweetener if you have it."

"Take your pick," he said, opening a little jar stuffed with three types of artificial sweetener.

"Thank you. This is all very nice. It's been awhile since I've seen a hutch that large."

"All hand-me-downs. My mother's stuff. I only buy what plugs in. But I like to use the nice stuff now and then, especially when I have dinner parties."

"Dinner parties?"

"Oh, you know. Special occasions, church events, birthdays, things like that. It's a chance to break out the sterling which I hate polishing but everyone seems to enjoy."

Steven sat back in his chair and observed his guest carefully. "So," he said, semi-sizing her up, "you're here to do a story. What about?"

"You...and your wife, of course."

"There's not much to tell. We got married. She was twenty, I was twenty-one. We had a great six months together. Then the accident."

"What happened? Do you mind me asking?"

"She was coming home from work and hit some black ice. Skidded off the road, hit a guardrail that deployed her air bag, but then kept on skidding and hit a tree head-on. By that time, the air bag had deflated. Hit her head hard against the window. Was in ICU for two months, then rehab for six. At least she woke up. I can look into her eyes now. But that was it. She was never functional again. That was twenty years ago."

Steven was well rehearsed in his story. It was obvious he'd shared it many times. "And that's your story."

"No," TJ interrupted. "That's not my story. *You're* my story."

"Well, what can I say? When you take vows, you take vows. I promised to love and cherish her until death parts us. So far, death hasn't parted us." Again, obviously well rehearsed.

TJ thought carefully before posing her next question. She felt she herself could be on thin ice. It was a tricky question. She tried to ask the question by making it sound more like a statement. Cautiously, "So...you've not felt the need to remarry."

He answered again as if it was pre-planned. "That's really what you want to know, isn't it?"

"I'm a little curious, of course."

"Terri, a lot of people ask me that question. Everyone wants to know why I, being relatively young, eligible and in good health haven't just put my wife away somewhere, gotten an annulment, and started my life over. Let me ask you a question."

"Fair enough."

"Have you ever really been loved? Now, I didn't ask, 'Have you ever been *in love*?' I asked, 'Have you ever *really* been loved?' I mean, truly, deeply, unconditionally loved by someone whom you love?"

For the first time during the interview, TJ felt uncomfortable. She was totally unprepared to be interviewed about her love life. "I...I'm not sure. No. I guess not. Not like what you describe."

"Exactly. That's why it's hard for someone like yourself to even conceive of my love for my wife. We knew each other two years before we got married. We were so precious to each other; we didn't do anything that would result in guilt in our relationship. We kept ourselves pure for each other and when we married, we enjoyed every minute of it. But it wasn't just the intimacy that made our marriage so wonderful. It was knowing, without a shadow of a doubt, that you were loved unconditionally by someone whom you yourself loved unconditionally. How can you not love someone who loves you that much? How can you *stop* loving someone who has loved you that much? Does that make sense to you?"

"I suppose it makes sense."

"Terri, that kind of love never fades. Sure, we don't have pleasure together any more, but the love is still there. It's a different kind of pleasure. It's actually much stronger and more lasting than before. In fact, I have to say that after twenty years I love her more than I did in the beginning. It's more alive now than it was twenty years ago. Did you know that the more you sacrifice for someone the more you love them?"

Seeing no need to be cautious any further, "Steven, how do you know she still loves you? What I mean is...can she express her love? Can she speak? Does she even know you're around? Is she aware enough of her surroundings to respond to your love?"

"You don't get it, do you?"

"What don't I get?"

"Whether she responds to my love or not isn't the issue. When she had her accident, she loved me and I loved her and that's the way it's always been and that's the way it always will be. Love isn't love if it doesn't last forever."

For this, TJ had no answer. After a pause, "May I see... I mean, meet... your wife?"

"Of course. She's in the master bedroom."

As they advanced down the hallway and approached the bedroom, TJ began to hear the sounds of the humidifier for her supplemental oxygen. Having avoided hospitals at all cost, TJ felt anything but comfortable.

"I'm sorry, but I didn't even ask your wife's name."

"It's Elisabeth. That's with an 's.'"

Steven walked over to Elisabeth, brushed her hair back gently, and kissed her on the cheek. Her eyes were open but her stare went nowhere. Steven reached down and kissed her again.

"Hi, sweetheart. I want you to meet a friend. Her name is Terri. She's a writer. She wants to do a story about us. Is that okay?"

What Terri heard shocked her. A low moan with awkward throat and jaw movements came out of Elisabeth's body. Her clawed arm flexed at the elbow as if in some rudimentary wave hello.

"Don't let that fool you," Steven said. "That was pure reflex. It's been determined that she is in a permanent vegetative state."

TJ came alongside the bed. She couldn't bring herself to take Elisabeth's hand and had no clue as to how to talk to her. She just stood by and observed Steven hold her and talk to her. After a while, she took pictures of Steven and Elisabeth, Steven leaning over the bed cheek-to-cheek with Elisabeth and smiling with a great grin. She then took some close-ups of Steven. Back in the living room, they chatted awhile about writing, sharing many things in common.

When the interview was over she asked, "Can I call you sometime if I have any more questions?"

"Of course. Any time. The pleasure's been all mine."

On many occasions like this one, TJ would always pick up a hint from a man that he *really* enjoyed the time spent together, and there was frequently that glint of sexual or mutual attraction. Not on this occasion. It was a clean goodbye and his eyes never drifted down.

It took her only two days to complete the article. It was an ironic title with the byline Terri Jacobson: "Yes, Terri, There *Are* Good Men."

*Bill Walthall*

*Chapter Seven*

# "Even Perfect Love Can't Please Everyone" (Love and Jesus Christ)

*"We love, because He first loved us."* (1 John 4:19)

The story of Jesus Christ is not about a beautiful life leading to death—it is about death leading to a beautiful life. The only means by which Christ's life can be appreciated, therefore, is through his death. The only means by which the death of Jesus Christ can be justified is by recognizing the love of God the Father. Therefore, the love of God and the death of Jesus Christ are intimately related. Apart from God's love, there would be no need for the death for Jesus Christ. Apart from Christ's death, the love of God could not be made fully manifest. Love is the ultimate motivation for the death of Christ, and the death of Jesus Christ is the ultimate manifestation of love. The true definition of the relationship between love and death, therefore, is found in the person of Jesus Christ.

In understanding love and Jesus Christ, we must first grasp the nature of the love of the God, for the love of the Father and the love of Jesus Christ cannot be separated.

## The Love of the Father

The apostle John states, *"...God is love"* (1 John 4:8). What does that mean? Does it mean that God is merely an abstract concept we call "love"? Does it mean that God does not really have "person," but is rather some impersonal force we describe as love? Or, does it mean that God has person, but that his nature is comprised solely of love, the other attributes, such as mercy, compassion, justice and righteousness, being merely various expressions of his love?

Throughout church history, theologians have formulated various doctrines and selected specific words to describe God, his nature and essence. Terms like communicable and non-communicable attributes are theological words used to help us conceptualize God's nature.[1] These attributes are sometimes referred to as "perfections."[2] All orthodox theologians agree with the basic doctrine of the Nicene fathers that there is one God but three persons comprising the Trinity: God the Father, God the Son, and God the Holy Spirit. (Other related terms include "Triunity," "the Godhead," or "the Triune God.") The doctrine of the Trinity preserves the explicit biblical teaching of monotheism ("The Lord our God is one Lord," Deut 6:4) and the divinity of both Jesus Christ and the Holy Spirit. Though separate and distinct in person, the members of the Godhead are identical (not similar) in essence and nature; that is, three persons, one God. (The Trinity is a mystical concept categorically found in Scripture, yet denied by some either because the word "Trinity" is not found in the New Testament or because the Trinitarian doctrine appears as a threat to monotheism. Moreover, in an attempt to explain the inexplicable, it has often resulted in heresy, even by those otherwise orthodox in their theology.) In describing what is called "the Godhead," therefore, attributes (or perfections) are used by such theologians as Charles C. Ryrie: eternal (no beginning and no end), independent (subject to no one or no thing), immutable (meaning unchanging), infinite (that is, unlimited), holy (ethically and morally perfect and transcendent), love (includes mercy and compassion), omnipotent (all-powerful), omnipresent (everywhere present), omniscient (all-knowing), simple (indivisible; not composed of parts), sovereign (supreme; the "chief Being" in the universe), righteous (which includes just), unity (one God but three persons) and truth ("includes the ideas of veracity, faithfulness and consistency").[3]

Love, therefore, is just one attribute of the Godhead. If God were only love, where would justice fit in? If God's nature was comprised only of love, how would readers of the Old Testament reconcile God's command to Joshua to annihilate entire people groups, and how would readers of the

New Testament come to grips with the wrath of God the apostle Paul writes of in the first chapter of Romans?

When John states, "...God is love," he is describing the attribute of God, the divine impetus, the driving force, the principle motivation, the relational focus, the underlying essence, the primary manner by which God relates to mankind. All interaction between God and man is based on love. Love was the primary reason God created man and woman in the first place, for God desired that his creation would be able to appreciate and participate in the love that exists among the persons of the Godhead. God's love is the principle manner through which God communicates and directs the affairs of man. Upon the Israelites, God's love is declared by Moses:

> *"...On your fathers did the Lord set His affection to love them, and He chose their descendants after them, even you above all peoples, as it is this day."* (Deut 10:15)

Note that there is no mention that the Israelites have earned God's love. To the contrary, they have not even sought God's love. Beginning with Abraham, God's love for them is a grace, not a recognition of their goodness. His love for them is unconditional, though the earthly blessings they can receive from his love are conditional. God doesn't love them because they're special—they are special because he loves them. They have neither earned nor deserved his love.

Even in the midst of Israel's disobedience, God told the prophet Jeremiah,

> *"At that time," declares the Lord, "I will be the God of all the families of Israel, and they shall be My people." Thus says the Lord, "The people who survived the sword found grace in the wilderness – Israel, when it went to find its rest." The Lord appeared to him from afar, saying, "I have loved you with an everlasting love; therefore I have drawn you with lovingkindness."* (Jeremiah 31:1-3)

Man's love for God is not what causes God to respond. It is God's love for man that ultimately draws a man or a woman to himself. It is God's love, not man's response, which ensures his perfect plan for humanity will be brought to fruition. The apostle Paul states this clearly in his letter to the church in Ephesus:

> *"But God, being rich in mercy, because of His great love with which He loved us, even when we were dead in our transgressions, made us alive together with Christ (by grace you have been saved), and raised us up with Him, and seated us with Him in the heavenly places in Christ Jesus, so that in the ages to come He might show the surpassing riches of His grace in kindness toward us in Christ Jesus."* (Ephesians 2:4-7)

In addition, it is the true understanding of who God is and his love for mankind that Jesus came to reveal.

No New Testament writer addresses God's love for humanity more directly than the apostle John.

> *"For God so loved the world, that He gave His only begotten Son, that whoever believes in Him shall not perish, but have eternal life. For God did not send His son into the world to judge the world, but that the world might be saved through Him."* (John 3:16-17)

> *"See how great a love the Father has bestowed on us, that we would be called children of God; and such we are."* (1 John 3:1)

> *"Beloved, let us love one another, for love is from God; and everyone who loves is born of God and knows God. The one who does not love does not know God, for God is love. By this the love of God was manifested in us, that God has sent His only begotten Son into the world so that we might live through Him. In this is love, not that we loved God, but that He loved us and sent His Son to be the propitiation for our*

**sins. Beloved, if God so loved us, we also ought to love one another. No one has seen God at any time; if we love one another, God abides in us, and His love is perfected in us."** (1 John 4:7-12)

All of the relational attributes of the Godhead, therefore, are based on love. Love is behind God's lovingkindness found throughout the Old Testament (Heb. *hesed*). Love is the basis for God's grace revealed in the New Testament (Grk. *charis*). Love is the impetus for God's mercy, compassion, patience, long-suffering, pity, goodness, benevolence, revelation of himself, the selection of Israel to be to be a light to the world, and his unconditional promises to them in spite of their past, present and future failings. It was God's love that established an everlasting covenant with Abraham. It was God's love that rescued the Israelites from the hand of Pharaoh and brought them into the Promised Land. It was God's love that allowed them the grandeur of Solomon's kingdom, and it was God's love that disciplined them for their unfaithfulness. Out of God's love, the Torah was given through Moses. Out of God's love, the prophets were raised up, not just for warning but also for hope. Out of God's love the seed line to the Messiah was preserved in spite of Satan's attempt to destroy from outside and from within the nation of Israel. Moreover, it was out of God's love that when the time was full, Jesus Christ was sent into the world.

Based, then, on the evidence from Scripture that God the Father and God the Son are identical in nature and essence though separate in person, each must have identical attributes. If God is love, then Christ also must be love, for without love, there would be no relationship. It was by love that God sent his Son into the world, and it was by love that his Son sent himself to the cross.

Love, therefore, is what defines the relationship between the Father and the Son, and, therefore, the Holy Spirit as well.

## The Love between the Father and the Son

The introduction of Jesus as the Son of God by John the Baptist introduces also the love relationship between God the Father and God the Son.

> *"After being baptized, Jesus came up immediately from the water; and behold, the heavens were opened, and he saw the Spirit of God descending as a dove and lighting on Him, and behold, a voice out of the heavens said, 'This is My beloved Son, in whom I am well-pleased.'"* (Matthew 3:16-17)

Again, this relationship is affirmed during Jesus' transfiguration.

> *"This is My beloved Son, with whom I am well-pleased; listen to Him!"* (Matthew 17:5)

These are two of the three incidents in the Gospels when the voice of God the Father is recorded, Jesus has plenty to say about the love relationship between himself and the Father.

> *"The Father loves the Son and has given all things into His hand."* (John 3:35)

> *"For the Father loves the Son, and shows Him all things that He Himself is doing; and the Father will show Him greater works than these, so that you will marvel."* (John 5:20)

> *"For this reason the Father loves Me, because I lay down My life so that I may take it again."* (John 10:17)

Perhaps the clearest affirmation of the Father's love for the Son is declared the night before Christ's crucifixion. In Jesus' prayer in the Garden of Gethsemane, he states:

> *"The glory which You have given Me I have given to them, that they may be one, just as We are one; I in them and You*

*in Me, that they may be perfected in unity, so that the world may know that You sent Me, and loved them, even as You have loved Me.*

*"Father, I desire that they also, whom You have given Me, be with Me where I am, so that they may see My glory which You have given Me, for You loved Me before the foundation of the world.*

*"O righteous Father, although the world has not known You, yet I have known You; and these have known that You sent Me; and I have made Your name known to them, and will make it known, so that the love with which You loved Me may be in them, and I in them."* (John 17:22-26)

The love that Jesus has for his disciples, therefore, is merely an extension of the love that exists between the Father and the Son. Christ is on the mission of recapturing for the Father what was lost in Paradise, the Garden of Eden. God intended man and woman to enjoy and participate happily in the love that exists among the persons of the Godhead. But that Paradise was lost due to sin, and mankind willfully chose to separate himself from God's love, protection and provision. Humanity's attitude that "We can do it on our own" affected every aspect of life, including relationships. From that point on, humanity had to relearn from scratch what is was to love God. It is due to the weakness of our flesh, our total depravity, that we must learn God's love even when it is against our nature to do so. Though the love of God for his creation has never ceased, man's attempts to return love to his creator always take a myriad of twists and turns, ending nowhere, hopelessly bogged down in the quagmire of self-love, quickened instead by love for the things of this world. It would take the love of Christ to show humanity the road back to God's love, and the ministry of the Holy Spirit to create in us a new nature to be able to respond. The lesson would not be without resistance on man's part and sacrifice on Christ's part, for the love of God is neither easily grasped, fully accepted nor gratefully returned.

## The Love of the Son — His Kenosis & Incarnation

How does one even begin to explain the love of Jesus Christ? It is too rich, too deep and too vast even to grasp, much less explain. Perhaps that is why it is easier sometimes to resort to feelings and emotions rather than attempt to put his love into words. Words always come up short and are never fully satisfying. It is a far better thing to experience the love of Christ rather than read about it. Nevertheless, writing of it is important to ensure that what we are experiencing is indeed the love of Christ and not some preconceived notions of our imagination, false teachings or, God forbid, Hollywood.

Jesus Christ is the ultimate manifestation of God's love revelation. He is more than just the personification of God's love. As God is love, he is love. For Christ, the mission of extending God's love into the world began at the incarnation and continues to this day. It will continue throughout all eternity, as we shall see.

A presentation on the incarnation of Christ actually begins in heaven. Under the inspiration of the Holy Spirit, Paul provides a glimpse in Philippians.

> *"Have this attitude in yourselves which was also in Christ Jesus, who, although He existed in the form of God, did not regard equality with God a thing to be grasped, but emptied Himself, taking the form of a bond-servant, and being made in the likeness of men."* (Philippians 2:5-7)

In Christology (that is, the theology of Christ), this event is called the *kenosis* based on the same Greek verb meaning, "to empty." Charles C. Ryrie sums up the definition of *kenosis* very succinctly in his *Basic Theology*:

> *"(The kenosis is) Christ's emptying Himself of retaining and exploiting His status in the Godhead and taking on Himself humanity in order to die."*[4]

Paul's statement does not mean that Christ gave up his divinity or his equality with God. It means that he willingly gave up his preincarnate state of being and condition with the Father in order to fulfill the Father's will to restore humanity to himself. Some of his attributes, such as omniscience, he voluntarily limited. Others, such as his holiness and righteousness, he retained. As one Christian hymn expresses it,

> *Thou didst leave Thy throne and Thy kingly crown when Thou camest to earth for me....*[5]

A paraphrase of Philippians 2:5-7 could go something like this:

> *"Have the same mindset in your thinking which was also in Christ Jesus, who, although existing in spirit form only in His preincarnate state, did not consider remaining in spirit form something to be selfishly retained, but gave up this preincarnate state of being and took on the form of humanity, even that of a servant, having been made in the likeness of man."*

Literally, Jesus left Paradise to muddy his feet in the quagmire of mankind.

Not only was the *kenosis* of Christ an amazing act of love, but his incarnation and his humble birth were incredible expressions of his love as well. John tells us in his Gospel, ***"And the Word became flesh, and dwelt among us, and we saw his glory, glory as of the only begotten from the Father, full of grace and truth"*** (John 1:14). In the original language of the New Testament, Greek, John uses the word *logos* to describe Jesus' preincarnate state. (Our English versions translate *logos* as "Word.") The basic meaning of *logos* in Greek is "a thought expressed," or simply "word" because words express thoughts, concepts and ideas.

John's use of *logos* is significant. John is stating with that one simple term that Jesus is the ultimate and complete expression of what God is like. That is, Jesus Christ is God expressed. Jesus is therefore the one true and divine revelation of God. To know Christ is to know God. To know God is to recognize Christ as the Son of God.

This truth is easier to understand than we may think. For example, consider the word "television." When you hear the word television, you immediately picture something...your TV! That is because the word television describes an object, something you can see, feel and hear, something you are already familiar with, something that has been "revealed" to you before. An image immediately comes to mind based on familiarity. On the other hand, consider the word "truth." What truth? Truth about what? A "truth" can refer to many things. Truth is a noun that refers to something abstract. You can say, "I have the truth," but you cannot put "truth" in a box and ship it away as a present. You can certainly see the results of truth, and you can see evidence of truth once it is put in a tangible form, but "truth" needs some means of expression, such as words.

Such is the case with *logos*. Consistent with Greek philosophy and Hebrew theology of his day, John chose a word that would capture the true concept of God expressed. We can neither see God nor touch him. All that was known about him was revealed in the Old Testament, and even then, there was some confusion. He is invisible to the naked eye, for he is spirit. Scanning the heavens will reveal only the work of his hands, but not God himself.

However, if God were to reveal himself fully...if God were to express himself in bodily form, manifested through words and actions...that form would be Jesus Christ. Jesus confirmed this by responding to Philip's request, "Lord, show us the Father, and it is enough for us." Jesus responded, ***"Have I been so long with you, and yet you have not come to know Me, Philip? He who has seen Me has seen the Father; how can you say, 'Show us the Father'?"*** (John 14:8-9) That means that the true knowledge of God comes only through Jesus. As John goes on to tell us, ***"No one has seen God at any time; the only begotten God who is in the bosom of the Father, He has explained Him"*** (John 1:18).

But isn't it odd that God would come in the form of the infant of a peasant girl? Luke informs us that his incarnation and birth were anything but worthy of his being:

*"And (Mary) gave birth to her firstborn son; and she wrapped Him in cloths, and laid Him in a manger, because there was no room for them in the inn"* (Luke 2:7)

What would cause Christ to do such a thing? That is, to leave his glorified condition with the Father, voluntarily set aside many of his divine attributes, and come to earth in the form of an infant delivered by a carpenter and his wife in a stable? The only answer would have to be love. Only a special kind of love would cause someone to make such a sacrifice, to leave every comfort for a future no more certain than an agonizing, unjust death. With full knowledge, Christ left everything heavenly in order to be born to die. That is love of the highest order. It is the definition of biblical love.

Though few earthly parallels can be found, a lovely acquaintance comes close. Once a senior vice president of one of the nation's largest banking corporations, my friend became a Christian through the influence of a co-worker. Immediately she began reading on a daily basis the Bible her friend had given her. Within months, she began questioning the course her life had taken and realized that if Christ had given up such glory to live in a meanly state and go to the cross for her sins, she ought also to do the same for him. By the end of a year, her husband had also become a believer—himself a successful corporate executive—and eventually both resigned their lucrative positions. They joined a mission organization and traded an expensive Manhattan townhouse for an apartment in a small California community. All their executive skills and talents were poured into the mission organization where their contributions cannot be measured. They left their "throne in Manhattan" for a "cave in California." They have never looked back, saying, "We wouldn't trade it for the world."

The true gravity of Christ's *kenosis*, however, cannot be grasped until we look at his ascension, which we shall examine shortly. Only then can we see how great a love the Lord has for us!

## The Love of the Son — His Earthly Ministry

Ask any pastor and he or she will immediately confess, "There's nothing more painful than rejection." Criticism, of course, goes hand in hand. The worst experience for pastors is that those who criticize, reject and eventually leave the church angry are often those in whom the pastor has invested untold hours in counseling, discipleship, visitation, encouragement and prayer. Those who are so quick to offer the praises and receive the blessings of the pastor are often the first to reject him. There is not a pastor in any church who has not experienced this kind of grief. It is a personal hurt that is frequently encountered, difficult to forgive and never forgotten.

Jesus, the Good Shepherd, was no exception. *"He came to His own, and those who were His own did not receive Him"* (John 1:11). This is an incredible statement. He who revealed God as a loving Father, preached good news to the poor and oppressed, who opened the ears of the deaf and loosened the tongues of the dumb, who healed all who came to him, who cast out demons, raised the dead, cleansed the leper and fed the multitudes was ultimately rejected and sent to the cross to die the painful death of a common criminal.

The rejection of Jesus' earthly ministry began at the top—Israel's spiritual leaders. As to his being the Messiah, those who should have been first to recognize him were first to reject him. The signs of the Messiah were clearly presented by the Old Testament prophet Isaiah.

> *"Say to those with anxious heart,*
> *'Take courage, fear not.*
> *Behold, your God will come with vengeance;*
> *The recompense of God will come,*
> *But He will save you.'*
> *Then the eyes of the blind will be opened*
> *And the ears of the deaf will be unstopped.*
> *Then the lame will leap like a deer,*
> *And the tongue of the mute will shout for joy.* (Isaiah 35:4-6)

When John the Baptist asked for confirmation from Jesus that he was the Messiah, Jesus responded primarily from the messianic prophet Isaiah:

> *Jesus answered and said to them, "Go and report to John what you hear and see: the blind receive sight and the lame walk, the lepers are cleansed and the deaf hear, the dead are raised up , and the poor have the gospel preached to them....*
> (Matt. 11:2-5)

These signs were clear for all to see, yet they were ignored by scoffers, taken for granted by the multitudes and rejected by the spiritual leaders.

Incredibly, the very miracles that should have convinced Israel's spiritual leaders that the Messiah had arrived were ignored, rejected and rationalized away. When Jesus cast out a demon from a mute, freeing his tongue and enabling him to speak for the first time in who-knows-how-long, the Pharisees rationalized the exorcism by saying, "He casts out the demons by the ruler of the demons" (Matt. 9:34). So much for caring about the man whose tongue had been set free!

During Jesus' earthly ministry, even after extraordinary miracles that only the Messiah could have performed, the reaction by the spiritual leaders was critical and hostile. For example, immediately after healing the man with the withered hand, "...the Pharisees went out and conspired against Him, as to how they might destroy Him" (Matt. 12:14). It was the spiritual leaders who premeditated Jesus' murder, and it was the spiritual leaders who took advantage of Judas Iscariot's betrayal.

> *Then the chief priests and the elders of the people were gathered together in the court of the high priest, named Caiaphas; and they plotted together to seize Jesus by stealth and kill Him.... Then one of the twelve, named Judas Iscariot, went to the chief priests and said, "What are you willing to give me to betray Him to you?" And they weighed out thirty pieces of silver to him. From then on he began looking for a good opportunity to betray Jesus.* (Matt. 26:3-4, 14-16)

The final rejection of Jesus by the spiritual leaders occurred at his trial before Israel's ruling council, led by Caiaphas the High Priest. After being accused of blasphemy, "...they spat in His face and beat Him with their fists; and others slapped Him, and said, 'Prophesy to us, You Christ; who is the one who hit You?" (Matt. 26:67-68)

For rejecting him in spite of all the evidence, Jesus pronounced a terrible fate for Israel's spiritual leaders.

> *"But woe to you, scribes and Pharisees, hypocrites, because you shut off the kingdom of heaven from people; for you do not enter in yourselves, nor do you allow those who are entering to go in..."* (Matt. 23:13)

> *"Jerusalem, Jerusalem, who kills the prophets and stones those who are sent to her! How often I wanted to gather your children together, the way a hen gathers her chicks under her wings, and you were unwilling."* (Matt. 23:39)

But Jesus' rejection was not limited to Israel's spiritual leaders. In spite of having generated fame through his healing and preaching ministry in Galilee, Jesus experienced rejection even in his own hometown.

> *And He came to Nazareth, where He had been brought up; and as was His custom, He entered the synagogue on the Sabbath, and stood up to read. And the book of the prophet Isaiah was handed to Him. And He opened the book and found the place where it was written, "The Spirit of the Lord is upon Me, Because He anointed Me to preach the gospel to the poor.*

> *He has sent Me to proclaim release to the captives, and recovery of sight to the blind, to set free those who are oppressed, to proclaim the favorable year of the Lord."*

*And He closed the book, gave it back to the attendant and sat down; the eyes of all in the synagogue were fixed on Him. And He began to say to them, "Today this Scripture has been fulfilled in your hearing."* (Luke 4:14-21)

Jesus continues speaking and prophesies that he will be rejected, even in his hometown, and that eventually the gospel, the good news, will be given to and received by the Gentiles. The response of his listeners was anything but enthusiastic.

*And all the people in the synagogue were filled with rage as they heard these things; and they got up and drove Him out of the city, and led Him to the brow of the hill on which their city had been built, in order to throw Him down the cliff.* (Luke 4:28-29)

Perhaps Jesus' final rejection was the most painful, if not ironic, of all. When presented to the mob at his palace, Pilate shouted to them, "'...What shall I do with Jesus who is called Christ?" They all said, 'Crucify Him!'" (Matt. 27:22)

It's one thing to be criticized...it's quite another to be rejected, especially by those whom you literally left Paradise to help. The rejection of Jesus' earthly ministry by those he loved and came to save can be attributed only to the very thing he came to save them from—spiritual blindness as a result of depravity and sin. Jesus was never forced to leave Paradise and take on humanity—he did that voluntarily. From the beginning, he knew he would be rejected, and that rejection would lead to a painful death. Yet he came anyway. He came with full knowledge that rejection by those he loved would lead to the cross, and the cross would be the means, the only means, by which men and women could be saved from themselves. There is one thing and one thing only that explains Jesus' actions—his love. To his love, only a few responded. It is no different today than it was during his earthly ministry. His love is what draws men and women to him today. Ironically, what caused men and women to reject him during his earthly ministry is the very thing that causes men and women to reject his love today—spiritual blindness. There can be no other explanation, for why would we reject so great a love as this?

## The Love of the Son — His Death on the Cross

Though it was nothing new to the people of Jesus' time, it took a movie to help people today see the agony of crucifixion. Years before "The Passion" played to theater audiences throughout the world, I had taught on the details of Roman crucifixion. The first occasion was a community "Good Friday Prayer Breakfast." Like most gatherings of this nature, the event was about 99% breakfast and 1% prayer. Though I was not a well-known pastor in the community, for reasons I cannot recall I was asked to deliver "a devotional" appropriate to Easter week. I took advantage of the opportunity to bring to light the true agony of Roman crucifixion. Most of my material I took from Jim Bishop's book, "The Day Christ Died."[6] My intent was not just to present gory details but rather to put the sacrifice of Christ in historical perspective. By doing so, I felt, we could better appreciate his sacrifice on the cross, the love behind his going there, and the reverence and humility we ought to show when we observe Good Friday.

I was not prepared for the reaction. Men and women squirmed in their seats. One lady had to excuse herself. Grown men buried their heads to avoid eye contact. Seasoned pastors glared at me as if I was committing heresy. The local free-lance reporter feverishly scribbled notes on a pad, later to show up on the front page of the local paper: "Pastor Describes Crucifixion." Of course, when the breakfast ended, there were the courteous handshakes and the routine, "That was a nice talk." Afterwards, one pastor confided in me, "It seemed a bit much for a prayer breakfast."

That was the last community prayer breakfast I was ever invited to.

I continued to teach on the details of crucifixion when I was an assistant professor of physical therapy. One of the classes I taught happened to be the evaluation and treatment of the hand. Even then, I was surprised how a few students found discussing Christ's crucifixion in medical terms offensive, as if "This is not the place for something sacred." Yet, a detailed medical assessment of $3/8^{th}$ inch nails being driven through the wrists and ankles confirmed the miracle of the resurrection to Christians and created interest and curiosity in those students who were skeptical of Christianity. After all, the nails were not sterilized, critical nerves and tendons in the hands and bones in the ankles would have been severely traumatized, infection would have set in, and hands and feet would have been useless for weeks if not months. And that's without going into details about the pain, suffocation and heart failure associated with this kind of death.

That Jesus knew what awaited him on the cross is all the more reason to acknowledge his love. Jesus did not go to the cross for himself—he went for us, and to comply with his Father's will.

Jesus prepared his disciples to recognize his love the night of his betrayal. In preparing them for his death, he said,

> *"Greater love has no one than this, that one lay down his life for his friends. You are my friends if you do what I command you."* (John 15:13-14)

And what was Jesus' command?

> *"A new commandment I give to you, that you love one another, even as I have loved you, that you also love one another. By this all men will know that you are My disciples, if you have love for one another."* (John 14:34-35)

It was love, therefore, that drove Jesus to the cross, and it was love that kept him there. Could not the one through whom the world was created have removed himself from the cross? One would think the greater the suffering the greater the temptation to take away the pain. Yet there he remained, struggling to catch his breath, literally suffocating to death. Unable to bear the knifing pain screaming up his legs, he found himself pushing up on his nailed feet to catch a breath of air, then slumping back down on his dislocating shoulders because the muscle spasms in his thighs could hold him up no longer.

Still, the rejection. As the Gospels record, soldiers threw lots for his only piece of clothing. Other soldiers mocked him saying, "If You are the king of the Jews, save Yourself!" One of the men crucified beside him "was hurling abuse at Him, saying, 'Are You not the Christ? Save Yourself and us!'" Jewish rulers "were sneering at Him, saying, 'He saved others; let Him save Himself if this is the Christ of God, His Chosen One.'" All but one disciple disappeared for fear they would suffer the same fate. Yet, even in the agony and abandonment, his love for us was never quenched. In spite of the sneering and mocking and abusing and rejection, he loved enough to say, *"Father, forgive them; for they do not know what they are doing."* (Luke 23:34)

## The Love of the Son — His Ascension

It is unfortunate that most Christians' acknowledgement of Christ's love ends with his death on the cross. Few realize that when he left his preincarnate state with the Father, he left it forever.

After his death and resurrection, Jesus met with his disciples over a period of forty days. During this time, "...He opened their minds to understand the Scriptures..." concerning the Old Testament prophecies about his suffering, death and resurrection. When the time for his departure came,

> *"He led them out as far as Bethany, and He lifted up His hands and blessed them. While He was blessing them, He parted from them and was carried up into heaven."* (Luke 24:45, 50-51)

Theologically, this is referred to as the "Ascension."

The apostle Paul later informs us that Christ's departure into heaven had a destination—the "right hand" of God.

> *These are in accordance with the working of the strength of His might which He brought about in Christ, when He raised Him from the dead and seated Him at His right hand in the heavenly places, far above all rule and authority and*

*power and dominion, and every name that is named, not only in this age but also in the one to come."* (Ephesians 1:19-21)

"...Seated at the right hand of God" does not refer to a literal heavenly chair next to God's literal right hand. The phrase "right hand of God" is a metaphor for a position of authority. In days of antiquity, the "right hand" of a ruler was a designated and trusted individual who carried out the daily affairs for the ruler. It was considered beneath the dignity of a ruler to spend his time running his kingdom. That responsibility would be delegated—to make a play on words—to his "right-hand man." Joseph became Pharaoh's right-hand man during his sojourn in Egypt. Daniel became Nebuchadnezzar's right-hand man in Babylon, as did Nehemiah in the form of a cupbearer to King Artaxerxes. With the responsibility of carrying out the affairs of the kingdom came the authority to do so; that is, the king gave not only the responsibility but also the authority to run his kingdom. When the ruler seated himself on his throne, his right-hand man usually sat at his right side, making the king's declarations, deciding who could or could not approach the ruler. Often, death was the penalty for one who approached the throne and spoke directly to the king. All discourse had to go through the one put in charge of the kingdom, seated at the king's right hand.

Jesus informed his disciples that God had placed him in a position of authority: "All authority has been given to Me in heaven and on earth" (Matt. 28:18). That is, God the Father placed all authority in heaven and on earth into the hands of his Son Jesus. How would Jesus carry out his responsibilities? John, as well as the other Gospel writers, reveals that to us.

*"I will ask the Father, and He will give you another Helper, that He may be with you forever; that is the Spirit of truth, whom the world cannot receive, because it does not see Him or know Him, but you know Him because He abides with you and will be in you."* (John 14:16-17)

*"These things I have spoken to you while abiding with you. But the Helper, the Holy Spirit, whom the Father will send*

*in My name, He will teach you all things, and bring to your remembrance all that I said to you."* (John 14: 25-26)

*"But when He, the Spirit of truth, comes, He will guide you into all the truth; for He will not speak on His own initiative, but whatever he hears, He will speak; and He will disclose to you what is to come. He will glorify Me, for He will take of Mine and will disclose it to you. All things that the Father has are Mine; therefore I said that He takes of Mine and will disclose it to you."* (John 16:13-15)

However, authority over heaven and earth is not the full extent of Jesus' heavenly ministry. There is more, much more. Upon his ascension, Jesus assumed a position of eternal mediator between God and man:

*"For there is one God, and one mediator also between God and men, the man Christ Jesus."* (1 Tim. 2:5)

When the second person of the Trinity, the *Logos*, came in human form through the incarnation, he became neither just man nor just God. That is, when he became a man, he did not take on a human nature absent of his divinity, nor did he exist on earth as a divine "phantom" without flesh as some Gnostics asserted. He was both fully divine and perfect humanity. Both natures co-existed in the man Jesus Christ. He, who had no human nature before his incarnation, took on human nature in addition to his divine nature. What many Christians fail to realize is that the human nature Christ assumed would never be lost. When Christ ascended to the Father, he did not leave his human nature behind. He not only ascended as fully divine and perfect humanity, but he will remain in that condition throughout all eternity. For, in that condition, he is able to serve as an eternal mediator between God and man, and in that condition, he serves as an eternal intercessor on behalf of his bride, the church. For, as the apostle Paul writes to the church in Rome, *"Christ Jesus is He who died, yes, rather who was raised, who is at the right hand of God, who also intercedes for us"* (Rom. 8:34). The writer of Hebrews confirms this, likening Jesus to the Levitical High Priest who annually interceded on behalf of God's people:

*"But Jesus, on the other hand, because He continues forever, holds His priesthood permanently. Therefore, He is able also to save forever those who draw near to God through Him, since He always lives to make intercession for them."* (Hebrews 7:24-25)

It is no wonder, then, that "the disciple whom Jesus loved" would want the whole world to experience the love of Jesus.

*Now before the Feast of the Passover, Jesus knowing that His hour had come that He would depart out of this world to the Father, having loved His own who were in the world, He loved them to the end."* (John 13:1)

The love of the Son was not diminished when he left his heavenly throne to be born into the world as a vulnerable, dependent human infant. The love of the Son was not tarnished by the continual rejection by those he came to save. The love of the Son was not destroyed when he died in agony nailed to a Roman cross. And the love of the Son was not left behind when he ascended into heaven to sit at the right hand of God the Father. The love of the Son has been with us all along, and it is the love of the Son that will escort us into eternal life.

---

1. E.g., Louis Berkhof, *Systematic Theology* (Grand Rapids, MI: Wm. B. Eerdmans, 1974).

2. Charles C. Ryrie, *Basic Theology* (Wheaton, IL: Victor Books, SP Publications, 1986), 35.

3. Ryrie, *Basic Theology*, 35-44.

4. Ryrie, *Basic Theology*, 262.

5.  Emily E. S. Elliott & Timothy R. Matthews, "Thou Didst Leave Thy Throne." From *Hymns for the Family of God* (Nashville, TN: Paragon Associates, 1976), 677.

6.  Jim Bishop, *The Day Christ Died* (New York: Harper & Brothers, 1957).

# *Vignette for Chapter Eight*

# *"Productivity"*

The two observers, one a supervisor and the other an intern, stood at a distance trying to make sense of what they were seeing: one man with a few interns and a large crowd gathering. Expecting the crowd to dissipate as the afternoon grew on, it only increased.

"This is good," the boyish intern said.

"Maybe, maybe not," the senior supervisor noted. "If you observe carefully, you'll notice that his productivity hasn't increased. There's a lot of down time going on. You'd expect that the more people who come the better the productivity. He spends a lot of time talking."

"Yes, but if the crowds increase, there's bound to be increased productivity as the days pass. I see it as an investment. Invest in the people and later you will be the recipient of their business."

"You would think so, but I'm not sure that's happening. Look, any good worker should have at least eighty percent productivity. My rough calculations indicate he's running less than fifty percent. That's completely unsatisfactory. There's a lot of non-productive time here."

"But doesn't it all depend on what you count as productivity?"

"Of course. But to be effective, you need productivity goals. No goal, no plan. No plan, less productivity. Less productivity, the greater the waste of everyone's time, including ours."

The two observers wandered over to a smooth boulder and sat down watching the crowd. It was a warm, sunny spring day without a cloud in the sky. There was a cool breeze from the west. The grass was newly sprouted and freshly green. People were passing them by on either side of the observers heading for the crowd. Suddenly there was a loud commotion from the center of the crowd.

"What's going on?" the intern asked.

"Well," the sup said, standing on the boulder and peering over the crowd, "it looks like he's cast a demon out of another lunatic. This is always a bad choice."

"Why?"

"You'd expect him to move on to the next person. Get the demon out, problem solved. But no, he spends the next twenty minutes talking to the guy. That's twenty minutes of poor productivity. It only takes him a few minutes to cast out a demon. He spends the next twenty talking. That's very poor use of one's time."

"I don't see it. Isn't the talking productive? After all, he must be teaching the guy something, and it's loud enough that everyone can hear."

"It's not the same. Look, here's how we measure productivity. You need to see visible results. If he spends time casting out demons or healing, that's visible, tangible results that you can definitely measure. How do you measure the results of teaching? Even if you ask the crowd to recite everything the teacher said, would that constitute productivity?"

"Maybe it just takes longer to measure. Maybe it's just measured differently."

"Not the same. Grapes and pomegranates. Look, here's what you want to learn. If you do something really spectacular in a person's life, like restoring sight or ridding him of leprosy, he'll be indebted to you for the rest of his life. He'll follow you wherever you go. He's bound to be the biggest giver, the deepest pocket. Without deep pockets, it's hard to sustain a ministry."

"But with teaching? Doesn't that change their way of thinking?"

"Of course. But teaching is always risky. A person may or may not accept the teaching. Look at it this way. Let's suppose you teach someone for an hour. Then they end up rejecting everything you teach. That's zero productivity. Case in point: those Pharisees and scribes over there. He argued with them for an hour and got absolutely nowhere. That's a terrible waste of time. Time is productivity and productivity is profit. Even if they were to accept half of what he taught, that's only fifty percent productivity."

"I think I see your point."

"But cast out a demon—that takes roughly five minutes—restore sight to a man born blind—another five minutes—and so on down the line...that's *real* productivity. Tangible, hard-evidence productivity that can stand up to any scrutiny by management. Heal for an hour, that's perfect productivity. Every hour not spent healing is an hour's lost productivity. And what's more, you get these people contributing to your ministry for the rest of their lives. Now *that's* productivity."

"Look, the crowd's moving."

They watched as the worker began walking up a hill to a small town on the ridge. The crowd followed instantly like a flock of sheep following a shepherd.

"*Now* what's he doing?" the supervisor wondered. "Ask someone."

After a few minutes, the intern came back with the answer. "Nothing much. He just heard that somebody died a few days ago. He's going to visit the family."

"Oh, my lord! How productive can *that* be? Well, we'd better go see what's going on. But I can tell you now that with this extended lunch break, productivity's going out the window. This is really going to be a lost day."

The two men followed the large crowd up the hill, along the road that led to the villa where the owner had died, and through the gate to the private cemetery.

"*Now* what's he doing?"

"He's talking to the family. One of the sisters, I believe."

"Make a note of this: Family training can be delegated to subordinates. Not a good use of one's time."

The two men watched curiously as the worker wandered over to the family cemetery and had some hired hands remove the stone entrance.

"How long has it been now," the supervisor asked. "About an hour? This is turning into a productivity disaster!"

Standing on the edge of the crowd, they heard the worker shout something. To their amazement, the dead man stood at the entrance to the cave where he had been placed four days earlier.

"Wow," the intern said. "This guy's good."

"Not bad," the other replied. "Not bad at all. This makes up for a lot of down time today."

"Better productivity?"

"You bet. This will win some followers. Raise a man from the dead. Now *that's* productivity. Wait till they hear about this at the managers' conference!"

*Bill Walthall*

## *Chapter Eight*

# "Gospel DNA"
# (Love and the Gospels)

*"For I say to you that unless your righteousness surpasses that of the scribes and Pharisees, you will not enter the kingdom of heaven."* (Matthew 5:20)

Two major themes parallel one another throughout the Gospels. Like the helix of a DNA molecule, the two themes are intrinsically wound and intimately connected. The first and most obvious theme is truth; that is, the truth about the person and work of Jesus Christ. As John states at the close of his Gospel:

*"Therefore many other signs Jesus also performed in the presence of the disciples, which are not written in this book; but these have been written so that you may believe that Jesus is the Christ, the Son of God; and that believing you may have life in His name."* (John 20:30-31)

The truth presented throughout the Gospels, therefore, centers on the person and work of Jesus of Nazareth. The truth is clear, profound and adamantine: Jesus is the Christ, the Son of David, the Son of God. He alone is the Jewish Messiah, the only one who can deliver us from our sins and offer abundant life on earth and eternal life in heaven. Jesus Christ is mankind's Savior and hope, and he is the only means of restoring a person to a right relationship to God. Jesus Christ is the one and only personification (incarnation) of truth. He is the Word, the *Logos*, the visible manifestation of invisible deity. The Gospel writers offer proof of this truth through Jesus' teachings, through his miracles, through the fulfillment of Old Testament prophecies, and through his death, resurrection and ascension. The most important teaching throughout the Gospels focuses on the truth of who Jesus Christ is.

There is a second theme, however, that is just as important and without which the first would be incomplete. The second theme is love. This theme presents the truth that the core of God's nature—and therefore Christ's nature—is love. It was out of love for a lost world that God sent His only Son into the world. It was love for the Father and love for sinners that drove Jesus to suffer agony and death on the cross. For Jesus' disciples, love would bind the church together in unity, and love for one another would be the primary means by which the world would recognize Jesus' disciples (John 13:35).

As has already been stated, the truth theme must be presented first, for without truth we would not know what true love is; that is, the love of God. Love cannot be properly understood until truth is disclosed simply because love requires definition. On the other hand, biblical truth points to, validates and discloses love because love is what biblical truth is all about. The purpose of truth is to direct us toward the love of God and God's love through Christ. Without love, truth has no means of incarnation, for it is truth that teaches us to respond to, live in, and offer God's love for a lost world. Love, therefore, gives body to truth. The purpose of biblical truth, then, is to point us to love, and therefore teach us how to act with biblical love.

In the chapter sub-titled "Love and the Ten Commandments," we learned that the Law, though valid, was insufficient to cover all the contingencies of life. How, then, does one become righteous? Jesus addresses this question in the Sermon on the Mount. He makes a seemingly outrageous statement: "For I say to you that unless your righteousness *surpasses* that of the scribes and Pharisees, you will not enter the kingdom of heaven." Any person in Jesus' audience would immediately interpret that as an impossibility. After all, the scribes and the Pharisees were the experts and the supreme keepers of the Law. The contemporary evangelical interpretation of Jesus' statement is this: when we commit our lives to Christ by faith, God declares us righteous. Our righteousness is imputed to us (justification) and through the ministry of the Holy Spirit, we become more righteous as we live out our Christian lives (sanctification). While this theology is correct within itself, I do not believe that is what Jesus had in mind when he called for his followers to be more righteous than the scribes and the Pharisees. It is the rest of the Sermon on the Mount that interprets the meaning of Jesus' statement. He shows his audience what a life more righteous than that of the scribes and Pharisees will look like, and it is all based around the second great commandment, "You shall love your neighbor as yourself" (Lev. 19:18). If the righteousness of the Pharisees is to be surpassed, one's moral code cannot be based on the Ten Commandments and the traditions of the elders alone. There is but one way to surpass the righteousness of the Pharisees and that is by basing one's behavior on the royal law (Jas 2:8).

The place of the royal law, however, was not well understood by the scribes and Pharisees. In Jesus' day, teachers of the Law, called rabbis, generally recognized that the Torah contained 613 commandments required to be kept.[1] Beginning about the time of Ezra and the Babylonian captivity, some four to five hundred years before Christ, scholarly Jewish priests began to realize that the commandments found throughout the Old Testament, and particularly those in the Torah, required interpretation in order to be practically applied. Thus, a body of oral tradition was developed alongside the Old Testament that included rabbinical teachings, commentaries and interpretations of the Torah. (Some believe the oral tradition dates to the time of Moses.) These oral traditions were later put in writing, the entire body of which would be called the Mishna and were eventually included in a larger work called the Talmud. Unfortunately, as stated earlier, these interpretations of the Torah began to be treated as equal in authority to the Law itself. By Jesus' time, about two thousand laws were in effect concerning the Sabbath alone; that is, what could or could not be performed on the Sabbath in keeping with the fourth commandment. As we briefly described in an earlier chapter, the scribes and Pharisees called these interpretations "the traditions of the elders" (Matthew 15:2). Jesus responded to the Pharisees and scribes that for the sake of their traditions, they were transgressing the commandments of God and invalidating God's word (Matthew 15:3, 6).

The point of the above review is this: even the Pharisees and scribes were realistic enough to discover that the 613 commandments found throughout the Old Testament were insufficient to cover all the situations and contingencies in life and relationships. Therefore, it was impossible to become righteous even if one *could* keep all the commandments, for the Law was insufficient and incomplete. The "righteousness" of the scribes and the Pharisees, who based their righteousness on the Law and the traditions of the elders, would need to be surpassed. How to surpass the righteousness of the scribes and Pharisees is the inspired centerpiece of the Sermon on the Mount. It is reflected in one way or another throughout the Gospels, culminating in the final teachings of Christ as provided to us through the apostle John.

## Love in Jesus' Teachings

The underlying message of love—the royal law—may be found embedded in nearly every part of Jesus' teachings. In many of his teachings, it is obvious. In others, it is not. Some are direct, others are very indirect and part of a larger picture of God's love. There are a few places, however, where the royal law is not only embedded but at the same time astonishing. Take, for example, a teaching found in the Sermon on the Mount.

> *"You have heard that the ancients were told, 'You shall not commit murder' and 'Whoever commits murder shall be liable to the court.' But I say to you that everyone who is angry with his brother shall be guilty before the court; and whoever says to his brother, 'You good-for-nothing,' shall be guilty before the supreme court; and whoever says, 'You fool,' shall be guilty enough to go into the fiery hell.*

> *"Therefore if you are presenting your offering at the altar, and there remember that your brother has something against you, leave your offering there before the altar and go; first*

*be reconciled to your brother, and then come and present your offering."* (Matthew 5:21-24)

A close look at this teaching by Jesus reveals three astonishing facts, none of which should be taken as exaggerations or metaphors. First, anger at others is akin to murdering them and therefore subject to sentencing in God's court of law. Second, demeaning others is even worse! Calling a person a "fool" (the contemporary equivalent would be labeling someone an "idiot" or a "jerk" in a condescending manner) is worthy of eternal condemnation. Why? Because it's not what goes into a man that defiles him, it's what comes out, and what comes out betrays a heart of hostility and hatred. Both of these truths taught by Jesus define love or, in one sense, the failure of it. If we truly loved others, we would not harbor anger toward them and because we show love, we would never refer to them in demeaning terms or treat them in a condescending manner.

The third truth, however, is even more astonishing: worshipping God is meaningless if you have not reconciled with your brother. Not surprisingly, the Pharisees and scribes were blind to this truth. That is because loving God meant merely loving the practice of religion. To the scribes and Pharisees, one showed love to God by obeying a rigid set of rules, such as dietary laws and laws of cleanliness, that may or may not have anything to do with relationships. In fact, the scribes and Pharisees majored in the laws having nothing to do with relationships and ignored those that did, such as honoring your father and mother and the commandment regarding adultery. What Jesus is teaching here is that the most important way to worship and love God is to first love your brother.

Applying this teaching to present-day practice, then, means that going to church religiously, reading one's Bible daily, tithing monthly, singing in the choir or decorating the altar, serving as an elder, a deacon, a bishop, a pastor or even a missionary, does not a disciple make. A disciple is one who follows Jesus Christ, not just in acknowledging biblical truths about him but in having biblical truths incarnated in such a manner that the end result is changed relationships based on love. A follower of Jesus Christ is one who loves his neighbor as himself. There is no incarnation of biblical truth, and there is no such thing as following Jesus, unless the disciple's behavioral changes permeate all relationships with biblical love. One can be saved by simply receiving Jesus Christ by faith, but the disciple of Jesus Christ is the one who loves. There is no such thing as following Jesus Christ without seeking with one's whole heart to fulfill the royal law.

These three truths, then, define what it means to keep the first and foremost commandment: "You shall love the Lord your God with all your heart, with all your mind, and with all your strength." We love God by loving others as he loves them. As John later affirms in his first letter:

> *"The one who says he is in the Light and yet hates his brother is in the darkness until now. The one who loves his brother abides in the Light and there is no cause for stumbling in him. But the one who hates his brother is in the darkness and walks in the darkness, and does not know where he is going because the darkness has blinded his eyes."* (1 John 2:9-11)

> *"If we say that we have fellowship with Him and yet walk in the darkness, we lie and do not practice the truth."* (1 John 1:6)

The Gospel of John, of course, is the Gospel that brings the theme of love to the forefront. John alone refers to love fifty-seven times throughout his Gospel. Most often, he uses the Greek word *agape* to describe the love to which he is referring. Although defined by some as "sacrificial love," the most important meaning of this Greek form of love focuses on the intrinsic value of the object of love. The simple interpretation is this: love is given, not because it has been earned or is deserved, but because of the recipient's intrinsic value. Therefore, when John writes, "For God so loved the world, that He gave His only begotten Son..." (John 3:16), he is teaching us that God loves us because of our intrinsic value, not because we have deserved his love. Out of his very nature and essence, he loves that which is unlovable, undeserving and unworthy. And he does so to the point of personal sacrifice—he gave of himself. It is with this kind of love that Jesus instructs his followers to love one another, and it will be due to this kind of love that Jesus' followers will sacrifice their own lives for those who have neither deserved it nor earned it. If God loves the sinner, then Jesus' followers are to love the sinner. It is on this basis and this basis alone that Jesus teaches, *"...Love your enemies and pray for those who persecute you, so that you may be sons of your Father who is in heaven..."* (Matthew 5:44-45).

The culmination of Jesus' teaching on love is recorded the same night of his ultimate betrayal of love by Judas Iscariot. In the upper room, during the Passover meal, Jesus teaches his disciples, *"A new commandment I give to you, that you love one another, even as I have loved you, that you also love one another"* (John 13:35). Jesus' commandment is simple to repeat but difficult to fulfill and requires a lifetime to learn. Disciples of Jesus Christ are to love one another in the same manner as he has loved us. This requires personal sacrifice, thus the definition, "sacrificial love." As Jesus is willing to lay down his life for his followers, his disciples are expected to do the same. By doing so, Jesus' disciples will reflect not only Christ's love, but God's: "...I have made Your name known to them, and will make it known, so that the love with which You loved Me may be in them, and I in them" (John 17:26).

Besides Jesus' teachings on love, there are the lessons on love learned through his encounters. There is no better place to start than the Gospel of John.

## Love in Jesus' Encounters

No incident in the Gospel of John better illustrates the rule of love over the Law than the one that describes the woman taken in adultery. This event is found in the eighth chapter.

> *Early in the morning He came again into the temple, and all the people were coming to Him; and He sat down and began to teach them. The scribes and the Pharisees brought a woman caught in adultery, and having set her in the center of the court, they said to Him, "Teacher, this woman has been caught in adultery, in the very act. Now in the Law Moses commanded us to stone such women; what then do You say?"*

*They were saying this, testing Him, so that they might have grounds for accusing Him. But Jesus stooped down and with His finger wrote on the ground.*

*But when they persisted in asking Him, He straightened up, and said to them, "He who is without sin among you, let him be the first to throw a stone at her."*

*Again He stooped down and wrote on the ground.*

*When they heard it, they began to go out one by one, beginning with the older ones, and He was left alone, and the woman, where she was, in the center of the court.*
*Straightening up, Jesus said to her, "Woman, where are they? Did no one condemn you?"*

*She said, "No one, Lord." And Jesus said, "I do not condemn you, either. Go. From now on sin no more."* (John 8:2-11)

There is no doubt that the woman sinned. It is not a false accusation. What is a greater fault than the woman's act of adultery, however, is the fault of the heart of her accusers. The scribes and Pharisees are not seeing the woman through the eyes of God's love. What the woman needs most is not God's wrath and judgment, but the knowledge of God's love for her, that she is of great interest to God, that she has intrinsic value in his eyes. She is seeking love in all the wrong places, leading therefore to sin in the form of a relationship not based on biblical love. If she were to experience the true love of God—the knowledge that he is more interested in her emotional, physical and sexual health than her condemnation—she would have a whole new perspective on life, particularly in regard to relationships. She would therefore seek out a relationship based on biblical love, which can only be determined by the truth of Jesus' teaching.

The hardened and darkened hearts of the scribes and Pharisees who value law over love is manifested in a glaring inconsistency: where is the woman's partner? Leviticus 20:10 clearly states, *"...the adulterer and the adulteress shall surely be put to death."* Although it is possible the partner ran off, the accusers seem intent on using the woman to destroy Jesus' reputation. They are not interested in healing, they are focused on hating. They are not concerned about the woman's well-being, they are more concerned about their religious *status quo*. They cannot see the love issues because they are blinded by law issues. They know that if Jesus stated the Law should be ignored, he would be seen as teaching contrary to Moses. If Jesus called for stoning, his love and compassion would be called into question. The point is that the woman's accusers are guilty of a failure to love—they love neither the woman nor Jesus. Ironically, they believe they are showing love to God by calling for her stoning and destroying Jesus' ministry. As Jesus clearly informs the scribes and Pharisees later in the chapter, *"If God were your Father, you would love Me..."* (John 8:42).

Many have speculated, therefore, about what Jesus wrote in the sand. Although we shall never know for sure, perhaps the best explanation is this: Jesus wrote down the sins of each of her accusers, unknown to anyone but Jesus and the accuser. It is conceivable that some of those sins were in themselves worthy of stoning, such as adultery or blasphemy. Whatever he wrote, it was enough to stop the accusers in their tracks. Jesus knew something about them they didn't want a soul to know. To pursue enforcement of the Law would result in the Law having to be enforced against themselves. It was enough to leave the woman to Jesus and bother him no longer with the Law.

The question remains, "Why didn't Jesus follow the Law by having the woman stoned?" It is because his righteousness surpassed that of the scribes and Pharisees. Though Jesus kept the Law perfectly, his righteousness wasn't based on the Law. Jesus' righteousness was intrinsic, having proceeded from the Father. The earthly expression of his righteousness, therefore, wasn't limited to keeping the Law, for he co-authored the Law. His earthly expression of righteousness was greater than the Law. In fact, his expression was the ultimate purpose of the Law, which is to love. Though not denying that the woman had transgressed the Law ("From now on sin no more."), Jesus instructs us that sin hurts us more than it hurts God. Indeed, one of the purposes of the Law is to keep us from hurting ourselves as well as to keep us from hurting others. We give laws to our children such as "Don't play with matches." The purpose of the rule is to keep the child safe, from being hurt. Those who commit adultery not only hurt themselves but all the people around them: their spouse, their children, the other spouse and other children, and, if a pastor or spiritual leader is the adulterer, all those who have trusted in the integrity of his or her leadership. Committing adultery is the opposite of loving, for it hurts everyone, especially those who become involved in it.

The Law was inadequate for keeping this woman from hurting herself. It didn't work because she needed something greater than the satisfaction of being a law-keeper. She needed true, biblical love. Jesus knew that a new perspective on love—specifically, his love—was the only thing that would enable her to experience life, and experience it more abundantly. When Jesus gave her his love, she would forevermore be indebted to him. Because of his love, she was healed emotionally as well as sexually. All of her relationships would be forever changed. By his love she was esteemed and affirmed, and made to feel like the person of intrinsic value she was. Her desire to sin no more would be motivated, not out of obligation, but out of gratitude, out of love. What the Law could not do, causing sin to come alive, love did. Love not only changed her behavior, her values and her relationships, it transformed her sense of purpose for living and loving. By inhaling and breathing God's love through the person of Jesus Christ, she became a new person, enabled to love as well as be loved. As Paul stated so clearly, "For while we were in the flesh, the sinful passions, which were aroused by the Law, were at work in the members of our body to bear fruit for death" (Romans 7:5). But it's love that heals and restores, and it's love that renews and transforms.

From this point on, not only would this woman sin no more, but her righteousness would surpass that of the scribes and Pharisees by light years.

Another incident also illustrates where the law-lovers were unable to grasp the value of God's love. In the seventh chapter of Luke, Jesus has been invited to dinner by a Pharisee named Simon (Luke 7:36-50). Simon no doubt invited his Pharisee friends and, in fact, may have been genuinely interested in getting to know better this healer and so-called prophet. There is a problem, however; he wants to sit on both sides of the table. He wants to know Jesus better but he does not want to appear that he supports his ministry. He quite rightly fears that the other Pharisees might see him going soft on them. (Even if there were no other Pharisees present at the dinner, surely word of this social engagement would have gotten out.) For this reason, though inviting Jesus to his home, Simon fails to extend to Jesus traditional common courtesies: hand and foot washing, normally done in the vestibule by a servant, a kiss of greeting and an anointing of oil on the forehead. It is a subtle sign of contempt.

Nevertheless, Jesus is reclining at the table, perhaps in theological discussion with Simon. During the meal, a woman described as "a sinner" enters the house and begins weeping over Jesus' feet. Wetting his feet with her tears and wiping them with her hair, she opens an alabaster jar and begins anointing his feet with perfume. It is possible she heard that Simon wouldn't stoop to the level of washing this itinerant preacher's feet—that would be a bit too much—but that Jesus deserved better treatment than what Simon was offering. Simon's waffling about who Jesus is comes out in his words: "If this man were a prophet He would know who and what sort of person this woman is who is touching Him, that she is a sinner."

According to the Law, to be touched by a declared "sinner" would result in the person being touched becoming unclean. Therefore, in Simon's lawful thinking, Jesus would not have allowed this woman to touch him if he knew she was unclean. Simon is unable to see the love principle because of his focus on Levitical law (e.g., Leviticus 15).

It is clear from the rest of the story that Simon is not stupid. When Jesus provides a parable about two debtors, one having been forgiven a small debt and one having been forgiven a great debt, Simon answers Jesus' question correctly: those who are forgiven much love much. Yet, Simon has a blind spot. He fails to see the connection between the parable and Jesus' encounter with the woman. He fails to see that her actions were actions of love and gratitude because of something Jesus did for her. His puzzlement extends when Jesus tells the woman, "Your sins have been forgiven." Simon fails on all accounts because he has never understood that the basis for the Law was love; that love is the foundation stone for all Old Testament law.

How should Simon have responded? What should Simon's evening have been like? First, had Simon understood that Jesus was the Son of God, the God of love, he would have welcomed him into his house and gone overboard with hospitality. He would have sent the servant away and washed Jesus' feet himself. He would have kissed his feet as well as his cheeks. He would have had available the most expensive perfume he could find, not that that would have impressed Jesus, but it would have demonstrated Simon's desire to give the Son of God his best. Instead of inviting his Pharisee friends to observe Jesus, he would have invited them to learn from him, to explain to them the relationship between the Law and Prophets and the Messiah. When he observed that a healed sinner was in his home, he would have provided her a place at the table. His love would have caused him to rethink his knowledge of what was then the truth; that is, the Law. And most important of all, when he observed that Jesus had the authority to forgive sin, he would have rushed to Jesus' feet and, bowing himself before him, begged that he, too, would have his sins forgiven. He would have leapt up and hugged the woman, congratulating her on the fact that she was no longer "a sinner" but a "saved" servant. Instead, he sat back and criticized the God of love because he mistakenly assumed he had no sin needing God's forgiveness, for he was not a "sinner" like that woman.

This incident in Luke is a tragic example of Simon's love being defined incorrectly because he failed to see that the basis for the Law and the Prophets was love. That even though truth trumps love, one must first know that truth's purpose is to enable all people to receive and give biblical love.

## Love in Jesus' Healings

It was a quiet, Sabbath morning somewhere in Galilee, perhaps in Capernaum. It was early summer and the grain fields were ripe for the first harvest, clothing the silent hills with a robe of gold. Jesus and his disciples have arrived at "church"; that is, the local synagogue. Having heard that Jesus and his disciples were in town, no doubt the synagogue was full to standing room only. Some came in great need, hoping Jesus would do one of his healings on them after sunset. Others just wanted a look at this new prophet who was causing such a stir. As a guest of honor, Jesus was asked to read from the Scriptures. What he read that particular Sabbath we don't know, but whatever he read he chose to expound and explain.

Instead of listening and learning from Jesus, however, present that Sabbath morning were scribes and Pharisees with other motivations. They were not there to worship but to see if Jesus would perform one of his healings on the Sabbath. If he did, they could accuse him of breaking the law of Moses. Ironically, healing on the Sabbath was not forbidden in the *Torah*. Acts of mercy, kindness and goodness were encouraged. It was rabbinic interpretations of the Law, the traditions of the elders, that forbade any healings but emergencies on the Sabbath. Why? Because routine healing was classified by rabbinic tradition as work. Physicians, therefore, were prohibited from practicing medicine on the Sabbath except in the case of a life-threatening situation. It was one of the two thousand or so rules dictating what an Israelite could or could not do to keep the Sabbath holy. In other words, it was the Sabbath itself that was being worshipped rather than the God who created it.

Also sitting in the synagogue listening to Jesus was a man with a withered hand. We know little about this man; we know neither the cause of his affliction nor how it affected his life and livelihood. His withered hand could have been a congenital condition or the result of an accident. One thing we do know, however—his condition was not what would be classified as an emergency. Therefore, instead of seeking help from Jesus, he sat quietly in his seat, hoping Jesus would not leave town before the morrow. That explains why Jesus had to call the man forward. He had been kept from coming to Jesus by the inflexible and unlawful rules imposed by the scribes and Pharisees.

We pick up the scene in Mark, chapter three:

*He said to the man with the withered hand, "Get up and come forward!"*

*And He said to them (the scribes and Pharisees), "Is it lawful to do good or to do harm on the Sabbath, to save a life or to kill?" But they kept silent.*

*After looking around at them with anger, grieved at their hardness of heart, He said to the man, "Stretch out your hand." And he stretched it out, and his hand was restored.*

*The Pharisees went out and immediately began conspiring with the Herodians against Him, as to how they might destroy Him."* (Mark 3:1-6)

There are few places in Scripture where Jesus demonstrates anger. The most obvious one, of course, occurs when he overturns the tables of the moneychangers who were making the Court of the Gentiles a "robbers' den" rather than "a house of prayer" (Matthew 21:12-13). In the case of the man with the withered hand, Jesus is said to experience two emotions—anger and grief. His anger is directed toward the religious leaders who chose not to answer his question, "Is it lawful to do good or to do harm on the Sabbath, to save a life or to kill?" They chose not to answer the question because by affirming the intent of the Law, they would expose their own malevolent intentions. By keeping silent, they were in effect saying that the rabbinical interpretations of the Law took priority over the Law itself, that demonstrating love for the man with the withered hand was a non-factor. As a result, the man with the withered hand—and no doubt countless others—had failed to seek Jesus' healing presence. Once again, the scribes and Pharisees chose law over love. Jesus was grieved because their hearts had become so hardened they cared nothing for the man with the withered hand. They cared only about their traditions.

By the actions of the Pharisees in verse six, it would seem to indicate that they had won a victory; they had caught Jesus in the act of doing work on the Sabbath. The irony is that Jesus did no work at all. He never touched the man with the withered hand; he merely instructed him to stretch out his hand. It was his words that healed him, not his work. The

Pharisees were so blinded by their hardness of heart they couldn't even see the inconsistency of their conclusions. Whereas Jesus' desire was to bring life to the downtrodden, the desire of the Pharisees was to take away Jesus' life as well as the lives of all those who would be touched by him.

We never hear again about the man with the withered hand. It would not take a great imagination, however, to speculate on the aftermath of his healing. Apart from the Pharisees and the Herodians who are huddled together outside the synagogue, the man whose hand was restored is getting more attention than the winner of American Idol. The entire synagogue—indeed, the entire town—is gathered around congratulating him on his new lease on life. Everyone wants to touch his new hand. "Squeeze my hand." "Make a fist." "Turn it over so I can see everything." And when he returns home, his family is astonished. The son they had known and loved all his life was no longer the object of jokes, ridicule and contempt. Whereas once his hand was a sign of God's judgment, now it is the recipient of God's love. If their son had been born with the affliction, whatever guilt the parents may have felt vanished in an instant. All the healers they visited, all the physicians who failed, all the tears shed over the misfortune of their beloved son were now past. It was a moment of love the Pharisees could neither understand nor experience.

There is one other point of significance about this healing that should not be overlooked. Luke informs us that the man's withered hand was his right hand (Luke 6:3). This has enormous implications in oriental custom. The right hand was considered more esteemed or "noble" than the left. The custom of the right hand having more esteem than the left permeated nearly every aspect of Jewish custom. This was because the left hand was used for personal hygiene, such as wiping oneself or blowing one's nose. Therefore, when a person ate, only the right hand brought food to the mouth and only the right hand passed food to another. The left hand, being offensive, was kept from view. The Jewish custom of right hand before left can be seen in the method of hand washing on the Sabbath, the details of a wedding ceremony, and in the reading and handling of the Scriptures. When taking another's hand, only the right hand was used because the left was considered the less clean of the two. With a useless, atrophied right hand, therefore, it was impossible to have a hand that was considered clean, thus resulting in a permanent state of uncleanness. If the man with the withered hand were a Levite, he would have been forbidden to make an offering to the Lord: "For no one who has a defect shall approach: a blind man, or a lame man, or he who has a disfigured face, or any deformed limb..." (Leviticus 21:18). When Jesus healed the man's withered right hand through his compassion and love, he not only gave him new life, he made him clean.

The contrast between Jesus' compassion and the Pharisees' compulsion are legend. What should have happened after Jesus healed the man? Had the Pharisees loved and cared about the man more than the Law, they would have leapt up and praised God for his goodness. They should have rushed out of their seats and given the man hugs of excitement and joy. They should have rejoiced with the man's newly found freedom, erasure of guilt, and restoration to life. They should have willingly walked him straight to the temple and gladly paid his tithe. They would have done that if they loved him more than they loved the Law. But, sadly, they didn't. They totally ignored the man and hurried outside to conspire against Jesus. In an attempt to defend "the truth," they overlooked the principle that God's love for man and God's desire that we love our neighbors as ourselves is what the truth is all about.

## Conflict in the Gospels

The Gospels are full of conflict. Most conflict surrounds the person of Jesus Christ. Is Jesus the Messiah or not? Did he blaspheme by making himself equal with God? Did he come to establish the kingdom of God, and if so, what form would it take? Would he restore Israel to its former glory, or was he a false hope? Did he come to bring peace or a sword, or both? And, perhaps most important of all, can he forgive sins?

There is another conflict throughout the Gospels, however. It is the conflict of Law and love. The two principles square off like heavyweights in a prizefight. In one corner, there is the keeper of the Law. He sees his responsibility as maintaining the integrity of the Law at all cost, even if it means defeating and destroying others in the process. When it comes to loving and obeying God, loving others is subservient to the point of irrelevance. After all, the Law is what defined Israel and the Jewish people. The Law is how God spoke to Moses and to the Israelites whom he rescued from Egypt. Without the Law, Jewish society would have unraveled and lost its identity. Law, too, was how one defined being right with God; that is, being righteous before God. All other so-called avenues to God were the creations of man. In short, they amounted to little more than idolatry. Little does this heavyweight realize that the whole basis for the Law he protects is based on love. That is because he has rewritten the Law to serve his own purposes, and in so doing, added layers and layers of fat to his body. He has taken what was given by God and made it to mean things God never intended. He has done this through the seemingly innocent method of adding laws to cover every contingency in life. In so doing, he has inadvertently covered God's Law with the unhealthy fat of his own layers of law. He has unwittingly committed idolatry by worshipping his laws above worshipping God. When Jesus came along, this heavyweight could no longer find God's true Law beneath the layers of his own creation. Like a fighter with bleeding eyes, he was blinded from seeing the power of his lean opponent, swinging helplessly and aimlessly, hoping to land the knockout punch. The very layers of fat he thought would protect him have now made him impotent. He is fighting for his life.

In the other corner is Jesus Christ. He is God's love incarnate. His training has been honed on the basics of the Law and none other. He has approached the Law as the God of love intended it to be. Not only has he added no layers of fat to the Law, but he is also strengthened by the essence of the Law's intent. He has summed up his training routine and his fight strategy to one simple rule—you shall love your neighbor as yourself. Against this offense, the law-keeper has no defense. He can neither see the punch coming nor block its power, but he refuses to go down without a fight. He is, after all, a heavyweight.

As the keeper of law, he will fight to the bitter end.

---

1. This list can be found at *www.religionfacts.com/judaism/practices/613.htm* (Accessed July 13, 2007).

# *Vignette for Chapter Nine*

## *"Pilate Revisited"*

Word got out that Political Science Professor Levy Schmidt, the champion of civil rights and a former lawyer for the ACLU, lay dying in the hospital from full-blown AIDS.

Greatly concerned for Professor Schmidt's soul, the leader of the college Christian group visited with him to share the gospel.

"I'm Jewish," Schmidt said. "I don't believe in your Christ."

"If you're Jewish, then certainly you believe in life after death."

"I'm an atheist Jew. I don't believe in God."

"You're going to die, you know. What's going to happen when you die?"

"When I die, I die. That will be the end. Now go away. I'm feeling weak."

Disheartened, the leader of the college Christian group went back to school, sharing with his student disciples how he had tried to share the gospel with this famous atheist but had failed. At least he had left a tract on the bedside table. They all got together and prayed for Levy's soul.

Two days later a local pastor from an evangelical church visited Levy. He, too, attempted to share the gospel but on a more intellectual level. For three hours, they debated religion, absolutism versus ethical relativism, the Christian Right versus humanism and the secular left. He earnestly tried to help Schmidt see the truth.

"What is truth?" Schmidt asked sarcastically.

"The Bible is the truth."

"That's your truth. Not mine. Even if I did believe in the Bible, my interpretation would be different from yours."

The pastor pulled out every apologetic argument and evangelical tactic he could to convince Levy that there was but one truth, but Schmidt would not budge.

"Thank you for coming, anyway. Now go away. I'm in a lot of pain."

Discouraged, the pastor from the local church went back to his congregation, sharing with his flock how he had tried to share the gospel with this famous secularist but had failed. At least he had left a Gideon's New Testament on the bedside table. At the Wednesday night prayer meeting, they all prayed fervently for Professor Schmidt's soul.

A week later, a charismatic pastor visited Schmidt. He had heard about him from the other pastor at the monthly pastors' prayer breakfast. He was quite sure that as a result of faith, he could bring about a healing.

When he entered Schmidt's room, he politely introduced himself and asked permission to pray for Levy's healing.

"Sure. Why not? What have I to lose?"

The charismatic pastor prayed fervently for about an hour, often speaking in tongues, interrupted only with the encouragement, "Just a little bit of faith, Levy. That's all that's needed. Just the faith of a grain of mustard seed. Jesus is ready to heal you."

But to no avail. Schmidt just lay there, unmoved. To him, the whole thing was rather bizarre.

"All you need is just a little bit of faith, Levy," the pastor said, obviously frustrated with Levy and implying that the reason there had been no healing was Levy's lack of faith.

"Can't muster it, pastor," Levy said matter-of-factly. "Wouldn't know it if I had it. But thanks for trying. Now go away. I'm feeling short of breath."

Disappointed, the charismatic pastor went back to the pastors' prayer breakfast the next month and shared how he, too, had attempted to bring healing to Schmidt. Alas, Schmidt just did not have faith. Not even a little. At least he had left Schmidt with the witness of tongues so that perhaps the Holy Spirit would open his mind to God's miracles.

One night, around 2 a.m., Levy woke up in great pain and found it difficult to breathe. His body was drenched in sweat. He reached for his nurse call button but could not find it. He felt he was suffocating.

"Nurse!" he tried to yell, but his voice was so weak he could barely utter a whisper. "Nurse!" He could feel his heart pounding, and now his head was beginning to throb.

An Hispanic aide happened to walk by his room. "Nurse!" he yelled as loud as he could. She stopped, turned and entered the room, switching on the night light.

"What's wrong, Mr. Schmidt?"

"Can't...breathe...pain...chest."

The aide quickly summoned the charge nurse and began taking his vitals. "His blood pressure's down—60 over 42. Heart rate 150 and irregular. Respiratory rate 28. Oxygen saturation is 84%."

"He may have a pulmonary embolism," the nurse said. "Lower his head and put oxygen on him at 10 liters a minute." She went to the nurse's desk and paged respiratory stat. "Call the EKG tech and have her run a strip. I'll call the doctor and see if he wants a chest x-ray and D-dimer."

It took four hours but eventually Levy was stabilized. His pulmonary embolism was confirmed and blood thinners were carefully administered. The Hispanic aide stayed with Levy, leaving his side only to do other necessary chores.

"You feel better Mr. Schmidt?"

"Much. Thanks. What's your name?"

"Natividad."

For the first time, Schmidt took a good look at the aide who had come to his rescue. She was strikingly obese; that is, morbidly obese. He couldn't see a wedding band on her finger and asked her if she was single.

"Yes and no. I have a little girl. She stays with my mother when I work at night. The father left when I got pregnant. He only married me for my good looks," she chuckled.

"I see you're wearing a crucifix. You must be Catholic."

"That's right. But I don't believe you have to be a Catholic to have God's love. *Dios te ama a ti sin causa.*" Levy discovered Natividad frequently peppered her English with Spanish phrases. He had no idea what she was saying.

There wasn't much said after that, either, for Levy and Natividad were both exhausted. The next night she was also on duty and passed by his room frequently. Every time he appeared uncomfortable, she would arrange his sheets and pillows, and kept his beside cup filled with cold water. Over the next few days, he came to the point of losing control of his bowels, and she would clean him, often several times during the night. She never let him lie in a soiled diaper. Every time he would thank her. Each time she responded, "*Dios es bueno. Como mi Dios es tan bueno conmigo, también lo deberia ser contigo.*" Of course, Levy was hesitant to ask what it meant. He supposed it to be Spanish for "Don't worry about it." He had no idea of the faith behind it.

"I'm not supposed to talk to you in Spanish," she said, "but once in a while, I like to say things my own way."

"You can say it anyway you want, Natividad."

The days passed by, the nights got longer, and Levy's visitors became fewer and fewer. Only Natividad was a regular. She took Levy under her wing and often held his hand when she prayed for him in Spanish, which he didn't seem to mind.

One night when Natividad was off, Levy reached for his water glass on his bedside table. Instead of the glass, his fingers rested on a small metal object that he quickly recognized as Natividad's crucifix. His reflex was to toss it but he had enough alertness to ask himself, "Why in the world would she leave it here without telling me?"

The longer he held it, the warmer it felt. He grasped it tighter until the edges of the cross made a mark in his palm.

He was beginning to understand Natividad.

*Chapter Nine*

# "Loving God Means *What*?"
# (Love and the Great Commandments)

*"Beloved, let us love one another, for love is from God;*
*and everyone who loves is born of God and knows God."*
(1 John 4:7)

There is an interesting insertion in Mark's Gospel that helps us understand the significance of Christ's death. Mark, Peter's missionary traveling companion, occasionally digresses from his narrative to offer explanation of Jewish tradition to the newly converted Gentile Christians. In chapter seven, the Pharisees object to Jesus' disciples' disregard for the tradition of ceremonially washing their hands before eating (Mark 7:1-5). Jesus scolds the Pharisees for being more concerned about their traditions and interpretations of the Law than the Law itself. Adhering to man-made traditions—which does not involve loving relationships—is easier than keeping the fundamental commandment to "Honor your father and mother" (Mark 7:6-13). The Pharisees, therefore, are hypocrites. They accuse Jesus and his disciples of failing to observe matters of lesser importance when they themselves fail to observe matters of utmost importance. In explaining the hypocrisy of the Pharisees, Jesus proclaims that it's not what goes into a person that defiles him, but what comes out (vv. 14-23). The reason is simple: regarding food and washing, what goes into a person passes into the stomach and is eventually eliminated. But what comes out—words, thoughts, choices and beliefs—come from the heart. What comes from the heart declares what a person is like on the inside.

In the middle of Jesus' explanation, however, Mark inserts an important theological teaching that could have come only from Peter's experience: ***"Thus He declared all foods clean"*** (v. 19). It was Peter who first learned this lesson in a vision before visiting the Gentile Cornelius (Acts 10:9-16).

This principle—that Jesus declared all foods clean—represents a radical change, and this change has to do specifically with the Law and not traditions. The Book of Leviticus specifically details as part of the Law which foods are clean and which are unclean (e.g., chapter 11). Mark is informing his readers that what a person eats has become a non-issue regarding his or her relationship to God. The apostle Paul confirms this teaching (Rom. 14, 1 Cor. 8, Gal. 2:11-14, 1 Tim. 4:4-5).

There is a greater law at work now that the Holy Spirit has come: it is the law of love. Whereas the Law required traditions and interpretations to apply, the law of love is universal and covers all law.

Think of the Law as a large block of ice. It is hard, cold and inflexible. You can put the ice block in a chest or refrigerator filled with food and, for a while, it will remain a solid unit. Leave the cooler lid or door open and exposed to the air, however, and the ice's state rapidly changes. Instead of being one solid, inflexible unit, it melts and becomes water. Whereas the ice block only filled a portion of the ice chest, now there is water everywhere. The entire bottom is covered with water. Anything coming in touch with the water becomes wet and saturated. Yet it is the same substance as was the ice, only in a different state.

The law of Moses—the Ten Commandments—is like a large block of ice. But the block has been melted by the New Covenant—specifically, the death and resurrection of Christ and the coming of the Holy Spirit. The ice's natural state, fluid, is revealed. The fluid water permeates and saturates everything.

Such is the comparison between the Law and love. The Law was non-fluid; therefore, the "fluid" had to be produced by interpretations of the Law by the scribes, by creating more laws, and by formulating traditions around the Law and therefore making them equivalent to the Law. Little ice cubes as it were. But such is not the case with love. Love has its own fluidity and can permeate every aspect of life and relationships. It is when love is attempted to be re-frozen that we run into problems, for it is easier to work with something solid than something fluid.

That is why the Great Commandments are what they are. The Great Commandments are fluid and can permeate any and all circumstances and situations. The Law cannot do this. What directs the flow of love, however, are the river banks of truth. Whereas love must be fluid, truth must be solid and inflexible. Only truth from the Scriptures can define and limit the boundaries of love.

Joseph Fletcher fell into the trap of ill-defined love. His book, *Situation Ethics: The New Morality* (previously cited in the chapter "Love and the Truth"), betrays the novelty of his hypothesis by unveiling his lack of understanding of the relationship between love and truth. The point of Fletcher's book is that the right thing to do in any given situation is the most loving thing. He goes so far as to actually say that Jesus was wrong and his disciples were right when the woman anointed him with costly perfume at Simon the leper's home (Matthew 26:6-13). Fletcher makes the same error as the disciples: it would have been more loving to sell the perfume and give it to the poor than to waste it on Jesus. Whether the disciples' pride was at stake or they were truly concerned about the poor is unclear. Nowhere else in the Gospels is there any indication that they were that compassionate for the less fortunate. More probably, they saw the use of the perfume as a waste of good money, and giving it to the poor as a way of justifying their disdain, either for the woman or for her actions. Jesus corrects the disciples by instructing them that anointing his head with perfume was not a love issue. The anointing of Jesus' head was a truth issue, for, unlike the woman with the alabaster vial, none of them believed he would really suffer and be crucified at the hands of the Gentiles (Matthew 16:21-23).

Fletcher's primary problem is that he fails to understand and define God's love with truth. Fletcher falls into the trap—as so many do—of making love itself the truth. Or, perhaps more accurately, he defines love according to man's interests rather than God's. He represents the epitome of situation ethics and relativism. He paints a portrait of love that has been imaged by his own knowledge and understanding. He betrays the wisdom of man rather than God. Only Scripture can define love because from

Scripture do we learn the Great Commandments. From the Scriptures alone, we learn truth.

So how is this love defined, and how is it presented in Scripture? Unlike a dictionary, the Scripture teaches love behind the scenes and only in a few places in the New Testament is the nature of love described. Yet love is everywhere. It permeates and saturates the Scriptures on nearly every page.

It is, of course, impractical in this book to comment on every instance in the Bible where love is an issue, but there are some important principles about love that can be established.

## The Great and Foremost Commandment

*"'You shall love the Lord your God with all your heart, and with all your soul, and with all your mind.' This is the great and foremost commandment."* (Matthew 22:37)

There is no question that the great and foremost commandment cited in the Old Testament (Deut. 6:5; 30:6) is affirmed by Jesus in the New (see also Mark 12:28-31 and Luke 10:25-28). However, with the death and resurrection of Christ and the baptism of the Holy Spirit, the interpretation and application of the foremost commandment is changed dramatically.

For an Israelite in Moses' day and a Jew in Jesus' day, the interpretation and application of the great and foremost commandment focused primarily on the Law. Up until the deportation to Babylonia, abstaining from idolatry was perhaps the key focus of showing one's love for God and for him alone. (After the return of the exiles to Palestine, in the four hundred years before Christ, idolatry became less a problem for the Israelites due to strict enforcement of isolation from other cultures.) In general, however, observing the laws, sacrifices and festivals of the Pentateuch, the first five books of the Old Testament, pointed toward a broader picture of what it meant to love God. In Exodus are found the Ten Commandments and the laws of the priesthood, the tabernacle and the Sabbath. In Leviticus the ritual, festival and sacrificial laws are detailed, as well as laws of what is clean and unclean. In Numbers are found the laws of genealogy, Levitical priesthood, and additional cultural and civil laws. It is clear, then, that to love God with all one's heart, soul, mind and might was to adhere to the Law put forth in these books. Even apart from the traditions of the elders, which began to be treated as equivalent to the Law in Jesus' day, to love God was to obey. If one's heart was in it, obviously that person would be at an advantage. However, even if one's heart was not in it, strict obedience was expected.

Therefore, to keep the great commandment meant a lifestyle of obedience and complete submission to Old Testament law. To love was to obey and to obey was to love. Whether one's heart was in it or not only determined if obedience was to be a blessing or a burden.

Unfortunately, even today, obedience to the Law specifically and to law in general is the common interpretation and application of the great and first commandment. To love God is to obey a set of laws and rules that springboard off the Ten Commandments. As in Jesus' day, when the traditions of the elders became equivalent to the Law, similar pitfalls exist today. Churches, pastors and well-meaning Christians establish social, religious and behavioral laws or rules—often softened with the term "guidelines" or "standards"—that help define the obedient Christian, and therefore the great and foremost commandment.

When I first became a Christian in 1959, evangelical Christians did not dance...period. I remember once when a local Christian camp faced a huge issue over whether or not to include square dancing as part of their evening activities for adults. Upon deciding in favor of including square dancing, a number of long-time supporters stopped donating and others stopped attending the summer camps. According to their theology, it was a huge breach of moral conduct.

I once preached a message on whether or not a Christian should drink alcohol (about half the church were closet drinkers). I shared that the New Testament did not forbid the use of alcohol, and that those believers who felt freedom to drink could do so without guilt so long as they did not become drunk or become a source of temptation for recovering alcoholics. After the message, before I had even left the pulpit, the mother of one of the members, visiting from out of town, came up and, pointing her finger angrily at me, said, "Satan had a field day in this church today! I can forgive you, but God will never forgive you for what you taught in this church today." Little did she know that her own daughter and son-in-law were among the closet drinkers! They just hid the booze when she was in town.

For so many Christians, to love God with all one's heart, mind and soul is a matter of obedience to some form of law, from keeping the Sabbath to compulsively having a daily quiet time, to not dancing or drinking or watching R-rated movies or, in the case of so many young people, abstaining from masturbating. Loving God is demonstrated by obeying law.

There are four problems with this belief system. First, to fail in one part of the law is to fail all the law (Gal. 3:10; 5:3; Jas. 2:10), regardless of the source of the law (Scriptural, church or self-imposed). Of course, the Christian deals with this failure by acknowledging that his inability to keep God's law, the laws of the church, or his own rules is accommodated for by faith in Christ; that failure to keep any law does not nullify one's salvation, for we are saved by grace and not by righteousness through law. What is the effect of the first problem then? Even though salvation is not at stake, guilt and bondage is. The belief that the great commandment is linked with law can only result in overriding guilt, defeat, frustration and self-recrimination.

The second problem with the belief system that loving God involves obeying law is obvious: what laws? Whose laws should one obey? Sabbath-keepers face divisions among themselves over everything from whether or not to eat eggs and dairy products to what activities are permissible on the Sabbath. (Is a child swimming in a pool on the Sabbath play or healthy rest?) Conservative evangelicals face divisions (i.e., denominations) over issues of what kind of musical instruments should be allowed during worship to whether or not musical instruments should be used at all. Moreover, there are strict rules as to what translation of the Bible a believer should use. For many, using any Bible other than a KJV Scofield Reference Bible is akin to idolatry and apostasy. (KJV stands for *King James Version*.)

The third problem with the belief that obeying law is necessary to show love for God is that this belief is no longer consistent with New Testament teaching. Paul makes this very clear in 1 Corinthians 7:19: "Circumcision is nothing, and uncircumcision is nothing, but what matters is the keeping of the commandments of God." But wait a minute. Wasn't circumcision a vital part of the Law and a commandment of God? Obviously, Paul has another commandment in mind than obeying the Law. There is another law, newer and greater, that is at work.

The fourth problem is that the whole concept of love and grace is distorted by law-dependent living. Demonstrating love through obedience to law alone is to remove all the blessings of personal relationship. For failing to love God's law perfectly, the joys of intimacy are supplanted by the fears of discipline. Without intimacy, God remains a distant relative. The believer's relationship with him is at best parochial. Love is equated to duty rather than desire. Blessing turns to bondage and peace to pacification. If one's relationship to God the Father is based purely on showing love through obedience, then one will never truly experience the blessings of intimacy and love.

Obedience to law, then, is no longer the answer to the great and foremost commandment. To love God with all one's heart, mind and soul must mean something other than what was assumed in Jesus' day.

As we shall see, upon the arrival of the Holy Spirit, *the great and foremost commandment is never again mentioned in Scripture.*

### *...And the second is like it... "You shall love your neighbor as yourself."*

Once again, Jesus affirms the Old Testament principle of loving one's neighbor as a significant part of the great commandment (Matt. 22:39; Mark 12:31; Luke 10:27). It is interesting to note that the Greek word chosen there does not mean "exactly alike," but "similar to." Thus, there is a clear distinction between loving God with all one's heart, mind and soul, and loving others as oneself.

The apostle Paul, however, throws a significant twist into the whole concept of the great and foremost commandment in his letters. For example, Paul states in Galatians 5:14: **"The whole Law is fulfilled in one word, in the statement, '*You shall love your neighbor as yourself*'"** (italics mine). The pattern of referring to love of one's neighbor only and not the great and foremost commandment (to love God with all your heart, mind and soul) is repeated too many times to be an ellipsis (that is, something purposefully omitted on the assumption that the reader will automatically inject it). Paul even goes so far as to repeat three times in Romans 13:8-10 that loving one's neighbor not only sums up the Law but also fulfills the Law. In Paul's letter to the Galatians, he states, ***"Bear one another's burdens, and thereby fulfill the law of Christ"*** (6:2). One wonders, then, why the apostle to the Gentiles did not include the great and foremost commandment.

James, too, repeats the pattern of omitting the great commandment. In chapter two, verse eight, he goes so far as to call the second commandment (to love one's neighbor as oneself) the "royal law" (literally, "the law of our King"). One wonders again why the Lord's half-brother, head of the Jerusalem church, probable leader of the more conservative Jewish Christians, did not include the great and foremost commandment?

The apostle John, though not quoting the great or second commandments in his Gospel or letters, approaches love almost exclusively from the aspect of the second commandment. Yet, "commandment" is a central theme of John's letters. In fact, the word "commandment" and its plural are used no less than seventeen times in his letters alone.

I am quite sure that if we were to ask Paul, James and John "Should we love God with all our heart, mind and soul?" they would of course answer in the affirmative. But I believe that what it meant to keep the great commandment, that is, its interpretation and application, had changed dramatically. That change was radical and had nothing to do with the Ten Commandments or the Law. That change is new, it represents a new revelation and it foreshadows the age to come.

## The New Commandment

*"A new commandment I give to you, that you love one another, even as I have loved you, that you also love one another. By this all men will know that you are My disciples if you have love for one another."* (John 13:34-35)

There are mysterious references by Paul and Peter that begin to shed light on the change in the great and foremost commandment.

Paul, writing to Timothy, instructs him to "keep the commandment without stain or reproach until the appearing of our Lord Jesus Christ" (1 Tim. 6:14). A simple question arises and in this case raises the possibility of an ellipsis: to what commandment is Paul referring? The context of the passage has to do with church issues: specifically, servants and masters, false teaching in the church, money and personal gain. Paul admonishes Timothy to "flee from these things...pursue righteousness...fight the good fight of faith; take hold of the eternal life to which you were called," and then, to "keep the commandment" (note, singular). Careful examination of the context fails to reveal an adequate antecedent for the commandment to which Paul is referring. It appears Paul is referring to a commandment that is familiar and obvious to Timothy. By deduction, it ought to be obvious to the reader. As in the next case, *it cannot be assumed by today's reader that the commandment to which Paul is referring is the great and foremost commandment.*

Peter presents us with the same dilemma in his second letter: "...You should remember the words spoken beforehand by the holy prophets and the commandment of the Lord and Savior spoken by your apostles" (2 Pet. 3:2). To what commandment (again, singular) is he referring? A clue is found in the immediately preceding verses: "For it would be better for them not to have known the way of righteousness, than having known it, to turn away from the holy commandment handed on to them" (2 Pet. 2:21). Once again, the commandment is not spelled out, but Peter is assuming that the reader knows what this "holy commandment" is. It cannot be assumed by today's reader that the holy commandment is the same as the great and foremost commandment, for nowhere else in the church letters is that commandment referred to.

Perhaps the answer to the question "What commandment?" lies in John's Gospel. John, more than any other disciple, details for his readers the last words of Christ. They form the basis for the future church's understanding of what will replace the Law that has been put to rest. The clear message from John's gospel and his subsequent letters is this: the first and foremost commandment has been superseded by a new commandment. John and the apostles never repeated the first and foremost commandment because all love for God could be fulfilled by loving one's neighbor as oneself—the royal law. To fulfill the royal law was to fulfill the first and foremost commandment *and* the new commandment to love one another. Why? *Because the first and foremost commandment was intimately tied to the Law, and the believer is no longer under the Law.* To love one another was tied to lovingkindness and grace. To love your neighbor as yourself was now what God was requiring to love him with all your heart, mind and strength. To love one another, and to love your neighbor as yourself, is to love God. Ironically, then, the first and foremost commandment is now summed up in the second great commandment.

This new teaching will pervade every aspect of Christian theology, from defining righteousness and sin to opening the door for a new understanding of the millennium.

# *Vignette for Chapter Ten*

# *"The Pastor's Wife"*

Pastor Norm loved being a pastor. Being a pastor was all he ever wanted to do. He never missed a class in seminary and the only times he wasn't in the pulpit was when he was on a family vacation. He loved preaching, he loved counseling, he loved visitations, he even loved church meetings. "They're the greatest entertainment on earth," he laughed. "Anything can happen!"

Pastor Norm was not the traveling kind. He liked staying at one church and loved "just plowing the field, sowing the seed" for years. In his forty years as a pastor, he'd been at only two churches.

Always with a smile on his face, never passing an opportunity to give a hug, he was well loved by his congregation. Only once had anyone ever hinted that it might be time to move on. Of course, the disgruntled elder and his wife eventually moved on themselves out of frustration. As they put it, "It's like talking to a teddy bear." As Pastor Norm put it, "I just wore them down."

He never planned to retire from being a pastor. "There's no such thing as a 'retired pastor,'" he often repeated. "It's an oxymoron. I want to die with my boots on." To him, the greatest way to die would be while preaching about the kingdom of God. "Just carry me out with the offering plates," he used to say at the end of every church meeting, and it always brought a laugh. Pastor Norm led a lively, happy, healthy church, the fruit of years of love and labor and the envy of many other pastors in the city.

But then came the foreign words, "Progressive supranuclear palsy." No, it was not his diagnosis...it was his wife's.

It started with him having a harder time understanding her at home. "You're mumbling," he would comment. But the mumbling became slurred speech, followed rapidly by periods of blurred vision which she never mentioned. Pastor Norm, always in a hurry, would become impatient with her as she trailed behind. He didn't recognize the pattern until one day she fell walking out to the car after church. It landed her in the hospital with a broken hip. "I just felt dizzy," she said. Subsequent tests and consultations eventually identified the rare brain disorder as PSP.

"It's the same problem Dudley Moore had," the neurologist informed them when he told them the diagnosis. Neither Pastor Norm nor his wife had ever heard of Dudley Moore.

"Is there a cure?"

"No. We can only treat the complications. First, we want to get you back on your feet."

"Will I walk again?"

"Probably. But it will be difficult. Eventually, you'll be confined to a wheelchair."

"And then bedridden, I suppose."

"Yes."

"How long do I have to live?"

The doctor, whose philosophy was always to state the facts, shared quickly. "Perhaps five years. Maybe more."

"Thank you for being honest."

The doctor left and Pastor Norm and his wife had a long cry together.

At the next board meeting, Pastor Norm gave the elders the news. "I never thought I'd say this, but I'm going to have to take an early retirement."

There was unexpected silence, but at the same time, expected understanding.

"We'll do everything in our power to help you through this, Norm," the head elder said.

And so Pastor Norm and his wife said their goodbyes to the church, and many tears were shed. "We're really going to miss you," they affirmed. "At least you'll be staying in town so we can see you often."

And for the next five years, rarely a day went by that someone from the church didn't visit, or drop off a meal, or bring over a bulletin. Pastor Norm would listen patiently to the complaints about the new pastor, but for the sake of the church, he never went back.

When he was unable to continue caring for his wife at home, she became a resident at a skilled nursing facility. He was always there at 7 a.m. to help get her dressed and wheel her in to breakfast. When she was no longer able to feed herself, he fed her. When she was no longer able to swallow without choking, he monitored the feeding tube and positioned her comfortably in bed so she wouldn't develop bed sores.

When she was no longer able to talk, she communicated by lifting her index finger for yes and her thumb for no. When she was no longer able to lift her fingers, he just sat by her bed, sometimes reading Scripture, sometimes reading to her the paper, sometimes reading to her some notes he had jotted down for the book he hoped to write.

When the end came, Martha's husband was at her side. You see, her husband loved being a pastor, but he loved more his dearly beloved Martha.

*Bill Walthall*

*Chapter Ten*

# "Don't Call Me
# Goody Two-Shoes"
# (Love and Righteousness)

*"Blessed are those who hunger and thirst for righteousness,
for they shall be satisfied."* (Matthew 5:6)

Righteousness has become a dirty word these days. For some reason, it has been placed in the category of "old-school Christianity." In churches that have shifted to a "seeker service" approach, righteousness, sin, blood and death are terms rarely heard from the stage. The purpose of omitting these words, it is taught, is to shelter visitors from being offended by negative images. Even in non-seeker-service churches, however, these terms are not heard as often as they used to be. The emphasis of preaching has shifted from expositional Bible teaching to addressing felt needs. A variety of factors may be involved. Perhaps one of the reasons the word righteousness is not heard as much in churches is due to fear of being labeled "self-righteous" by the world. Self-righteous, of course, has a very negative connotation. The term implies a holier-than-thou attitude, a judgmental demeanor, or a religiously prideful spirit that is insensitive to others and short on self-evaluation.

If there is any term that has biblical validity but has been invalidated by poor interpretation and application, the term righteousness may win the prize. Jesus validated the term clearly and poignantly when he stated to the multitudes, "Blessed are those who hunger and thirst for righteousness, for theirs is the kingdom of heaven," and "For I say to you that unless your righteousness surpasses that of the scribes and the Pharisees, you will not enter the kingdom of heaven" (Matt. 5:6 and 5:20, respectively).

For years, the typical evangelical interpretation of the second verse is that Christians can only exceed the righteousness of the scribes and Pharisees by virtue of being in Christ. That is, Christ alone surpassed the righteousness of the law-keepers and for those who are "in Christ," righteousness is imputed to them by God the Father. Although righteousness is indeed imputed to the believer by grace through faith (Rom. 3:21-26), it is an improper application to Jesus' statement in the Sermon on the Mount.

Let's take a moment, however, to see how righteousness is typically defined by evangelicals.

## Law — the Old Standard of Righteousness

Biblical righteousness refers to a standard of morality that reflects the very nature of God himself. God alone establishes the standard of righteousness for man. From man's perspective, the standard of righteousness is established and communicated through God's laws. When referring to the righteousness of God, however, the scope of righteousness transcends the Law and reflects his holiness and perfection. On his own, therefore, man can never hope to achieve the same level of righteousness that exists with God. And, as made clear by the apostle Paul, man cannot achieve righteousness even by keeping the Law (Gal. 2:16).

Here is a definition of righteousness from one of my favorite classical evangelical theologians, Merrill F. Unger.

> *Righteousness (Heb. şĕdĕq; Gr. dikia), purity of heart and rectitude of life; the being and doing right. The righteousness or justice (q.v.) of God is the divine holiness applied in moral government and the domain of law. As an attribute of God it is united with his holiness as being essential in his nature; it is legislative or rectoral, as he is the righteous governor of all creatures; and is administrative or judicial, as he is a just dispenser of rewards and punishments. The righteousness of Christ denotes not only his absolute perfection, but is taken for*

*his perfect obedience to the law, and suffering the penalty thereof in our stead. It is frequently used to designate his holiness, justice, and faithfulness.... The righteousness of the law is that obedience which the law requires.... The righteousness of faith is the justification (q.v.) which is received by faith.... The perfect righteousness of Christ is imputed to the believer, when he accepts Christ as his savior....[1]*

It is quite clear that this classical but complicated evangelical standard of righteousness is interpreted in the shadow of Old Testament law.

When I teach on the subject of righteousness, or when the word appears in the biblical text, I attempt to simplify the meaning by saying that righteousness simply means, "to be right with God." It is, of course, an oversimplification to some degree, but it serves the purpose, especially when teaching new believers or when witnessing to unbelievers. Rather than asking, "How does one become righteous?" I ask, "How do we become right with God?" Or, "What must we do for God to say to us, 'You're okay'?"

When the words "justify" or "justification" appear in the biblical text, I explain that they are simply different forms of the word for "righteous." Whereas "righteous" is the noun form in the Greek (*dikaios*), "justify" is the verb form (*dikaioo*; "justification," *dikaiosis*). Therefore, to justify someone before God (*dikaioo*) is to make that person righteous (*dikaios*).

The New Testament clearly teaches the following things about righteousness. First, no one is righteous before God (Rom. 3:10). Regardless of social, economic, moral or religious background, no one is capable of meeting God's standard of righteousness. The best of good people fall infinitely short of the standard of righteousness, or perfection, that God has established. An analogy is this: the best professional basketball player in the world, no matter how hard he trains, cannot jump high enough to break free of earth's gravity. If he were to stand on the top of Mt. Everest and jump as high as he could, he would fail to break the earth's pull. And so it is with man's attempt to break free from his unrighteousness. It is a futile and impossible task. The gravitational pull of sin is just too great.

Second, keeping the Law, no matter how precisely, cannot make one righteous, and therefore, cannot make one righteous before God (Rom. 3:20). This is because no person is capable of keeping the Law perfectly. And what of sacrifices in the Law? Sacrifices are offered not only to acknowledge that we have *not* kept the Law perfectly, but that we are indeed *incapable* of keeping the Law perfectly. Old Testament Law was never intended to make us righteous. Indeed, the Law's purpose was to reveal to us our sins. James informs us that if a person fails on one point of the Law, that person fails the Law completely (James 2:10). Furthermore, even if we *could* keep the Law perfectly, it would be of little avail simply because humanity is unrighteous *by nature* (Eph. 2:2). We were born in a state of unrighteousness, alienated from God, bound by an earthly force we cannot overcome (Rom. 5:12, 18-19).

Third, only one man was born righteous and kept the Law perfectly— Jesus Christ. By means of the Virgin Birth, Jesus was born without an unrighteous nature, the stain of "original sin" and "total depravity" shared by all humanity. Additionally, he kept the Law perfectly and was therefore sinless (John 8:46). As the writer of Hebrews states, Christ was *"...One who has been tempted in all things as we are, yet without sin"* (4:15). Thus, by being righteous before God, Jesus fulfilled all the points of the Law (Matt. 5:17), and by fulfilling all points of the Law, validated his righteousness before God. Thus, in the letters of the apostle Paul, we find the freeing presentation of what it takes to be right with God. There is but one way to be right with God: believing in, putting one's faith and trust in, and receiving Jesus Christ as the Son of God, the Righteous One, the Messiah, the Savior of the world (John 1:12; Rom. 3:21-24). That a person can become right with God by simply receiving Jesus Christ through faith in spite of sin is a free gift from God offered through grace (Eph 2:8-9). Therefore, being right with God is not something that can be earned or achieved; it is offered as a gift from God and accepted by faith. Nor is it deserved. Paul states, *"But God demonstrates his own love toward us, in that while we were yet sinners, Christ died for us."* (Rom. 5:8)

Lastly, when a person receives Christ by faith, God *imputes* righteousness to that person. To "impute" means to attribute or ascribe. In legal terms, it means to make a legal declaration that in itself becomes law. It is a wonderful thing. When someone receives Christ by faith, God imputes to that person the righteousness of Christ. It is as if the righteousness of Christ is transferred onto the other person. It is as if God is saying, "If you receive my Son by faith, I will cover you with his righteousness. You will be accepted into my presence unconditionally. I will give you all the rights and privileges of someone who had never sinned; indeed, the inheritance I have reserved for my Son. It will be as if you had never been born with a sin nature and as if you had gone through your entire life without ever sinning." True, the person who receives Christ is still unrighteous by nature, but from a legal and spiritual perspective, from God's perspective, the righteousness of Christ is attributed to the person who places his or her faith in Christ. For all intent and purposes, and from the perspective that most counts, the one who places faith in Christ is declared righteous by God. That means the person's sins will no longer be counted against him or her. That means all sins are forgiven. That means the person is right before God and in good standing with God even if he or she commits more sin.

The most amazing aspect about being declared righteous is that, in truth, we are not actually righteous. Our righteousness is through Christ, not ourselves. It is declared, not earned. It is given through grace; it is not deserved. Therefore, many theologians differentiate between "imputed righteousness" and "imparted righteousness." Whereas imputed righteousness is a legal declaration by God that makes a person righteous in his eyes, imparted righteousness is the life-long process by which Christians, through the sanctifying work of the Holy Spirit, change to *act* righteously. That is, to begin living as if they are actually righteous people; to live in such a manner that an outsider might say, "*There* is a righteous person."

The subject is complex, but this illustration might prove helpful. Let's suppose you are born with blue eyes, but blue eyes have been outlawed all over the world. You have tried your best to disguise your blue eyes—you've worn sunglasses, you've bought colored contacts, you've closed your eyes when the eye-patrol comes around, and you've lied about the color of your eyes on your driver's license and job applications. In short, not only is your very existence against the law, but everything you have done, albeit with good intentions and seemingly harmless, has been against the law. One day the eye-patrol catches you and the blue-eye judge sentences you to prison for life. There is nothing you can do to escape the sentence, for you are who you are. The color of your eyes cannot be changed and because of who you are, you've committed plenty of illegal acts, just one of which was bad enough to send you to prison for life. By law, you are, in fact, guilty. Now you're stuck in prison for life until you die. Even worse, because your eyes are blue, you are scheduled for "eye-cleansing." Your eyes will be surgically excised from your head and you will be blinded for life. You're in a real fix from which you cannot escape!

But something wonderful happens. The world's government is defeated by a powerful benevolent leader. This new leader immediately changes the law of the land and nullifies the law prohibiting blue eyes. He declares that all those who have been imprisoned for the color of their eyes may go free. There is but one condition—they must be willing to acknowledge and accept the new leader as the lord of the land and therefore the ruler of their lives. Acknowledgements from the heart by faith are accepted.

When the lord comes around, you choose to make such an acknowledgement and the doors of the jail fly open! The color of your eyes hasn't changed, yet you are free to go. In fact, you are free to go in spite of the color of your eyes.

Now, no illustration is perfect, to be sure, but it serves its purpose. Accepting Jesus Christ sets us free from the penalty of who we are (sinners) and what we have done (sin). As Paul writes in Romans 8:1-2, "Therefore there is now no condemnation for those who are in Christ Jesus. For the law of the Spirit of life in Christ Jesus has set you free from the law of sin and death."

But some interesting questions arise from the above illustration, questions that must be asked of all Christians. Once out of prison, how do we then live? Do we begin living again according to the blue-eye laws? (Old habits are hard to break.) Do we live as if the eye-patrol is watching our every move? (Old beliefs are hard to change.) Do we live in fear that if we are not careful, we will have to face the blue-eye judge once again? (Old fears are hard to overcome.)

This is where the issue of love and righteousness meet face to face. What many Christians miss is that righteousness is no longer defined by Old Testament law, or any law for that matter. Living righteously no longer depends on keeping a moral standard or conforming to the Law. Living righteously does not mean doing a better job of keeping the Law, regardless of whether it is the Old Testament laws or ecclesiastical laws or a church's laws or even personal laws. There is a new standard for righteousness, the measure of which is not law, but love. The measure of righteousness is determined by biblically defined love, and to live righteously is to love our neighbor as ourselves.

## Love — the New Standard of Righteousness

It is human nature to choose the easier, more traveled path. Yet, it is this human nature we are trying to leave behind. The "old self" (as the apostle Paul labels it in Romans 6:6) "was crucified" when we received Christ by faith. ("Was crucified" is in the *aorist* tense in the Greek, meaning that the act occurred in the past and is completed and finished.) Crucifying the old self was part of the imputation of righteousness. In its place a "new self" has been created through the indwelling Holy Spirit (Eph 4:24, 30). Furthermore, we know from Paul's letter to the Ephesians that the old self has left its mark on our being—our body, our mind, our emotions, our belief systems, our habits. Therefore, it is the responsibility of the Christian to "lay aside the old self" and "put on the new self" (Eph. 4:22-24). The critical question is, *what form does "putting on the new self" take*? How does the Christian put on the new self? In what manner will the Christian's behavior and belief system change?

The answer is found—not in Old Testament law—but in New Testament love.

There is a trap that many Christians, even evangelicals, fall into. It is the trappings of law. Our human nature tends to gravitate toward that with which we are most familiar, Old Testament laws. The weakness of our flesh draws us to that which the crowd dictates as the traditional standard of righteousness, the Ten Commandments. We make covenants and promises and pledges, declaring, "I will now comply more fully with God's laws. That is how I will live the Christian life, that is how I will live in such a manner as to please God, and that is how I will put on the new self." The trap in this kind of thinking is that turning to Old Testament law, or any law for that matter, often results in compartmentalizing our Christianity, becoming preoccupied with our keeping rules, ignoring the critical relationships around us, and doing exactly as the scribes and Pharisees did...picking and choosing what laws we can keep that will make us feel righteous.

But that is not the way of the New Testament. That is not what the apostles and prophets teach regarding putting on the new self. That is not what Christ meant when he told his disciples, "A new commandment I give to you, that you love one another..." (John 13:34).

Learning to love biblically is infinitely harder than learning to obey rules. Rules are inanimate; biblical love always involves relationships. Laws are black and white; biblical love requires "...knowledge of His will in all spiritual wisdom and understanding..." (Col. 1:9). Keeping a law requires discipline; offering biblical love requires sacrifice. Obeying the law depends only upon oneself; having love received depends entirely upon another. With laws, one can measure success; the measure of success in biblical love is only that it is offered. Laws are made so no one must think; biblical love requires wisdom and insight into God's Word. Laws are created so no decision must be made; biblical love cannot be offered without discernment. With laws, there is no grey area; with biblical love, all is grey. Laws must continually be created to cover all contingencies in life. The only contingency required for biblical love is the creativity with which it is offered. Laws are always conditional: if you keep them, you are rewarded, but if you disobey them, you are punished. Biblical love, however, is unconditional; it is the offer of love that is its own reward. Keeping a law offers immediate gratification; the outcome for sacrificially loving another may never be known. To do what is right concerning the law is to obey the law. To do what is right concerning love is to do the most loving thing, biblically defined. There are no risks involved in keeping the law; offering love always involves risks. Obedience to the law makes one feel self-important; biblical love always considers another more important than oneself. To resort to law is to resort to the old way of doing things; to resort to biblical love is to do all things differently. In one sense, keeping laws comes naturally; biblical love, by its very nature, does not come naturally—it must be learned.

If biblical love, then, is the new standard for righteousness, how is it learned and in what manner is it expressed?

There is a simple answer to what appears to be a complicated question. The answer is this: all behaviors, beliefs, actions and values can be measured, directly or indirectly, in the context of relationships. They are measured in terms of relationship to God, to one's family, to one's neighbor, to one's friend, to one's enemy, to one's co-worker or fellow student or boss or employee. They are measured on a corporate level as well as a personal level. They are measured toward oneself as well as toward one's significant other. They are measured as surely with a government as with a friend. All of life, one way or another, involves relationships.

There are literally hundreds of instructions (imperatives) in the New Testament on proper Christian living; they all involve relationships. In the context of righteousness, righteous Christian behavior can *only* be measured in the context of relationships. The common denominator is that, directly or indirectly, *all New Testament imperatives involve relationships*, whether with others or with God. If biblical love is manifested in those relationships, therefore, righteousness will prevail quite apart from any law.

The onus, therefore, is upon the Christian, the disciple of Jesus Christ, to live as one called to love. Indeed, as those who are set free from the bondage of the Law, Christians are set free to love. Christians are called to love biblically, and this biblical love must be learned as a part of putting on the new self. There is only one absolute source for this learning, and that is the word of God. The Christian must look for the love message in every book, in every chapter, in every verse of God's word. Only in this manner will the righteousness of God be manifested through his people, a people known, not for their obedience to law, but for their unconditional and sacrificial love and compassion.

The New Testament, then, teaches its adherents a new standard of righteousness. Righteousness is no longer based upon Old Testament law but on New Testament love. And here is the most amazing thing of all: the righteousness that is imputed to followers of Jesus Christ is a righteousness that considers us as having the same kind of love as Christ himself! When God imputes righteousness to a believer, he is treating us as if we have a perfect loving nature, even though we do not.

But actually gaining that loving nature is what God desires for us. By practicing biblical love, we will then be able to experience and express the love of God.

This is where *imparted* righteousness comes in. The Holy Spirit is sent into believers' lives to teach us how to love like Christ. As a result, Paul informs us in Second Corinthians 5:17, the Holy Spirit creates in us a new nature, a new person, a new self with the ability to learn to practice biblical love, to learn to love like Jesus loves. Does being able to love like Christ seem an impossible task? If that were the case, Jesus would never have said to his disciples, "This is My commandment, that you love one another, just as I have loved you. Greater love has no one than this, that one lay down his life for his friends" (John 15:12, 13; italics mine). By learning to love like Jesus, we begin to conform to the righteousness and love imputed to us. We do not practice biblical love in hopes that God will someday declare us righteous. We practice biblical love because God has *already* declared us righteous; we practice biblical love out of gratitude, not out of fear. Additionally, we do not become more righteous by practicing biblical love; in God's eyes we are already as righteous as we will ever be. We love because he has already declared us righteous, he has set us free from the laws that kept us from loving, and, through the Holy Spirit, he has created in us a new nature with the ability to love like Jesus loves. We do not earn God's favor by loving; we become biblically loving people because we already have God's favor. We love because he first loved us, and by loving, we conform to the righteousness declared.

Would you like to become a more "righteous" person? Then love your neighbor as yourself. Would you like to become more holy? Then love one another. Would you like to be the saint God declared you to be? Then love like Jesus loves.

How, then, does our righteousness surpass that of the scribes and Pharisees? By loving our neighbor as ourselves. And how, then, do we live righteously? By loving one another as Christ has loved us. How do we show God we love him? By loving one another.

The new standard of righteousness, then, is love.

---

1. Merrill F. Unger, *Unger's Bible Dictionary* (Chicago: Moody Press, 1957), 927-928.

*Bill Walthall*

# *Vignette for Chapter Eleven*

# *"Lover Girl"*

"I'm a lover girl. That's me!" Paddy giggled. "Love just seems to come natural for me. I can't explain it—I just love everybody. I've never met a person I haven't found some way to love. Black or white, rich or poor, educated or illiterate; I've always found a way to love anyone and everyone."

Paddy loved to host the women's group as well. Because she was such an excellent hostess, the ladies were glad to let her. Her house, though cluttered, was dustless. Food was plentiful and homemade, always getting, "These are wonderful! Don't tell me you made these from scratch!" And Paddy was always ready for the group by the time the first member arrived. Chairs were set up comfortably in a circle, extra Bibles were readily available, and name tags had been printed ahead of time with extras for guests. If the leader couldn't make it that Tuesday, Paddy was great at filling in. She always had a tear-jerking personal story ready that almost everyone laughed and cried at simultaneously. Therefore, tissues were also strategically placed. It seemed that at one time or another every Tuesday, someone would have a good cry. The other women genuinely loved Paddy, a nickname of endearment adopted by her late husband because, he would confess privately, "She's like a big, fluffy pillow." And Paddy, always full of fun and laughter, didn't mind. In fact, she rather liked the name. "I can identify with that," laughing hoarsely.

Her husband, Paul, was alluding to Paddy's only real flaw: she was quite overweight. Other than her weight, Paul had always known that, in spite of it, he had married a jewel. She gave more love and empathy than anyone he had ever known. She was sensitive, caring, empathetic, showing mercy to all. He had always felt Paddy had the gifts of helps and giving, almost to a flaw. Once, she gave so much to a visiting children's African choir that Paul had a hard time paying bills that month. She and Paul spent the next three months juggling bills to get back on budget. And, especially important to him, she was a good lover as well. He affectionately called her his lover girl. She never said no to him, and did a fine job raising two happy children who could survive on their own.

It was when Paddy developed Type II diabetes that her son and daughter became concerned. Her daughter, a registered nurse, had always been after her about her weight.

"Mom, I'm just worried about you," she said every time she visited with Paddy's grandson.

"You don't need to worry about me. I can take care of myself. God's looking after me. I have more faith in Him than you'll ever have, honey."

Her son, a physical education teacher, was less tactful: "You're packin' on the pounds, Mom. One of these days, you're going to fall and not be able to get up. Then what?"

And it wasn't as if Paddy didn't know. She just didn't care. Oh, yes, she'd tried a diet or two here and there, but it was all too complicated, all "Too depressing. It takes away the only pleasure I have!"

Once, her children thought they had controlled her eating habits, buying only healthy foods and spending hours preparing balanced meals. Little did they know that the women's group was very accommodating to Paddy's pleas and bringing from the store sweets that were cleverly hidden from her children.

No matter how many times her children tried to warn her, she tuned them out. Until, that is, she had to have both knees replaced because the pain was so severe from the wear and tear of degenerative arthritis. It took her months to find an orthopedist who would do the risky elective surgery on a morbidly obese patient.

She followed her dietician's advice on weight management for about a month, but once she realized her knees didn't hurt anymore, she went right back to her old habits.

Next came the cholescystectomy for an infected gall bladder, and then a prolonged hospitalization for cellulitis and swelling in her legs and feet. Because of her diabetes, she had lost nearly all feeling in them. That made her more prone to falling when she tried to walk.

The worse she got the more time her children had to spend on her. During her multiple hospitalizations, they would take turns feeding the cats, paying the bills and watering the plants. Finally, they got her home, each one taking turns spending the nights. One day, home alone, Paddy tripped over the cat she refused to give away and, falling, broke her hip in a very bad place.

"You can't put any weight on that leg for six to eight weeks," the orthopedist instructed her. Of course, unable to stand on one leg because she couldn't lift her own weight, she was sent to a skilled nursing facility for rehabilitation.

In the course of her stay there, one therapist and two aides hurt their backs trying to roll her or transfer her. She was too heavy for the mechanical lift that had a weight limitation of 350 pounds. The nursing home wasn't happy because they had to rent an expensive heavy-duty bed with specialized air mattress, and a heavy-duty wheelchair which she used only twice. The children quickly became faced with the fact that Paddy would need to stay long term. Realizing she would never return home, they sold the house and got rid of most of her things. She fought them all the way, of course. "You can't get rid of that. I've had that since your father and I married." Living under an umbrella of guilt heaped upon guilt, they paid monthly to have her things stored.

The nursing home wasn't pleased, either. Her medical problems were causing it to lose quite a bit of money, as reimbursements from the insurance company were capped and all extra costs were passed on to the facility. All Paddy could talk about, however, was how terrible the food was. To compensate for her "deprivations," Paddy had her loyal church ladies sneak in candy and cookies which she cleverly hid in her bedside table and imbibed at night when the aides weren't around.

Paddy spent the rest of her life in the nursing home, paid for by Medicaid. She was sent to the hospital at least once a month for problems ranging from cellulitis flare-ups requiring extensive wound care, to angina from her coronary artery disease, to a bowel obstruction for which she required surgery, and eventually a stroke. In spite of all the efforts of the nursing home, she died with bedsores on her massive bottom.

"So," Paddy's son asked his sister when they were looking at headstones, "what do you think we ought to write on it?"

Paddy's daughter, who had taken the burden of the care giving responsibilities, who had spent nights and weeks away from her own family, who fought with the insurance companies and the nursing home over medical costs and coverage, who had visited her mother daily and listened to all the complaints about nursing, and who, along with her brother had to fork up personal savings for a 4x-oversize casket, looked harried, worn down and exhausted. She was still struggling with the grief of her mother's passing and the gladness that it was finally over.

"I'm not sure," she pondered, recalling the stress of the last few years. "But there's one thing I definitely won't have written on it."

"Oh? What's that?"

"Lover Girl."

*Chapter Eleven*

# "When 'Missing the Mark' Misses the Mark" (Love and Sin)

*The one who says he is in the Light and yet hates his brother is in the darkness until now. The one who loves his brother abides in the Light and there is no cause for stumbling in him.* (1 John 2:9, 10)

Sin has been defined in a number of ways. Ask any discipled evangelical Christian what sin is and he or she will give you the standard definition taught repeatedly from the pulpit: "The Greek word for sin—*hamartia*—means 'to miss the mark.' It is based on a military term meaning that a soldier's arrow fails to hit the bulls-eye. Sin is anything short of God's standard of perfection. His holiness requires that humanity hits the bulls-eye every time. Anything less is sin."

The evangelical theologian Charles Ryrie examines the definition of sin in *Basic Theology*. He cites eight Hebrew words used for sin in the Old Testament and no less than twelve in the New Testament. Ryrie sums up the definition and describes sin this way:

*...Sin has generally been defined as lawlessness (from 1 John 3:4). This is an accurate definition as long as law is conceived of in its broadest sense, that is, defection from any of God's standards." And in the following paragraph, "Sin may also be defined as against the character of God (from Rom. 3:23) where the glory of God is the reflection of His character.*[1]

Ryrie also draws from other evangelical sources. For example, "(Augustus) Strong furnishes an example when he defines sin as 'lack of conformity to the moral law of God, either in act, disposition, or state.'"[2] Another source Ryrie cites is James Oliver Buswell: "Buswell defines sin in this way: 'Sin may be defined ultimately as anything in the creature which does not express, or which is contrary to, the holy character of the Creator'"[3] As we can observe, all of the above definitions relate back to a standard that is usually interpreted in the light of Old Testament law. Even if the Ten Commandments are not mentioned directly, that standard is implied.

It is interesting that the subject of love is never mentioned specifically in the above definitions. By inference, love is implied in statements like, "...defection from any of God's standards," or "...against the character of God...." If the absence or perversion of love is implied by all the above definitions, it is surprising that few if any evangelical theologians specifically refer to love directly when it comes to defining sin. Perhaps it seems too simplistic. Unfortunately, a failure to love is treated by theologians more as an *effect* of sin rather than the *cause*. It is the purpose of this chapter to encourage Christians to view sin through a broader paradigm; that is, that all sin can be interpreted in the context of biblical love. It is either a failure to love God in a manner he prescribes or a failure to love one another in a manner biblically defined. It is also possible, of course, to fail to love oneself, but this inevitably leads to failure to love others.

Therefore, I would like to introduce a much simpler definition of sin that encompasses every definition of sin in both the Old and the New Testaments: *sin is a failure to love biblically.*

There are many who will take issue with this definition, calling it simplistic or incomplete. But I believe the above definition is very accurate when taken in light of what I have written in earlier chapters concerning the Law and in light of the royal law. Let me explain.

If Satan is the architect of all evil, as the Scriptures clearly states, then he is the origin of all sin. His purpose for creation is twofold. First, to blind all of God's creatures from seeing, believing or accepting the biblical truth that God is love, that it is his nature to love, and that his love is freely, unconditionally offered to all. The result of this blindness, therefore, is to cause people not to love God in return, or to love God in a manner other than what God intended; that is, to love God according to a man-made standard of acceptability, a designer love as it were. Satan's second purpose, then, is to cause people not to love one another and to live in hate instead, for he is our adversary, the liar and deceiver, the destroyer, and a "murderer from the beginning" (John 8:44).

Though Satan is the origin of sin, we know from Scripture that he is not the *instrument* of all sin. The instrument of all sin is each and every one of us; that is, all humanity. Every man and woman has inherited a nature that is predisposed to sin. (This is also called "original sin.") Because of this "old nature," as the apostle referred to it, we cannot help but sin. It is in our nature to sin. Why is that? If we were to translate original sin in terms of biblical love, we would see that at the root of all sin is self-love. Our natural tendency is to love ourselves before we love others. Whereas biblical love is self-less in nature, sin is ultimately selfish in nature.

We have already placed love issues as the foundation of the Ten Commandments. It would perhaps be helpful here to focus on some specific examples from the New Testament to see that ultimately, all sin is a failure of biblical love.

## Examples from the Gospels: The Temptation of Jesus (Matt. 4:1-11; Mark 1:12-13; Luke 4:1-13)

*Then Jesus was led up by the Spirit into the wilderness to be tempted by the devil.*

*And after He had fasted forty days and forty nights, He then became hungry.*

*And the tempter came and said to Him, "If You are the Son of God, command that these stones become bread."*

*But He answered and said, "It is written, 'Man shall not live on bread alone, but on every word that proceeds out of the mouth of God.'"*

*Then the devil took Him into the holy city and had Him stand on the pinnacle of the temple, and said to Him, "If You are the Son of God, throw Yourself down; for it is written, 'He will command His angels concerning You'; and 'On their hands they will bear You up, so that you will not strike Your foot against a stone.'"*

*Jesus said to him, "On the other hand, it is written, 'You shall not put the Lord Your God to the test.'"*

*Again, the devil took Him to a very high mountain and showed Him all the kingdoms of the world and their glory; and he said to Him, "All these things I will give You, if You fall down and worship me."*

*Then Jesus said to him, "Go, Satan! For it is written, 'You shall worship the Lord your God, and serve Him only.'"*

*Then the devil left Him; and behold, angels came and began to minister to Him.* (Matt. 4:1-11)

Without opening the theological discussion of *posse non pecare* (able not to sin) versus *non posse pecare* (not able to sin), Satan's temptations of Jesus are clear: derail Jesus' ministry and God's plan for the redemption of humanity. Any of the three temptations can lead to sin: the first temptation, the sin of using divine powers for personal pleasure; the second, to violate the first commandment to worship God alone; and the third, to test God.

However, all three temptations also are rooted in tests of love. Does Jesus love the Father enough to overcome the temptations, and does he love the world enough to suffer for it? It seems so simple just to classify the temptations as tests of obedience. Apart from theological analysis, the underlying theme of the temptations of Jesus is one that tests his love.

In the first temptation, does Jesus love God more than himself? Does that love translate into trust that his Father in heaven will provide for all his needs, even at the point of death? On the other hand, will Jesus love himself more by taking care of his own needs and wants at Satan's prompting? If Jesus puts his own needs first, he will fail to love the Father by rejecting the purpose for which the Father sent him. This would not only be a failure of love toward the Father, it would be failure of love for a lost world.

In the second temptation, does Jesus love God more than the world and all its riches and pleasures? Whereas the crux of the first temptation was needs versus suffering, the second temptation is comfort and pleasure versus suffering. Jesus could bypass his suffering on the cross by accepting Satan's legitimate offer. By saying no to Satan, Jesus was effectively condemning himself to a life of material and physical suffering culminating in the cross.

In the third temptation, does Jesus love the lost enough to die for their sin first before appearing to them in glory? The Jews were always looking for signs, and Satan's subtle temptation is that if the crowd at the temple, including the priests, saw Jesus descending out of nowhere, they would immediately believe he was the Messiah. But that was not God's plan. The forgiveness of sins must come before the kingdom of glory. Jesus knew God's plan clearly: ***"The Son of Man must suffer many things and be rejected by the elders and chief priests and scribes, and be killed and be raised up on the third day"*** (Luke 9:22), the necessity of which the apostles would not grasp until after the resurrection (Luke 24:46, 47; Acts 3:18). By resisting Satan's temptation, Jesus declared that his love for a lost world not be derailed by showmanship.

## Problems of the Heart (Matt. 15:15-20)

The scene is a confrontation between Jesus and the Pharisees over the tradition of hand washing. The Pharisees considered eating with unwashed hands sinful, yet Jesus informs the Pharisees that they themselves are committing true sin by not taking care of their parents. (As we have seen, it is a failure to love). During the confrontation, Jesus provides first a principle followed by a parable for his disciples: "It is not what enters into the mouth that defiles the man, but what proceeds out of the mouth, this defiles the man" (v. 11), and "Every plant which My heavenly Father did not plant will be uprooted. Let them alone; they are blind guides of the blind. And if a blind man guides a blind man, both will fall into a pit" (vv. 13-14).

Peter asks for an explanation. Jesus explains in verses 17-20:

> *Do you not understand that everything that goes into the mouth passes into the stomach, and is eliminated? But the things that proceed out of the mouth come from the heart, and those defile the man. For out of the heart come evil thoughts, murders, adulteries, fornications, thefts, false witness, slanders. These are the things which defile the man; but to eat with unwashed hands does not defile the man.*

There are a number of lessons here. First, it is clear that eating with unwashed hands is not sinful. Why? First, there is nothing in Scripture defining it as sin. Second, it is not defined as sin in Scripture because it has nothing to do with love. All of the items listed in verse 19 are failures of love: "evil thoughts" which comprise devious plots against others; "murders" which result from hating another; "adulteries" which violate the trust and love of others and do irreparable damage to families and children; "fornications" which result in using others as objects to satisfy one's lust; "thefts" which are failure to care enough about another to honor their possessions; "false witness" which is lying, and therefore harmful to others; and "slanders" which are malicious, unloving words against another. All of the examples Jesus gives are defined somewhere in the Old Testament as sin, but above all, they are examples of failure to love others.

## The Rich Young Ruler (Matt. 19:16-26) and Zaccheus (Luke 19:1-10)

It is truly one of the tragic stories in Scripture. A young man is invited by the Lord himself to become a disciple, but he rejects the offer. The question is, "Why?"

The young man, obviously from a wealthy background, desires the assurance of eternal life. He essentially asks Jesus, "Have I done enough? Am I guaranteed eternal life?"

Jesus meets him on his level by referring to that with which the young man is familiar, the Ten Commandments. It is interesting, however, that the only commandments Jesus mentions are those pertaining directly to relationships and acts that would be interpreted as loving one another (the second tablet). Jesus also includes the second great commandment, "You shall love your neighbor as yourself."

It is quite certain that the young man took a deep sigh of relief, for in his mind he had kept the letter of the law; that is, up until now.

He ventures to ask Jesus, "What am I still lacking?" Or, "Is that enough to ensure me eternal life?"

Jesus provides the young man with a new challenge that will test, first of all, his definition of "neighbor," and second, his love for others.

"If you wish to be complete," Jesus says, "go and sell your possessions and give to the poor, and you will have treasure in heaven; and come, follow Me."

The young man has a choice to make. Does he consider "the poor" his neighbor? Does he care enough about them to sell off his vast possessions on their behalf? How much does he really love his neighbor? Up to this point, he has never been confronted with what he is doing with his possessions. Now, face-to-face with Jesus, the love issue comes to the forefront.

It is important to note that the word "sin" is never mentioned here. Nor is the issue of sin brought up. And it cannot be stated for certain that to *not* sell his possessions would constitute a classic evangelical theological definition of sin. The issue was not sin but a failure to love. He loved himself and his possessions more than he loved the poor, and therefore, did not possess biblical love. Sin or not, the results are the same. A failure to love results in separation from God.

In contrast, the story of Zaccheus in Luke 19 is a heartening story that has an opposite ending. Zaccheus, face-to-face with Jesus, deals both with sin (fraud which is tantamount to stealing) and with whether or not the poor are worthy of his possessions.

"Behold, Lord, half of my possessions I will give to the poor, and if I have defrauded anyone of anything, I will give back four times as much" (v. 8). Jesus' response? "Today salvation has come to this house...."

Again, only part of Zaccheus' actions was directed toward the issue of classic sin: "You shall not steal." The rest of his actions were clearly motivated by biblical love.

It is interesting to note as well that the rich young ruler refers to Jesus as "teacher" while Zaccheus refers to Jesus as "Lord." Was it seeing Jesus as his Lord that prompted him to act in love, or was it the ability to love that caused him to recognize Jesus as his Lord?

## The Woman Caught in Adultery (John 8:1-11)

Let's look again at the story of the woman caught in the act of adultery. It is the perfect blend of truth and love as it relates to the subject of sin. The issue of sin runs throughout the story and is never compromised. The overlying love principle, however, cannot be overstated.

As we recall, the story begins early one morning in the temple courtyard. The scribes and Pharisees bring to Jesus a woman caught red-handed in adultery. The Pharisees are not the least bit interested in the woman's welfare; their real intent is to trap Jesus concerning his position on the law of Moses. The woman is a mere pawn in a game of power and truth.

Having been caught in adultery—not denied by the woman and apparently witnessed by more than one person—she is obligated to be stoned to death according to Mosaic Law. There is a glaring hypocrisy, though. Where is the other guilty party, the man? Leviticus 20:10 clearly states that *both* should be stoned. One would almost suppose the woman was set up by the Pharisees.

Jesus neither refutes the law of Moses nor states that the law is no longer valid. Nor does he deny she has sinned, rationalize her sin away or make excuses for her act. Twice in the passage Jesus refers to her act as sin; that is, a violation of the seventh commandment.

Jesus does not condemn the woman because her greatest need was to experience God's love. She desperately needed love, but because truth trumps love, experiencing love in an adulterous relationship was not the kind of love God wanted her to experience. God wanted the woman to experience and learn to express biblical love. The love she thought she was gaining through adultery could only result in pain to herself, and possibly her family and to the other party and his family. She was seeking love and heading toward a bottomless pit of pain and despair. Instead of condemning her, Jesus chose to show her biblical love, giving her the opportunity to experience true love for the first time in her life.

Jesus knew that beneath the sin was a failure of biblical love. The only cure would be to experience real love, true love, God's love. God's love would be expressed in mercy, in forgiveness, and in grace, expressions greater than anything she could experience in the flesh. It was most likely a failure of love that brought the woman to the point of adultery; it was Christ's love that would restore her to life. It was a failure of love that caused her no concern for the other party; it was Christ's love that taught her to care. It was a failure of love that made her believe physical intimacy would satisfy her needs; it was Christ's love that opened her eyes to her greater need, to receive love and to give God's love.

It is the law that condemns; it is love that restores life. Paul is later to write about this in Romans 8:1-3: "Therefore there is now no condemnation for those who are in Christ Jesus. For the law of the Spirit of life in Christ Jesus has set you free from the law of sin and death. For what the Law could not do, weak as it was through the flesh, God did...."

Where the law was ineffective at resolving the woman's problem, love was present to begin redemption. Where sin was limited by its definition, love was unlimited by its application. Where the Law was in the process of judging relationships, love was in the process of restoring relationships. Where the Law failed, love prevailed.

Ultimately, as was the case of the woman caught in adultery, sin is a failure of love.

## An Example from the Book of Acts
## The Death of Ananias and Sapphira (Acts 5:1-11)

Without a proper definition of love, the incident of Ananias and Sapphira is difficult to understand. The incident is somewhat long, but it is included here for those who may not be familiar with it. The scene begins with a disciple named Barnabas.

*Now Joseph, a Levite of Cyprian birth, who was also called Barnabas by the apostles (which translated means Son of Encouragement), and who owned a tract of land, sold it and brought the money and laid it at the apostles' feet.*

*But a man named Ananias, with his wife Sapphira, sold a piece of property, and kept back some of the price for himself, with his wife's full knowledge, and bringing a portion of it, he laid it at the apostles' feet.*

*But Peter said, "Ananias, why has Satan filled your heart to lie to the Holy Spirit and to keep back some of the price of the land? While it remained unsold, did it not remain your own? And after it was sold, was it not under your control? Why is it that you have conceived this deed in your heart? You have not lied to men but to God."*

*And as he heard these words, Ananias fell down and breathed his last; and great fear came over all who heard of it. The young men got up and covered him up, and after carrying him out, they buried him.*

*Now there elapsed an interval of about three hours, and his wife came in, not knowing what had happened. And Peter responded to her, "Tell me whether you sold the land for such and such a price?" And she said, "Yes, that was the price."*

*Then Peter said to her, "Why is it that you have agreed together to put the Spirit of the Lord to the test? Behold, the feet of those who have buried your husband are at the door, and they will carry you out as well."*

*And immediately she fell at his feet and breathed her last,
and the young men came in and found her dead, and they
carried her out and buried her beside her husband.*

*And a great fear came over the whole church, and over all
who heard of these things.* (Acts 4:36 – 5:11)

As the church began to grow, early disciples were selling their possessions and delivering them to the apostles for distribution to the needy members of the church, many of whom were quite poor. One such person was Barnabas, a Levite who, according to the law, should not have owned land in Judea in the first place. Nevertheless, Barnabas sold his tract of land and "laid it at the apostles' feet" (4:37). There was obviously some recognition brought upon Barnabas for his act of generosity.

Ananias and his wife Sapphira also sold a piece of property. Instead of bringing the entire sum to the apostles, however, they withheld a portion for personal use. Perhaps their problem was that they were giving the appearance in front of the church of having brought the entire amount.

Peter immediately confronts Ananias and Sapphira. As a result, Ananias, and later, Sapphira, pay the price of death.

Without a correct definition of love, their sentence seems harsh. Wouldn't the more loving thing to do be to help them understand their mistake, carefully warn them of the consequences and give them a second chance? Peter's harsh judgment seems in stark contrast to "love your neighbor as yourself."

Careful observation of the event reveals some important insights that help the reader see that evil, sin, truth and love are all components of this intriguing story.

First, it is clear that Satan has entered into the picture in an attempt to bring evil into the church. This is the first mention of Satan in Acts and it is clear that he is attempting to get a foothold in the church through his usual tactic of lies and deception. Satan did not force himself upon Ananias, but instead found an opening through the weakness of Ananias' flesh. It is probable that Satan tempted Ananias in a similar manner to the way he tempted Jesus in the wilderness, and Ananias took the bait. Why would Satan want to introduce lying into the church? Because at the core of the church's purpose is the issue of truth: objective truth about the person and work of Jesus Christ, and truthfulness in terms of how the church is going to function among the members of its body.

Second, a sin has been committed by Ananias and Sapphira. Leviticus 6:3 and 19:11 clearly state that lying is wrong, but, in the case of deception or defrauding, restitution was to be made to the offending party and a guilt offering presented to the Lord. On the other hand, capital punishment was not a punishment for lying. But Ananias and Sapphira were lying—not just to the church—but to the Holy Spirit and "to God." Whereas Barnabas brought all of his property to the church (which was a sign of love), Ananias and Sapphira brought a lie (which is a failure of love).

Third, the element of truth is at stake. It must be carefully noted that Peter is not the executioner. In the case of Ananias, Peter says nothing about his fate. There is no indication that he knows what is going to happen to Ananias. In the case of his wife, Peter simply draws from experience. The party acting as executioner is neither Peter nor the church—it is the Holy Spirit. Most likely, the Holy Spirit took Ananias and Sapphira's judgment out of Peter's hands, for it is possible that Peter would have shown leniency. The issue of truth was so crucial at this point in the church that allowing deception to creep in was unacceptable. This is a clear case where truth must trump love.

The fourth element, then, is love. Beneath the sin of Ananias and Sapphira is a failure of love. It is a failure of love for those in need, it is a failure of love toward the church, and it is a failure of love for Christ who gave himself up for the church. The pretentious show of love by selling the property and publicly bringing the proceeds to the apostles was an ill-defined love, conceived alongside greed, and jeopardizing the core integrity of the very institution that God designed to be the beacon of truth and love.

## Love in the Letters (Briefly)

An entire book would be required to point out the relationship between sin and love in the rest of the New Testament. We will briefly look at a few sections of Scripture, for the point is easily made.

> *Now the deeds of the flesh are evident, which are: immorality, impurity, sensuality, idolatry, sorcery, enmities, strife, jealousy, outbursts of anger, disputes, dissensions, factions, envying, drunkenness, carousing, and things like these...* (Gal. 5:19-21)

It doesn't take long to see the relationship between sin and the failure to love in most of these. But a few are worth some clarification.

*Impurity*: This is not a term used to describe a failure to wash hands before a meal or eat food off the floor. In the New Testament, it is usually used in the context of sexual immorality. Whereas immorality is an act, "impurity" includes everything else. In today's context, internet or cable TV pornography would certainly fall into this category. Such impurity is always a failure to love. Why? Because that which is lusted for is viewed as an object of pleasure rather than the holy creature God intended. It's a pure case of selfish lust over biblical love.

*Sorcery*: The number one reason people involve themselves in sorcery is to gain power: power over another person (jealousy, vengeance or sexual pleasure) and power to have money. There is no such thing as biblical love associated with sorcery. Additionally, resorting to sorcery is a blatant failure to trust God, and therefore, a failure to love him.

The rest of the list should be self-evident. Sins like these will be addressed in much more detail in book 3 of this trilogy, along with the *positive* side of biblical love in Christian behavior.

In summary, then, all sin, in both the Old and New Testaments, can be identified as a failure of biblical love. I believe that a failure of love and the ability to love is not the effect of sin, but rather the cause. The road out of a sinful life, however, is not just to decide to love biblically. The road back to a restored life can only go through the person of Jesus Christ, the One who is full of grace and truth. But Jesus cannot be approached truthfully unless one is willing to acknowledge personal sin, repent of it, and receive Jesus Christ as the Son of God, the only One who can save us from our sin and our failure to love. Once a person is in the right relationship to God, restoration can begin, and it should always begin by learning biblical truth and expressing biblical love. Only then can we overcome "the sin which so easily entangles us..." (Heb. 12:1).

---

1. Charles C. Ryrie, *Basic Theology* (Wheaton, IL: Victor Books, a division of Scripture Press Publications, 1986), 212.

2. Ryrie, 212, citing Augustus Strong, *Systematic Theology* (Philadelphia: Judson, 1907), 269.

3. Ryrie, 212, citing James Oliver Buswell, *A Systematic Theology* (Grand Rapids: Zondervan, 1962), 1:264.

# *Vignette for Chapter Twelve*

# *"On the Ferry to Kowloon"*

"I can't believe we're back here again," said the doctor's wife merrily, sitting in an empty bench on the ferry to Kowloon. "How things have changed. Look at all the skyscrapers. Hong Kong has grown so much! Oh," she mused, snuggling against her husband's shoulder, "this is so romantic."

"It wasn't so romantic the first time we were here," he said, shaking his head.

"You got over it."

"No, *we* got over it."

Thirty years earlier their ferry was pulling away from Hong Kong Island to cross Victoria Harbor on the way to Kowloon. It was late but warm. There were only a few passengers on the first class deck that night. Some Chinese businessmen were reading the afternoon Star. Four American sailors in their liberty whites sat huddled together in the forward section where the breeze was strongest. Halfway back sat another sailor with his arm around his Cantonese date dressed prettily in her *cheongsam*. Behind them had sat the doctor and his wife.

"Do you remember what we talked about that night?" the doctor asked.

"I remember *exactly* what we talked about, dear. I said…"

"John, I don't think I can take much more of this."

"Take much more of what, my love?" not really wanting to hear the answer.

She shook her head, tears misting her eyes. "Those poor people. The children. Everywhere. Everywhere we go."

An anniversary gift of a Mikimoto pearl necklace and matching earrings, a Colinda original, a delightful dinner at Jimmy's Kitchen weren't enough to erase yesterday's emotional trauma. It was just more of the same ugliness they had passed by in Calcutta, in the Tondo in Manila, and on the river in Bangkok. What was to be the getaway of a lifetime was turning into a depressing, agonizing guilt trip.

John knew Laura was thinking back to yesterday's lunch. The morning had been clear and fresh and sunny and they had decided to ride over to Aberdeen to lunch on one of the floating restaurants. He remembered the expression that crossed Laura's face as the taxi descended the winding road toward the fish cannery and into the shelter for the *tanka*, or water people, and the clean fresh air suddenly turning into the sickening odor of decay and waste. He remembered how, as they stepped out of the cab alongside the quay for the water taxis, the bright reflection of the sun on the bay had been choked by the thousands of drab brown and grey wooden junks, huddled tightly alongside each other in endless rows, bobbing up and down in the briny debris of the dark water. The city of tiny junks and sampans, which were the homes and backyards and front yards and businesses of the *tanka*, sat clustered together like maggots in a stagnant pond. He remembered that, as they rode in the water taxi on the way to the Tai Pak restaurant, all they could see around them were small junks with whole families living on board, laundry strung across the masts and small fish drying on the decks. He remembered how the smoke drifted up from the lip on the stern of the junks, the lip serving both as the kitchen and the toilet, and that sometimes you could see the waste drop into the water and float up beside the hull. He remembered the woman who was rowing her own taxi with three small children aboard. He remembered how, as they approached the Tai Pak scores of children in their tiny dinghies hollered and yelled for them to toss coins in the water to dive for. He remembered how Laura, in their scant conversation at lunch, tried to ignore the constant smell from the *tanka* and the cannery that settled on the breezeless shelter like an early morning fog. They had walked through Aberdeen after lunch and he recalled how the thin, dark-skinned children with watery, jaundiced and often puss-filled eyes and pale lips, distended stomachs and sore-covered bodies wandered barefoot and half-naked about the junks and sampans and onto the streets to beg noisily at the gawking, perturbed tourists. Moving about the quai among the drying fish were water people with cancers and tumors and crooked limbs and people who looked like the relics they rowed. John knew Laura would never forget what she had seen, just as she hadn't fully recovered from what she had seen and smelled and touched in Calcutta or Manila or Bangkok. He knew she couldn't get the images out of her mind, thinking about that now, sitting beside him on the ferry, crossing the breezy harbor to the lights of Kowloon.

To distract her, John suggested they take the hydrofoil out to Macao to do a little gambling.

"Not interested," she mumbled.

"Look, honey, there's lots of other things to see. We haven't been to Happy Valley yet, or to Repulse Bay, or to Victoria Peak at night. They say those are very lovely places and we shouldn't miss them while we're here."

Laura sat quiet, gazing across the harbor at the lights of the silent freighters and the pitching and rolling lights of the walla-wallas and cargo lighters that passed alongside the ferry.

"There are some really fine things we haven't done yet," he rambled, hoping for a response. "We haven't eaten in a *yum cha* restaurant and we haven't seen the Tiger Balm Gardens. And we really haven't done enough shopping for you. We won't worry about Customs. We just won't claim so much. Of course, we may have to rip out a few labels...."

"John?"

"What?"

"Don't."

"Don't what, my love?"

"Don't let's keep fooling ourselves."

Thirty years ago, almost to the night, the doctor had first thought Laura meant one thing before he realized she meant quite another. All she had to do was turn and face him and he knew exactly what she meant. Unable to respond, a sudden fear had come over him. Thirty years ago, the fear had been as strong as the warm, moist wind descending across the harbor. It rushed down at him and he could not look at Laura steadily.

When the ferry docked, the fear followed him up the quai and through the terminal and outside onto the street. As they walked along the street toward the Empress Hotel, he had held Laura closer to him than ever before, the fear swirling around him.

And the new life he thought this fear might bring all but took his breath away.

"Now, really, it wasn't so hard after all, was it?" Laura quipped. "Tell me you haven't loved being a doctor for the mission."

John smiled in quiet acknowledgment. More than anything, he noticed, the fear was gone.

*Bill Walthall*

## Chapter Twelve

# "So Why Does Loving Seem So Hard?" (Love and the Flesh)

*He who has found his life will lose it, and he who has lost his life for My sake will find it.* (Matthew 10:39)

You're frustrated. You woke up in the morning feeling pretty loving toward everyone but by the end of the day you've gossiped about a neighbor, criticized your spouse, yelled at the kids and entertained some really sinful fantasies about a co-worker. You sit down to watch the evening news and the lead story is about a famous TV evangelist who leads a lavish lifestyle and routinely uses his private jet to visit the woman with whom he is having an affair. Embarrassed for born-again believers, you quickly change the channel. The news story is focused on mass genocide taking place between warring tribes in Africa. Another channel is reporting on recent suicide bombings of innocent civilians in the Middle East. You choose an educational channel. The PBS station is presenting a detailed account of 9/11. Another channel is completing a series on World War II and the discovery of Nazi concentration camps. You try a sitcom. The audience is laughing hysterically about the fact that the lead homosexual character is upset that his domestic partner had a tryst with his sister. You finally turn off the TV in disgust and take some comfort in the fact that—except for your words—at least you haven't murdered anyone today, although the next-door neighbor's barking Dalmatian is edging up higher on your list. The more the dog barks the angrier you become with your neighbor for letting it bark day and night and destroying your peace and quiet. Fleeting thoughts waver between poisoning the dog and burning down your neighbor's house. At the moment, you are too angry with your neighbor and too disillusioned with the world to consider what might be the most loving thing to do. You realize, of course, that no evil action ever has a good outcome, so you try to numb yourself to it all and sit there listening to heartbreak songs from the 24-hour Country station. You finally regain your emotional composure and decide that reading your Bible might be the very thing you need. Just as you begin reading and realigning your thoughts spiritually, the telephone rings. It's your sister in New York. Her entire family has just been killed in a head-on with a drunk driver. Hearing the news, the last emotion you feel is love.

Manifesting biblical love seems so logical and reasonable in concept but so impossible and inadequate in real life. Why is that? It's one thing to come to the conclusion that God wants us to live a life characterized by experiencing and expressing biblical love; it's quite another to have to live it throughout each day and apply it to the really rotten things that go on in the world around us.

While we cannot control the world around us, and we cannot control what others believe or do, we can control ourselves. Learning to reshape our beliefs and behaviors to experience and express biblical love is the whole purpose behind crucifying the old self and putting on the new self. The apostle Paul wrote to his disciple Timothy instructing him on the goal of discipleship: *"But the goal of our instruction is love from a pure heart and a good conscience and a sincere faith"* (1 Tim. 1:5).

So, what's the problem? Why can't we Christians just start loving? What's blocking us from being the loving Christians we ought to be? What is it that keeps us from experiencing and expressing biblical love? Why does loving seem so hard?

It's difficult to imagine that biblical love is intimately tied to death, but it is true. Without a willingness to die to self, biblical love is impossible.

In the preceding chapters, we have seen that love is an expression of God and a revelation to humanity. We have determined, therefore, that biblical truth must always trump love because love requires definition. We have called the love revealed "biblical love." We have seen that the foundation for all Old Testament law—specifically, the Ten Commandments—is love. We have seen how biblical love is dramatically developed in the New Testament and perfected in the person and work of Jesus Christ. We have also seen that Christians are no longer under law, that is, the Mosaic Law, and instructed by the apostles to live according to what James referred to as the royal law, an instruction confirmed throughout the letters of the New Testament writers. We have observed that whereas the Ten Commandments are tangible and inflexible, the royal law of biblical love is entirely fluid. The Old Testament laws require additional laws and traditions to account for all the contingencies of life, whereas the royal law is a single principle that can be applied to all situations in life.

A legitimate question must be asked, however. If the royal law is a single principle that can be applied to all situations in life, why do we not see more of it? Why is it so hard to demonstrate consistently sacrificial, selfless, biblical love? In other words, why is it so hard to love?

The answer to these questions begins with understanding the problem of the flesh. The flesh, we will discover, is the enemy of love. Understanding the flesh will explain why fulfilling the royal law is neither something that comes naturally nor is a behavior easily learned.

## The Problem of the Flesh — Self

All Christianity can be summed up in two words: truth and love. If truth is accessible, and love is possible, why don't Christians show more of both? Contemporarily, as well as historically, not all Christians grasp the truth and not all Christians display love. Why? The answer is the same for both: the flesh. It would be helpful to define the flesh before condemning it as the culprit.

An examination of the New Testament indicates that there is but one Greek word that should be translated "flesh" (*sarx*). That word is used 147 times but is sometimes translated other ways depending on the context. In the NASB (*New American Standard Bible*), it is translated "flesh" (and "fleshly"), "body" ("bodily," "bodily condition"), "earth" (and "earthly"), "fellow countrymen," "man" (and "mankind"), "nation" and "personality."

The vast majority of times (129) *sarx* is translated simply as "flesh"; even then it has various meanings and theological implications. Charles Ryrie, for example, explains it this way: "Though flesh sometimes refers to tissue (Luke 24:39) or to the whole material part of man (1 Cor. 15:39; Heb 5:7), when used of a facet of the immaterial nature it refers to that disposition to sin and to oppose God (Rom. 7:18; 1 Cor. 3:3; 2 Cor. 1:12; Gal. 5:17; Col. 2:18; 2 Peter 2:10; 1 John 2:16). Both the believer and unbeliever possess this capacity."[1] This is a helpful explanation but incomplete.

Unfortunately, many pastors teach that the terms "flesh" and "sinful nature" are identical and interchange the two terms. This mixing of terms has even taken place in some modern translations.[2] The evangelical should understand that the term "sinful nature" occurs nowhere in Scripture; that is, in the original languages. "Sinful nature" is a theological term that has, over the years, been adopted to mean "flesh."

The Greek word translated "nature" (*phusis*) can be found but twice in the New Testament when it is used in reference to believers. Ephesians 2:3 states, "we were by nature (*phusis*) children of wrath." Peter also uses the term referring to our new self: "…so that…you may become partakers of the divine nature (*phusis*)…" (2 Peter 1:4). The nature associated with our former selves, children of wrath, is an expression of the old nature; that is, the sinful nature or the old self. The nature associated with our new selves, "partakers of the divine nature" is an expression of the new nature; that is, the new self or new creation of 2 Corinthians 5:17. Ephesians 5:8 states this clearly: "…You were formerly darkness, but now you are light in the Lord; walk as children of light." The clear implication is that Christians have a new nature and are capable of walking as children of the light.

If one desires to tag the theological term "sinful nature" to a New Testament concept, a better match would be what the NASB translates as "old self" (Rom. 6:6; Eph. 4:22; Col. 3:9; or, in some translations, "old man").

Here, Neil T. Anderson is helpful. This explanation is lengthy but provides important insights into the origin and nature of the flesh.

> The term (flesh) speaks of the tendency within man's soul that centers one's interests on himself. An unsaved person functions "in the flesh" (Rom. 8:8), worshipping and serving

*the creature rather than the Creator (Rom. 1:25). Such persons in the final analysis "live for themselves" (II Cor. 5:15), even though much of what they do may have an appearance of selflessness and concern for others.*

*Since the fall, every person is born physically alive but spiritually dead. This unregenerate man learns how to live his life independent of God. This learned independence makes the flesh hostile to God. Self-serving, self-justifying survival techniques known as defense mechanisms are what characterized the flesh. The flesh serves self....*

*What was appealed to (Eve, in the garden) was 'the flesh,' that capability of the soul to act in one's own behalf, to serve self. The advent of sin in the world changed everything. The flesh became perverted into selfishness. While having physical appetites, visible possessions, and personal self-esteem are not wrong in themselves, the introduction of sin into the picture twists these legitimate desires into crass expressions of man-as-his-own-god. The flesh now exists in opposition to God. For this reason we are told that, "the mind set on the flesh is hostile toward God; for it does not subject itself to the law of God, for it is not even able to do so" (Rom. 8:7).*

*The crucifying of the flesh, the putting to death, the considering dead (by means of the Spirit) is the believer's responsibility on a day-by-day basis. What makes this possible is the already completed fact that our old self was crucified with Christ. God changed our nature in regeneration; it is our responsibility to change our behavior. Growth in Christ (the process of sanctification) is predicated on the complete and perfect work of the Atonement, dealing fully with the 'old self' and uniting the believer in Christ (II Cor. 5:21). The Christian, complete in Christ (Col. 2:10), enabled by the Spirit to understand his true identity in Christ, must choose to walk in this truth. The Christian begins to experience what it means to "walk in newness of life" (Rom. 6:4), and "serve in newness of the Spirit" (Rom. 7:6). Again, the problem is our walk, not our existence or essence.*[3, 4]

The flesh, then, is in its essence neutral. It is programmed at birth by the sinful nature (what we call "original sin") and remains that way as long as the sinful nature sticks around.

Having defined some terms, let us now look at Scripture to see what it says about the flesh in relation to the old self. For this, we'll refer to Romans 6:1-7.

*What shall we say then? Are we to continue in sin so that grace may increase? May it never be! How shall we who died to sin still live in it? Or do you not know that all of us who have been baptized into Christ Jesus have been baptized into His death?*

*Therefore we have been buried with Him through baptism into death, so that as Christ was raised from the dead through the glory of the Father, so we too might walk in newness of life.*

*For if we have become united with Him in the likeness of His death, certainly we shall also be in the likeness of His resurrection, knowing this, that our old self was crucified with Him, in order that our body of sin might be done away with, so that we would no longer be slaves to sin; for he who has died is freed from sin.*

There is a startling principle in this section of Romans: *Christians no longer have a sinful nature.* Why? In verse six Paul states, "our old self *was* crucified...." The term "was crucified" is in the aorist tense in the Greek, meaning that it is a completed action in the past. It's done with...it's over with. When we first believed, that old self, to which we will now attach the theological term "sinful nature" died. It is no more. Believers no longer have an old self, a sinful nature. Instead, believers, by virtue of their faith in Christ are given a new nature, a divine nature (2 Cor. 5:17; Eph. 4:24; 2 Peter 1:4).

The logical question to ask here is, "Okay, if I no longer have an old self (sinful nature, old man), why is it that I still sin?" The reason is simple. The flesh has been programmed throughout life by the sinful nature. Therefore, even when the sinful nature or old self is gone, its impact is still there: old habits, old thought patterns, old belief systems, old values. They continue to work in our flesh reflexively until they are somehow changed.

You might say, "So what's the difference if, as believers, we call our tendency to oppose God the weakness of our flesh or the depravity of our sinful nature?"

That's an important question, but there is an equally important answer. With the sinful nature gone, the flesh is no longer *obligated* to follow it. And, in addition, there is a new nature present, a divine nature, a new creation brought about by the presence of the Holy Spirit. *That means that we are no longer obligated or compelled to sin.* That is why Paul can say in Romans 6:12-14:

> *Therefore, do not let sin reign in your mortal body so that you obey its lusts, and do not go on presenting the members of your body to sin as instruments of unrighteousness; but present yourselves to God as those alive from the dead, and your members as instruments of righteousness to God. For sin shall not be master over you....*

The principle is crucial. *With the presence of the Holy Spirit, believers have the ability to change.* Christians, through the power of the Holy Spirit, have the ability to re-program the flesh. That means, too, that the Christian can learn about and begin to express biblical love.

But there are other factors. The flesh was born with the sinful nature (original sin). Therefore, the flesh is forever polluted and corrupted. It is tainted forever. The analogy, though imperfect, is like a deadly virus that gets into the body. As of this writing, once a person acquires HIV (human immuno-deficiency virus), it is there to stay. Inevitably, it will result in death. Medicines may delay the onset of AIDS, but eventually this virus, with rare exceptions, will kill you because once there, always there.

And so it is with the sinful nature. It has forever polluted the flesh. Therefore, even though Christians can change, we can never be entirely sinless. Though we are not obliged to sin (Romans 6:12-14) and no longer have to be mastered by the flesh (Roman 8:12), we will never be sin-free. The flesh, by virtue of having been tainted by the old nature, has a death sentence. That is why we must all die physically. Without physical death, we cannot rid ourselves of our earthly flesh and receive the new body that is immortal and imperishable (1 Cor. 15:50-54).

During this earthly life, then, God has provided a way to alter the intentions of the flesh; that is, through the power of the indwelling Holy Spirit. If Christians could not change their behavior, why then would the Scriptures instruct us to live a different kind of life? (E.g., Romans 12:3-21.) The results of the flesh's being forever corrupted with all the tendencies and selfishness of the old self, though it is dead, remain firmly implanted in the flesh. Therefore, the believer is warned against living according to the flesh (Romans 8:9-13). Living according to the flesh is behaving according to the old self.

An illustration I like to use is this. In his late teens, a man was convicted of having committed a violent crime and sentenced to life imprisonment. All he experienced most of his life was imprisonment—guards, a regimented day, other inmates and their habits, confined quarters and a whole lifetime of negative experiences. Therefore, he lived and shaped his lifestyle accordingly. It was all he ever knew. When he was in his forties, however, a judge reviewed his case, concluded that the man's punishment was too harsh and set him free. He was set free into a life and world that was totally foreign to him. After a week out of jail, he wanted to go back! Being in jail was the only life he had known and the life he was most familiar with. Finally, a Christian at a halfway house found him, took him in and provided for him the care and guidance that was needed. He helped the ex-con adjust to a new way of life. It took years before the ex-con began to rid himself of his former life and begin living the life of one who had been set free.

In Romans, Paul is telling Christians, "You have been set free from imprisonment and the bondage of sin. Don't go back to that old lifestyle even though it is your natural bent. You now must live according to a new way of life, and you have the ability and the freedom to do so."

This is the good news: *Christians are not obligated to live a life directed by the flesh, but can choose to live lives directed by the Holy Spirit* (Gal. 5:16). Nevertheless, the flesh is still present; as long as we live, the flesh will always be with us. The presence of the flesh, then, is what interferes with our ability to learn and express biblical love.

The flesh, then, is the greatest enemy to expressing love. Why? Because the flesh was programmed by the sinful nature to love itself, and to love others only to the extent that it would be beneficial to itself. The flesh is self-serving. The flesh seeks its own pleasure, enjoys its greed and lusts, considers others as things rather than God's children and is at the very least self-aggrandizing, self-edifying, self-glorifying and self-exalting. The flesh is self-absorbed, self-confident, self-conscious, even self-destructive. The flesh seeks to esteem itself, affirm itself, indulge itself. The flesh is, therefore, at its very core, selfish. This was the work of the sinful nature, and this selfishness is the very opposite of biblical love. The enemy of love is self.

The good news is that, even though Christians will never be perfect, there is the God-given power to put self aside and live in love. If it were not possible, Jesus would not have commanded us to love.

Christians will always love imperfectly because we are not perfect. Love will always fall short of what it could be because Christians must dwell in a fleshly body until death. Perfect love cannot be experienced in an imperfect being. Unfortunately, because of the flesh, love can never be perfected. That is the hope of the coming age.

So how do we begin to learn to love? The answer is simple and clear. We begin with truth.

## The Solution for the Flesh — Truth

As I write this section, I am reminded of a joke I heard once. It goes something like this:

> *A psychiatrist was taking some young interns through a psychiatric ward. He was pointing out various patients and their disorders.*
>
> *"Now there's an interesting patient," he said. "He believes he's dead."*
>
> *Carefully they approached the patient for the interns to see for themselves.*
>
> *"Mr. Jones."*
>
> *"Yes, that's me."*
>
> *"I understand you believe you are dead."*
>
> *"That's right. I am dead."*
>
> *"How do you know you're dead?"*
>
> *"Well, it's just one of those things you know."*
>
> *"So," the doctor said, "there's no way I can convince you you're not dead?"*
>
> *"Nope."*
>
> *"Let me ask you this. Do you believe dead men don't bleed?"*
>
> *"Of course. I believe that dead men don't bleed."*
>
> *"Can I see your hand?"*
>
> *"Sure."*
>
> *Quickly the doctor grabbed Mr. Jones' hand, pulled out a small needle and stuck it into his thumb. The thumb started bleeding profusely.*
>
> *"Now do you still believe you're dead?" the doctor asked.*
>
> *"Oh my gosh," Mr. Jones shouted. "I've been wrong all along. Dead men do bleed!"*

The problem with our flesh having been controlled by the sinful nature is that our belief systems are programmed wrong. What we believe, how we believe, indeed, our very thought processes themselves are influenced and shaped by the old nature, the old self. Incorrect thinking patterns and errant belief systems are at the heart of all heresies and false religions. Believing lies is what motivates a suicide bomber to kill himself and dozens of innocent people. Believing falsely results in Christians donating millions of dollars to charlatan faith healers and heretical TV evangelists. Exchanging truth for error often leads to preaching false doctrines, such as the prosperity gospel. Tainted by original sin handed down from the Fall, our minds just don't work right spiritually. We do not naturally believe correctly. We believe things that are not true, and we fail to believe the things that are. The Bible calls this spiritual blindness (2 Cor. 4:4).

At the heart of biblical revelation is truth. Here are some words Jesus had to say about the importance of truth:

> *"If you continue in My word, then you are truly disciples of Mine; and you will know the truth, and the truth will make you free."* (John 8:31-32)

> *Jesus said to him, "I am the way, and the truth, and the life; no one comes to the Father but through Me."* (John 14:6)

> *"But when He, the Spirit of truth, comes, He will guide you into all the truth..."* (John 16:13)

> *"Sanctify them in the truth; Your word is truth."* (John 17:17)

The apostle Paul also emphasized the necessity of truth. Here are just a few passages.

> *"For the wrath of God is revealed from heaven against all ungodliness and unrighteousness of men who suppress the truth in unrighteousness.... For they exchanged the truth of God for a lie and worshiped and served the creature rather than the Creator, who is blessed forever."* (Romans 1:16, 25)

*"As a result, we are no longer to be children, tossed here and there by waves and carried about by every wind of doctrine, by the trickery of men, by craftiness in deceitful scheming; but speaking the truth in love, we are to grow up in all aspects into Him who is the head, even Christ..."* (Eph. 4:14,15)

If we were to trace the theme of truth throughout the New Testament, we would quickly discover that truth is at the heart of the gospel message. If we do not believe Jesus is whom he said he is, he cannot help us. If we fail to believe the facts of the crucifixion and resurrection, we will never experience saving faith. If we do not believe that the Bible is the word of God, we will never see that Jesus is the Savior—the only Savior—of humanity. And if we do not seek to conform to biblical truth, it will be virtually impossible to experience or express biblical love.

Therefore, the answer to experiencing and expressing biblical love is knowing and believing the truth. The answer to overcoming the flesh is appropriating biblical truth. Furthermore, the only way we will ever be willing to put self aside and learn to live selflessly is by devoting ourselves to biblical truth. And here is the biblical truth that is key to expressing biblical love: we must die to self.

Here is the way Jesus taught it:

*"...He who does not take his cross and follow after Me is not worthy of Me."* (Matt. 10:38)

*And He was saying to them all, "If anyone wishes to come after Me, he must deny himself, and take up his cross daily and follow Me. For whoever wishes to save his life will lose it, but whoever loses his life for My sake, he is the one who will save it."* (Luke 9:23, 24)

*"Truly, truly, I say to you, unless a grain of wheat falls into the earth and dies, it remains alone; but if it dies, it bears much fruit. He who loves his life loses it, and he who hates his life in this world will keep it to life eternal."* (John 12:24,25)

It is impossible to live for oneself and fully express biblical love. Why? Because expressing biblical love requires selflessness; in other words, it requires the death of self. Living for self is antithetical to showing biblical love.

Dying to self may seem gloomy, unappealing and, quite frankly, impossible, but God is gracious. He would not ask us to do something that is impossible, and he would not ask us to pay such a price without promising wonderful benefits in exchange. Here are a few.

First, learning to overcome self is a life-long process. The theological word for this is "sanctification"; that is, becoming more set apart for God's purposes. Sanctification does not come as a result of learning to conform to the law or some standard. Sanctification results from learning to set our own needs aside and practice the royal law. By becoming sanctified, we become more Christ-like, more holy, more righteous. All righteousness comes from experiencing and expressing biblical love.

Second, the key to selfless living is learning to believe. Learning to believe means a willingness to change our belief systems and our thinking patterns. It involves *what* we believe as well and *how* we believe. Through the power of the Holy Spirit, our minds can be renewed in order to live selflessly.

See if you can trace this pattern in the following selection of scriptures.

*"...The mind set on the flesh is death, but the mind set on the Spirit is life and peace..."* (Rom. 8:6)

*"Therefore I urge you, brethren, by the mercies of God, to present your bodies a living and holy sacrifice, acceptable to God, which is your spiritual service of worship. And do not be conformed to this world, but be transformed by the renewing of your mind, so that you may prove what the will of God is, that which is good and acceptable and perfect."* (Romans 12:1, 2)

*"...We have the mind of Christ." by virtue of having the Holy Spirit;* (1 Cor. 2:16)

*"But you did not learn Christ in this way, if indeed you have heard Him and have been taught in Him, just as truth is in Jesus, that, in reference to your former manner of life, you lay aside the old self, which is being corrupted in accordance with the lusts of deceit, and that you be renewed in the spirit of your mind, and put on the new self which in the likeness of God has been created in righteousness and holiness of the truth."* (Eph. 4:20-24)

Third, not until we begin dying to self do we begin living fruitfully for Christ. The reward Jesus offers us in return for our lives is—not prosperity—but the ability to truly experience and joyfully express biblical love.

Jesus requires from his followers a fundamental change in human behavior, one that is not natural and cannot be learned from the world. He has commanded, "Love one another as I have loved you." Loving one another as Christ has loved us will demand putting aside oneself and fervently believing the truth the New Testament teaches. Because of the flesh, we will never love perfectly...but we can always love better. The fact that the apostle John writes so much of love in his Gospel and letters is because love is the one area besides truth that Christians should work the hardest on and be the most committed to.

Are you fearful of dying to self? You need not worry, for *"There is no fear in love; but perfect love casts out fear..."* (1 John 4:18).

The good news is this: there will come a day when experiencing and expressing biblical love will come naturally. It will not have to be worked at, prayed for, studied or learned. Every creature on earth will live and abide in love. Love will come as naturally as breathing and sleeping. Expressing biblical love will no longer need God's command to fulfill it. Biblical love will characterize the whole world. We call that day the millennium.

1.   Charles C. Ryrie, *Basic Theology* (Wheaton, IL: Victor Books, a division of Scripture Press, 1986), 199.

2.   E.g., *The New International Version* (Grand Rapids, MI: Zondervan, 1995). See Romans 7:18 and 7:25, though 7:18 is appropriately footnoted "Or my flesh." Other verses include 8:3-5, 8-9, 12-13; Gal. 5:13, 16-17, 19, 24.

3.   Neil T. Anderson, *Spiritual Conflicts and Biblical Counseling* (La Habra, CA: Freedom in Christ Ministries, 1989), 10-12.

4.   Credit should be given where credit is due. Most that is written in this chapter concerning the neutrality of the flesh, the difference between the old and new natures, and the theology of Romans 6 come from Dr. Neil T. Anderson, to whom I am gratefully indebted. I have simply taken the basic concepts I learned from him and applied them to the area of biblical love.

*Bill Walthall*

# *Vignette for Chapter Thirteen*

# *"His Perfect World"*

All Craig Lawson was looking for was some peace and quiet. "Knock it off in there!" he shouted angrily to his sixth-grade twin boys, sprawled out on the floor during a wrestling match. "Can't you see I'm trying to have my quiet time? Go outside if you're going to horse around. And Kristi?"

"Yes, dad. What now?"

"A little quiet, that's all I'm asking for. Can you turn down that god-awful music?"

"It's Christian music, Dad, and my name is Kristina."

"It's heavy metal music, *Kristina*. Heavy-metal Christian music is an oxymoron."

"Are you calling me a moron?"

"Forget it. Just put your headphones on."

"It messes up my hair."

"Well, your music messes up your mind. Now do as I say or you're grounded."

"I'm already grounded."

"Okay, then, you'll be grounded times two."

Craig Lawson—successful accountant, excellent provider, daily jogger, avid outdoorsman, chairman of the board at his kids' Christian school—had recently joined a men's discipleship group even though he had been a born-again Christian for two decades.

"You need some Christian men-friends," his wife Cynthia chided him one day, "and *I* need a spiritual leader in the home. You're still a baby Christian, Craig dearest."

Thoroughly insulted and, in his words, "castrated," Craig signed up for a men's group at their church. Though they'd routinely attended the same evangelical megachurch for years, reading the Bible had never taken hold, although he owned three, all gifts. You see, Cynthia considered herself the spiritual leader in the home.

She was often gone three or four nights a week for food distribution, worship team practice and, of course, numerous women's ministries.

One of the things that made Craig very nervous about the men's discipleship group was that the leader, Pastor of Men's Discipleship Groups (Ages 35-45), asked all the men to sign a covenant. Craig didn't like being put in an "accountability" situation. Being accountable meant that he would have a daily "quiet time" of Bible study, Scripture memory, devotional reading and prayer. *Daily?* That meant *every* day. He initially thought his biggest hurdle would be trying to have a quiet time on his weekend hunting or fishing trips. He was surprised to find out later that he faced his biggest hurdles at home.

Nevertheless, Craig, being the perfectionist that he was, poured his energies into the men's group. To his surprise, he began to stand out. It so happened that he was the only man among men who *always* had all the reading done, who *always* had the verse memorized perfectly, and who was always there.

"After all, I signed a covenant, didn't I?"

Cynthia was very proud of him and told him so. "Craig, dearest, you're the *man!*"

"The only thing I still struggle with is prayer. I think it's the noise around here that makes it hard for me to concentrate."

"You could always get up earlier, before anyone else."

"Are you kidding? That's my jogging time. If I get up any earlier I'll fall asleep at the computer."

Craig came up with a plan. It was an expensive one, to be sure, but it would guarantee him the peace and quiet he needed to really focus on his spiritual growth. With Cynthia's tacit approval, Craig bought a second RV and parked it by the side of the house. But this was no RV off the showroom floor. He had it custom ordered to include bookshelves for his swiftly growing Bible library, extra insulation to block the outside noises, and interior colors to reflect his Christian theology—blue represented the Holy Spirit, crimson the blood of Christ, white meant sanctification, and so on. He had a special room built inside the RV for prayer with a custom-made, solid-oak prayer bench installed. He purchased an array of monk's habits with a separate hood and cowl to stay warm in the winter.

"This will be my mobile sanctuary," he explained to his men's group. "I'm finally going to nail down this prayer thing."

And nail down the prayer thing he did. At first, every evening was spent in the mobile sanctuary, much of the time on his knees. One night, however, he never came into the house.

"I didn't hear you get into bed last night, dearest."

"I didn't get into bed. I retired in my sanctuary."

"Where did you sleep?"

"On the floor. I ordered a monk's mat from a monastery."

"How'd you sleep?"

"Every time I woke up, I just prayed."

"Well, I guess you've finally got that prayer thing down."

The more Craig Lawson got into his prayer thing, the less time he spent at home. He used up all his vacation time at work traveling to isolated places to meditate and pray. He finally gave up on his men's group.

"I'm sorry, guys. God's just got me on this indescribable path. For the first time in my life I know what it means to be one-on-one with God."

One of the men questioned Craig about his home life. "What do your wife and kids think about all this?"

Craig sighed deeply and became pensive. "You know, Dan, one thing I've learned is that people are the problem. I don't mean to sound harsh, but people—no matter who it is—can keep us from growing spiritually. Now, don't get me wrong...I love my family. But I've discovered that they just don't see things like I see them now. We all live in an imperfect world. I've come to believe that God wants us to live in a perfect world. Why should we wait for Christ to return to have heaven on earth? I've created my own heaven on earth. I've created a near-perfect world. No interruptions, no phone calls, no loud Christian music, no complaining, no demands—just God and me. Things are almost perfect."

"What's it going to take to make it perfect?" Dan asked.

Not long after the meeting with his men's group, Craig quit his job.

"Don't worry, honey. The government's loaded with welfare benefits. Just ask around. You'll find them."

The last thing Cynthia heard from Craig was that his mobile sanctuary had broken down in Denali National Park in Alaska. He had bought an old ranger cabin and set it up as his new sanctuary. When they last talked, she didn't have the courage to tell him that his daughter Kristina had become pregnant out of wedlock and both boys had been suspended from school for starting fights.

"Not so mobile any more," he wrote in his last letter. "But the birds. You can't believe how noisy the birds are up here. The wind's always blowing and making a terrible fuss. The mosquitoes are so big you can hear them buzzing around at night. I need to find another mobile home."

He never got that chance. One day he was out chopping wood and a grizzly ate him.

*Chapter Thirteen*

# "Will I Ever Love My Neighbor As Myself?" (Love and the Millennium)

*Blessed and holy is the one who has a part in the first resurrection; over these the second death has no power, but they will be priests of God and of Christ and will reign with Him for a thousand years. (*Revelation 20:6)

You cannot have been a born-again, evangelical Christian for very long without hearing about the millennium. Premillennialism, the most prominent end-times teaching among evangelical Christians, teaches that the millennium refers to the literal thousand-year reign of Christ on earth after his return in glory.

There are, of course, varieties of theological viewpoints concerning the end times. (The study itself is called Eschatology.) Although it is beyond the scope of this chapter to describe the various millennial theologies, this writer takes a "premillennial" position. That is, at the end of the church age—and only God knows when that will be—Christ will return in glory. In a final showdown at Armageddon, Christ will return with his angels and resurrected saints, destroy the armies of the Antichrist, and banish Satan to the abyss. Christ will then establish his throne in Jerusalem and establish his kingdom on earth. The millennium will be a period of lasting peace and prosperity. Earth will become like the Garden of Eden and the way God intended earth to be in the beginning. Paradise will be restored. There will be no more war, no more strife, no unrighteousness and no evil. Peace, goodness and righteousness will prevail. The return of Christ is the great Christian hope.

There is scant detail in the New Testament as to the exact nature of the millennium. Jesus says very little about the millennium other than he will come "with great power and great glory" and will reserve his kingdom on earth for the righteous only (Matt. 24:30).

> *"But when the Son of Man comes in His glory, and all the angels with Him, then He will sit on His glorious throne. All the nations will be gathered before Him; and He will separate them from one another, as the shepherd separates the sheep from the goats; and He will put the sheep on His right and the goats on the left.*
>
> *"Then the King will say to those on His right, 'Come, you who are blessed of My Father, inherit the kingdom prepared for you from the foundation of the world. For I was hungry, and you gave Me something to eat; I was thirsty, and you gave Me something to drink; I was a stranger and you invited Me in; naked, and you clothed Me; I was sick, and you visited Me; I was in prison, and you came to Me.'*
>
> *"Then the righteous will answer Him, 'Lord, when did we see You hungry, and feed You, or thirsty, and give You something to drink? And when did we see You a stranger, and invite You in, or naked, and clothe You? When did we see You sick, or in prison, and come to You?'*
>
> *"The King will answer and say to them, 'Truly I say to you, to the extent that you did it to one of these brothers of Mine, even the least of them, you did it to Me....'"* (Matt. 25:31-40)

Most of what is given to the church in the New Testament, therefore, is how Christians are to live *until* the second coming of Christ. The followers of Jesus Christ are called to live in a manner that will reflect to the world what the millennial reign will look like.

The more detailed account of the millennium comes to us from the Old Testament in prophets like Isaiah and Ezekiel. (The reader may be interested in reviewing these Scriptures in detail. See Isaiah 2, 35, 49, 60, 66; Ezekiel 39-48; Micah 4) Though these Scriptures refer generally to Jerusalem and Israel, they are taken by premillennialists to refer to the earth in general. From these Scriptures, we learn the following.

➤ Nations will put down their arms and wars will cease (Isa. 2:2-4; cf. Mic. 4:3).
➤ The wilderness and deserts will be lush and fruitful (Isa. 35:1-3, 7).
➤ Those who are blind, mute, deaf and lame will be healed (Isa. 35:5-6).
➤ Dangers will cease to exist (Isa. 35:9).
➤ Those who live in the millennium will be filled with joy (Isa. 35:10).
➤ There will be no more hunger or thirst (Isa. 49:10).
➤ The nation of Israel will not be forgotten and will receive compassion (Isa. 49:14-15).
➤ All the ends of the earth will see the salvation of God (Isa. 52:10).
➤ The glory of the Lord will shine throughout the earth, and the nations will respond favorably to him (Isa. 60:1-3).
➤ All Israel will recognize Jesus as the Messiah and repent (Isa. 60:15-22; cf. Zech. 12:10).
➤ Israel, the temple, temple worship and a dedicated priesthood will be restored to serve the Lord on his glorious throne and the geography of the land will be utterly changed (Ezekiel chapters 39-48).

If there is one word that consistently characterizes the millennial kingdom of Christ on earth, it is "peace." Peace is what we long for: freedom from fear, freedom from persecution and affliction, freedom from crime and freedom from the violence of war.

The purpose of this chapter, however, is to ask the question, "What brings the peace?" Before we answer that question, it is important to examine a theological term that is not well known—progressive revelation. Applying progressive revelation to the advanced concepts of love in the New Testament will help us understand that God's desire for his children to experience and express his love, has been there throughout the ages.

## The Progressive Revelation of Love

It had been there all along. What the scribes and Pharisees were unable to see, what the disciples had yet to learn, what the people couldn't imagine was there in plain view throughout the Old Testament.

Before coming in glory, the Messiah must first suffer and die.

The fact that a Messiah was coming to save Israel, to bring righteousness and peace on the earth, and to bring an end to suffering, misery and tyranny was something even the casual student of the Law and the Prophets could predict. What was clear to a very few, however, was that before the glory God's Servant must suffer. Sin must be dealt with before God's kingdom would be established on earth.

The disciples particularly had difficulty with this truth. When Jesus blessed Simon Peter for first uttering the fact that Jesus was indeed the Messiah, the Christ, he went on to share with Peter and the others his fate.

*From that time Jesus began to show His disciples that He must go to Jerusalem, and suffer many things from the elders and chief priests and scribes, and be killed, and be raised up on the third day.*

*Peter took Him aside and began to rebuke Him, saying "God forbid it, Lord! This shall never happen to You."*

*But He turned and said to Peter, "Get behind Me, Satan! You are a stumbling block to Me; for you are not setting your mind on God's interests, but man's."* (Matthew 16)

Peter simply echoed what most Jews at the time believed: the Messiah would come in glory and establish his kingdom on earth. The prophets Isaiah, Ezekiel, and Zechariah especially wrote abundantly about the nature of the Messiah's kingdom. Even John the Baptist wondered: "Are

You the Expected One, or shall we look for someone else?" His hopes were high, as were the multitudes that followed Jesus.

But a few Jews knew that the glory could not come before the suffering. When Jesus was taken to the temple in Jerusalem for his circumcision and Mary's purification (Luke 2), a man named Simeon was waiting.

> *There was a man in Jerusalem whose name was Simeon; and this man was righteous and devout, looking for the consolation of Israel; and the Holy Spirit was upon him. And it had been revealed to him by the Holy Spirit that he would not see death before he had seen the Lord's Christ. And he came in the Spirit into the temple; and when the parents brought in the child Jesus, to carry out for Him the custom of the Law, then he took Him into his arms, and blessed God, and said, "Now Lord, You are releasing Your bond-servant to depart in peace, according to Your word; for my eyes have seen Your salvation, which You have prepared in the presence of all peoples, a light of revelation to the Gentiles, and the glory of Your people Israel."*
>
> *And His father and mother were amazed at the things that were being said about Him.*
>
> *And Simeon blessed them and said to Mary His mother, "Behold, this Child is appointed for the fall and rise of many in Israel, and for a sign to be opposed—and a sword will pierce even your own soul—to the end that thoughts from many hearts may be revealed."* (Luke 2:25-35)

That the Messiah must suffer first before he would fully establish his kingdom on earth was something the disciples wouldn't grasp until after the resurrection. Luke records for us Jesus' encounter with two of his disciples on the road to Emmaus: "Was it not necessary for the Christ to suffer these things and to enter into his glory?" (Luke 24:27). Later, when

Jesus met with all the disciples, he began showing them this truth from the Scriptures.

> ***Then He opened their minds to understand the Scriptures, and He said to them, "Thus it is written, that the Christ would suffer and rise again from the dead the third day, and that repentance for forgiveness of sins would be proclaimed in His name to all the nations, beginning from Jerusalem."***
> (Luke 24:45-47)

No doubt Jesus shared with the disciples Isaiah 53, Psalm 22 and Jonah.

That the disciples, and especially Peter, finally grasped the truth is reflected in Peter's second sermon after Pentecost (Acts 3).

> ***"And now, brethren, I know that you acted in ignorance, just as your rulers did also. But the things which God announced beforehand by the mouth of all the prophets, that His Christ would suffer, He has thus fulfilled. Therefore repent and return, so that your sins may be wiped away, in order that times of refreshing may come from the presence of the Lord."*** (Acts 3:17-19)

Peter and the other apostles began to understand that before the Messiah would come in glory to establish his kingdom on earth and bring judgment against every kind of unrighteousness, there would have to be the opportunity for the forgiveness of sin. This could only be done "*in the name of Jesus,*" not, as before with John the Baptist, in the name of *Adonai* (Acts 2:37-38).

This truth, that the Messiah must first suffer for the sins of mankind, had been present all throughout the Law and the Prophets. They just hadn't seen it.

The apostle Paul, too, needed a revelation from Jesus on a previously "hidden" truth; that is, the inclusion of the Gentiles into God's kingdom. This message was first introduced to Paul by Ananias immediately after his conversion: "But the Lord said to him, 'Go, for he is a chosen instrument of Mine, to bear My name before the Gentiles and kings and the sons of Israel...'" (Acts 9:15). Though it was Peter who first officially introduced the gospel to the Gentiles (Acts 10), Paul was the specific instrument God used to carry out the mission. Paul addresses his mission and the promise behind it in Ephesians 3:

*For this reason I, Paul, the prisoner of Christ Jesus for the sake of you Gentiles—if indeed you have heard of the stewardship of God's grace which was given to me for you; that by revelation there was made known to me the mystery, as I wrote before in brief. By referring to this, when you read you can understand my insight into the mystery of Christ, which in other generations was not made known to the sons of men, as it has now been revealed to His holy apostles and prophets in the Spirit; to be specific, that the Gentiles are fellow heirs and fellow members of the body, and fellow partakers of the promise in Christ Jesus through the gospel, of which I was made a minister, according to the gift of God's grace which was given to me according to the working of His power.*

*To me, the very least of all saints, this grace was given, to preach to the Gentiles the unfathomable riches of Christ, and to bring to light what is the administration of the mystery which for ages has been hidden in God who created all things; so that the manifold wisdom of God might now be made known through the church to the rulers and the authorities in the heavenly places.* (Eph. 3:1-10)

That the Gentiles would be included in God's promises can also be found in the Old Testament, though it is not as obvious as the truth that the Messiah must suffer. Simeon's quote from Isaiah at Jesus' presentation at the temple was prophetic, though at the time he probably didn't know it. On five occasions, Isaiah prophesies that the Messiah, the Suffering

Servant, will be a "light to the nations" (Isa. 9:2; 42:6; 49:6; 51:4; 60:1-3). Amos also refers to this hidden truth (Amos 9:12). Of course, these verses could be interpreted many ways. Most Jewish leaders would simply say that the Messiah would be the *source* of truth to the nations, or that Israel herself would be God's beacon of truth. The Gentiles ("nations"; Heb *goyim*) would always remain in a subservient role to God's kingdom through the nation of Israel. It would take a revelation to help Paul see that not only would the Gentiles be recipients of the light, but be recipients of the promise for inclusion into God's kingdom.

The revelation given Paul that the Gentiles were included in the promise did not sit well with many Jews. (A foreshadowing of this opposition occurred early in Jesus' ministry when he read from the Book of Isaiah in the synagogue at Nazareth, Luke 4:16-28.) In Pisidian Antioch, on Paul's first missionary journey, opposition arose to the point that the missionary team was driven out of the city (Acts 13:44-52). A similar disruption occurred in the next city they visited, Iconium (Acts 14:1-7). When Paul returned to Jerusalem after the first missionary journey, he and Barnabas shared with the church council the marvelous work God was doing among the Gentiles. Nevertheless, even some Christian Jews were having difficulty accepting Gentiles into the church unconditionally (Acts 15:1-5). Finally, Paul's mention that God was taking his promise to the Gentiles as well resulted in a riot in Jerusalem (Acts 22:21-22).

The truths mentioned above are just two examples of what is called "progressive revelation." Progressive revelation is the theological term used to specify that God does not reveal everything all at once. Revelation about himself and his eternal plan is spread out over the ages. It is similar to what a student is exposed to in school. A third grader learning the basics of arithmetic cannot be taught the finer points of calculus. Building blocks are needed before higher mathematics can be grasped.

I believe progressive revelation is true about love in the Bible.

The point is this: God reveals his plan through progressive revelation. That is, he does not reveal his complete plan and intentions all at once. God often foreshadows his plans through historical types, through prophecy, even through the Law. God did not reveal his complete plan for the nations in the Old Testament, but provided prophecies so that when the time came, his people would recognize the plan and realize that it was *his* plan, not the plan of men. That the Gentiles would be included in God's promises was hidden throughout the words of the Old Testament, but it took a vision to Peter and a revelation to Paul to see that truth. Even though God provided exquisite details concerning his plan for the coming Messiah, his people were blinded to the truth until the truth actually happened. That the Messiah must first suffer and die was thoroughly revealed in the Old Testament, but it took Jesus to open the eyes of the disciples to help them see that truth.

I believe there is another truth that is being revealed to the church today in these end times. It is the revelation of love.[1] We will begin to see this as we more thoroughly examine love and its biblical revelation.

## The Mark of the Millennium

Certainly one might say the Lord's glory on earth and the absolute rule of Christ on his throne will ensure that peace reigns. But I believe there is something far greater and far more wonderful in store for those who live in the millennium.

There will be peace on earth because the love of God will abound in each and every person. Everyone who lives will love because everyone will be healed by Christ's presence, or perhaps even the touch of his hand. But how will love abound? Will love abound simply because it is decreed by the Lord to abound? Will love abound on the earth because Christ will see to it that his command to love one another is fulfilled? I don't believe that is the case. Love will abound throughout the earth because the Lord will heal every man, woman and child, and that healing will involve all those weaknesses of the flesh that cause us to be selfish. His healing will free us from the bondage of the flesh and enable us to experience and express biblical love. All the emotional, physical, biological, genetic and environmental barriers that keep us from loving one another will be healed and made whole. There will no longer be a need for "defense systems," either personally or governmentally. All the memories and hurts and pain that have resulted in hate will be erased and resolved. There will be no more need to hate; only the desire to love. A man and a woman will be healed emotionally so that love may abound. There will be no more envy, for we will be satisfied with what we have. There will be no more rejection and abuse, for these things will be unnatural for the person of love. There will be no more crime because murder and rape and theft are not the loving thing to do. There will be little if any sickness because the Lord will heal everyone, and the world's resources will be placed into restoration rather than into war. There will be no more mental illness because all minds will be healed by truth and love. There will be no more confusion over gender, for all will love in the manner prescribed by the truth. There will be no more unrighteousness because righteousness is defined by love, and love will prevail. It is not that all people will be emotionless or without emotions; it is that all emotions will be perfectly aligned and the nature of a man and a woman will be to love. There will be no need for violence, for everyone will treat one another with love. The Ten Commandments will be written on the heart of every man and woman because every man and woman will live a life of love. Envy, strife, jealousy, bitterness and wrath will be put away from all mankind because these things are the antithesis of love. Emotions that cause harm will be healed. Emotions that result in joy and peace and harmony will prevail because the new nature is to love.

It is the love of God that heals, and it is the love of Christ that brings healing to the world.

There will be no more war because there will be no more hate. There will be no more crime because love of one's neighbor will overrule coveting of the neighbor's property or person. There will be no more adultery because the love of a man and a woman will be pure and faithful and lasting, and the love of one's neighbor would not allow lust for another's wife. There will be no more hate crimes; there will be only love deeds. There will be no more abortions because love will dictate that each and every person, including the unborn, are of great value. All who become pregnant will have done so out of love and not lust, and that love will encircle even the unborn. There will be no more homosexuality because the emotional, chemical or genetic imbalance causing the distortion will be healed.

What was lost in the garden was the ability to love purely. What will be restored in the millennium is the natural ability to love one another and to love one's neighbor as oneself.

Because love rules, there will certainly be the end of war. It will be a time of peace because God's love reigns on the earth.

There will be no fear in the millennium because perfect love casts out all fear, and the millennium will be a time of perfect love. Everyone living during the millennium will be able to experience and express biblical love. Love will no longer be something to strive for; love will be something to enjoy. Love will no longer need to be commanded; love will happen naturally as a part of our healing.

The millennium will be the fulfillment of God's progressive revelation of love. Whereas the Old Testament was the age of Law, and the New Testament the age of grace, the millennium will be the age of love. The passages on love in the New Testament will no longer require obedience. Just as the Old Testament prophecies concerning the church age were fulfilled in the first coming of Jesus Christ, the New Testament admonitions for the church to love will be fulfilled in the millennium.

The wonderful news for the Christian is this: we will all be a part of the millennium. Whether we return with Christ at his second coming, or, for some reason, we remain alive on earth after his return, the results will be the same. The earth will be restored to the Garden of Eden, and we shall live in it. One day, one way or another, we will all be healed. The weakness of our flesh will exist no more, and the glory of our new body will abound in love.

In the meantime, there is today. Today, how do we then love?

---

1. By making this statement, I do not mean to put myself on the same footing as the disciples and Paul. That is, to imply that I have been given special revelation to see into the mysteries of God which have hidden through the ages. One must remember that neither the disciples nor Paul had a complete New Testament. They were, in fact, in the process of producing it through the superintending of the Holy Spirit. But today we have the complete New Testament and the presence of the Holy Spirit to interpret and apply it. I am doing nothing more than what the average preacher or theologian does

on any given Sunday: interpreting and applying the word of God. I am not a prophet, I've had no vision, no special revelation, no visits with angels (with the exception of my wife), and no encounters with demons (with the exception, of course, of my cat who, along with most cats, at times appears quite possessed).

# *Vignette for Chapter Fourteen*

# *"The Love Track"*

Dean Wright was finally enjoying his newly renovated office. Since he added the walnut bookshelves to accommodate his enormous library, finding references was much easier. Not every professor had taken the time to label and arrange all of his books according to the Dewey Decimal System, a habit he had begun as a seminary student and maintained throughout his doctoral programs. As the dean of the Department of Theology and now the newly appointed dean of the prestigious evangelical seminary, he needed every moment he could find. Now, thankfully, he would waste no more time searching for books.

The admiration was suddenly interrupted by his intercom.

"Dean Wright, your nine o'clock has arrived."

"Thank you, Sarah." As was his custom, he went out to the lobby to greet his visitor.

"Good morning, Mr. ..."

"Jeremiah," Sarah quickly intervened. "Paul Jeremiah."

"Paul Jeremiah. That's an appropriate name," he smiled, shaking the second-year seminarian's hand.

"My parents thought it would be a good idea to blend the old with the new."

"Well, they did a good job. Let's go into my office, shall we?"

The young seminarian picked up his backpack and entered into what seemed like a well-lit library with a desk in the middle. The bookshelves were stacked from floor to ceiling with every theology, church history, Bible commentary and ancient language book imaginable. It seemed like a replica of the university's own theology section. A little overwhelmed, he sat down in the chair across from Dean Wright's massive executive desk.

"Jeremiah...Jeremiah," Dean Wright echoed. "That name strikes a contemporary bell. Are you related to Walter Jeremiah on the university's board of directors?

"He's my dad."

Dean Wright perked up. "I see. What brings you here today, Paul?" hoping for the best but anticipating the worst.

"Well, Dean Wright, I'm a little concerned about my seminary training," he stammered, obviously not confident about the question he was about to raise.

"It *is* going to be the worst," Dean Wright thought to himself. "And I was so enjoying my bookshelves." He leaned forward on his desk and clasped his hands. "How's that?" he asked attentively. He pretended not to be worried.

"It's about love, sir."

"Love? Oh, I see," Dean Wright said with a silent sigh of relief. "Let me guess. You're in love and your love life is interfering with your studies."

"Well, no sir. I mean, the subject of love—biblical love. I'm not sure I really understand what biblical love really is. I don't think I really know *how* to love biblically. I'm feeling that I won't be prepared to be a good pastor when I graduate from seminary and take a church. I need someone to teach me all about love. Otherwise, I won't be able to teach others."

Dean Wright sat back in his chair with a long sigh. "Interesting. Go on."

"Well, sir, I've decided to take John 13:34-35 seriously. I've come to the conclusion that Christians are to be known by their love. But when I go looking, I can't find anything in the school's curriculum that actually teaches about love, especially how to love. The school's doctrinal teachings here are right on and the professors are great. I'm loving Hebrew and Greek, and believe it or not, I'm really enjoying church history. But I suddenly realized during my quiet time a few weeks ago that I'm not getting trained to love."

Dean Wright didn't respond immediately. He wasn't sure how. "Have you mentioned this to your dad?"

"Oh, no sir. We don't see each other very often. He's pretty busy. His company made Fortune 500 this year, you know. He's gone a lot."

"I see."

"Please don't think I'm complaining. I love my seminary education. But it just suddenly dawned on me that there's this one area of my Christian life that seems lacking. And I'm not coming today expecting any answers. I'm just sort of sharing my concerns. I really don't know where else to go."

"I appreciate your honesty, Paul. Thank you for opening up to me."

"You're welcome. Like I said, I'm not complaining. I'm just feeling a little shaky about going into a pulpit and telling people they ought to love one another when I'm not sure I have the faintest idea how."

"That's an interesting point you're making," Dean Wright stalled, digging into his library of prepared answers when the ambiguities of theological studies crept up. "You know, Paul...and I don't want to seem like I'm punting on this issue...seminaries can't be expected to teach *everything*. There're a lot of practical elements of Christian development that we rely upon the churches to provide."

Dean Wright wasn't prepared for the young seminarian's response.

"That's exactly what my pastor said. He said, 'You know, Paul, the church doesn't have the resources to teach *everything*. That's what we send young men like you to seminary for.' That's why I'm a little confused."

"I can see why you're confused," Dean Wright pondered, realizing the seminarian had a point. His computer-like mind categorically surveyed every good evangelical church he was familiar with and couldn't recall any of them providing discipleship on love. Many churches had great outreach and community projects going on, and many others had 'adult electives' on marriage and family, divorce recovery, literacy programs, feeding ministries and so on, but what about the ins-and-outs of everyday interpersonal relationships based on biblical love? In even less time, he concluded there were no evangelical seminaries, Christian universities or even Bible schools offering courses on how to love one another.

"You know, Paul," he said sincerely, "I think you've brought up a good point. It's a terrific observation, and I mean that. Now that I look back on my own theological training, in all the years no one ever offered me a course in loving. Isn't that odd?"

"Yes sir, it is."

"Boy, you've really stimulated my thinking." He leaned over toward his intercom. "Sarah?"

"Yes, Dean Wright?"

"Cancel all my appointments this morning. I have some work to do before the faculty meeting this afternoon." He released the button on his intercom. "Paul, I can't tell you how much I appreciate your coming this morning. You've opened up a whole new dimension to my thinking about seminary education. It's something I need to discuss with the faculty." He got up from his chair, walked around his desk and gave the young student a warm hug. "You've been an inspiration to me this morning."

Young Paul Jeremiah was a little overwhelmed. "Well, thanks. Thanks for listening to me. Did you want me to tell my dad about today?"

"That won't be necessary. I'll probably end up talking to him myself."

"Well, then, thank you again." He picked up his backpack and exited quietly. "Have to get ready for a Greek quiz."

"I understand completely." Dean Wright returned to his desk. "Sarah?"

"Yes sir?"

"No interruptions, no phone calls till faculty meeting, please."

"Except your wife?"

"Of course. Except my wife or kids." He quickly opened his top drawer, pulled out a legal pad and pen, and began feverishly jotting down notes.


"There's one more subject I want to address that's not on your agenda," Dean Wright announced, approaching the podium and laying his legal pad perfectly in the middle. He could tell his faculty was growing a little restless. "I had a fascinating conversation this morning that I want to share with you all." The dean shared enthusiastically with his faculty as many details as he could recall from his conversation with Paul Jeremiah. He did not mention Paul's name or that his dad was on the board of the university.

"So, I'm going to make a bold proposal and I'm requesting your feedback. I propose that we form a committee to establish an entire curriculum based on John 13:34-35. As a seminary on the cutting edge, we have an opportunity to be trendsetters. I believe with all my heart, however, that this young student has a valid point. At what point in preparing young men for the ministry do we teach them how to love, and teach them how to teach others how to love?"

There was a long pause among the members of the faculty. Finally, someone spoke up. "Dean, I think we should revisit the concept that it really is up to the local church to address this issue."

Dean Wright responded immediately. "And how do we expect the pastors of the local church to teach these truths if we aren't preparing them?"

"I know what we can do," blurted out one of professors. "Let's ask our wives to put together a class."

There was an immediate outburst of nervous, ironic laughter. Dean Wright didn't even acknowledge the remark.

"I'm serious, ladies and gentlemen. I really want to look into this matter."

"But Dean," another objected, "we're already packed out in our curriculum. There's no room for expansion. We'd end up cramming in another required class."

"I'm thinking about an entire semester," the dean responded. The room gasped.

"That would put us at odds with every other seminary in the country," someone said.

"Of course it would!" the dean reacted. "We would need more than *a* class on love. We would need a couple of classes to provide the biblical foundation and then have labs and field ministry to help the students put into practice what they've learned. It would require input from mission organizations, humanitarian relief groups like Samaritan's Purse, urban renewal ministries, racial reconciliation advocates, and so on."

"We already hear from groups like that," one professor objected.

"That's right," the dean answered. "We 'hear from.' We do not 'teach with.'"

"Nobody would want to sign up for a longer MDiv program," another objected. "Recruiting would be a disaster."

"Who would teach it? I certainly couldn't."

"Not my bag, either. How about Professor Wong? She's always open to new things."

"I like the idea," she said, "but I don't have any more time than you do."

"I barely have time for publishing as it is," exclaimed an apologetics professor.

"How in the world would we test for it?" a church history professor asked. "How do you measure love?"

"How do you design an entire curriculum on love?" asked a practical theology professor.

After the grumbling had subsided, Dean Wright waved his hand.

"Dear faculty. I'm not proposing we start this year. It will take planning, lots of planning. For now, I just want us to put our academic heads together and brainstorm this idea. Now, who wants to volunteer for the committee?"

Two years later—too late for young Jeremiah, unfortunately—the "Love Track" became required curriculum for the Master of Divinity degree. The introductory class was appropriately called "Love 101"; it was jointly taught by Dean Wright himself and his wife Julie who had become an adjunct faculty member.

Curriculum restructuring precluded the need for an additional semester. As word got out, enrollment in the MDiv program increased 40 percent over a three-year period. Additional faculty was added to meet the increasing needs.

Dean Wright sat back in his chair, pondering the success of the Love Track. He perused his precious library and admired how organized it was. The walnut shelves still glowed, dusted weekly by Sarah even without his asking. His thoughts wandered back to his encounter with young Jeremiah.

Paul Jeremiah was the one book Dean Wright didn't have in his library.

# Chapter Fourteen

# "How Do We Then Love?" (Love and the Christian)

*...Having loved His own who were in the world, He loved them to the end.* (John 13:1)

Before answering the question, "How do we then love?" it would benefit us to review the major truths presented thus far in Book 1. Understanding the biblical truth about love is important because learning to love biblically comes neither naturally nor easily. Only truth can set us free from our misconceptions and misgivings about love, and only biblical truth can be the standard by which we know love. The truths presented in the previous chapters open the door both for experiencing and expressing biblical love.

In chapter one, we established that love is not something that evolved naturally. Biblical love, later defined, runs contrary to the laws of evolution. As Christians, we believe that love is a revelation from God. The general revelation of love is evident throughout creation. The specific revelation of love is given through God's word, the Bible, and culminates in the person of Jesus Christ.

We then learned that love existed among the members of the Godhead, the Trinity, before creation (chapter 2). There was perfect harmony, perfect unity and perfect love among the Father, the Son and the Holy Spirit. When God created man and woman, that love was a part of their creation. God wanted them to experience the love that existed in the Godhead, and he wanted them to experience that love between each other.

Unfortunately, when Paradise was lost, so was the ability to experience and express the pure love God had created in them. The remaining history of the Bible focuses on restoring humanity to a right relationship with God. Included in that restoration, however, is the restoration of God's children to experience and express perfect love. God has a wondrous love he wants to share (chapter 3).

In chapter 4, it was necessary to pause and define biblical love. We determined that love in the Old Testament was equated with obedience to the Law. God established a treaty with his people full of conditions and consequences. If the Israelites obeyed the Law, then they would receive earthly, material blessings. If they failed, then they would experience terrible consequences. The terms of the treaty were conditional and their love for God was measured in terms of their obedience. God's love for his people, however, was unconditional. If his people disobeyed or sought after other gods, they might lose his protection and his blessings but they would never lose his love. God's love for his people is unconditional; God will never stop loving his children.

Also in chapter 4, we witnessed in the New Testament a dramatic development in the revelation of love. We witnessed that the revelation of love in the New Testament vastly exceeds the revelation of love in the Old. We saw that biblical love is to be extended even to enemies. However, we also saw that love, though greatly advanced in nature, still requires obedience. We raised the question: "Will biblical love ever become natural?"

We then took a brief look at love in relation to Old Testament law; specifically, we examined the Ten Commandments (chapter 5). We raised the important question, "Are the Ten Commandments still binding on Christians today?" We concluded that the foundation for all the commandments is love, and by fulfilling "the royal law" Christians will fulfill all the Ten Commandments. Therefore, it is important for Christians to fight the right battles when it comes to becoming involved in the political arena.

Chapter 6 examined the role of truth in relation to love. The important point to remember concerning truth is that truth must always trump love. That is because, as we saw in chapter 4, love requires definition; biblical love requires biblical definition, and biblical definition must be based on truth. Any other definition of love falls short. We also made the point, however, that all truth points to love and that love is what the truth is all about. Because we live in an imperfect world, however, and "see through a mirror dimly," we cannot always settle all conflicts between truth and love. For that we will have to wait for the millennium. Until then, Christians should treat each other in a loving manner even if their interpretations of Scripture are diametrically opposed. We may adamantly disagree with other Christians' theology, but that does not give us the right not to love them.

Whereas biblical love is presented and demonstrated throughout the New Testament, it is in the person of Jesus Christ that love is incarnated (chapter 7). We looked at the love of the Father, the love that exists between the Father and the Son, and the Son's love as manifested through his incarnation, his earthly ministry, his death and his ascension. We also concluded that apart from the person of Jesus Christ, the love of God can never be fully experienced or expressed.

In chapter 8, we took time to look at love in the Gospels and determined that the royal law—to love your neighbor as yourself—is embedded throughout. We saw this in Jesus' teachings, his encounters with the Pharisees, his healings and with his conflicts over the Law. The point is clear: the foundation for the royal law was being laid by Jesus himself and would be clear and evident throughout the rest of New Testament writings.

The points made in chapter 8 were taken a step further in chapter 9. In this chapter, the great commandments were addressed specifically. We realized that, after the Gospels, the first and great commandment is never again mentioned. That is because the apostles realized that to fulfill the second great commandment was to fulfill the first. The new commandment given by Jesus—"love one another"—summarizes the second great commandment. That is, we show our love to God by showing love to others.

We then raised the question of righteousness (chapter 10). Is righteousness something that is a part of what we call love? After a close look at the definitions of righteousness, we realized that all previous notions of righteousness have been Law-dependent. We realized that all of our assumptions of what it means to be righteous have been based on Old Testament Law. The royal law changed all that, however. Given the preceding explanations, we came to the conclusion that the only valid measure of righteousness is love, not the Law.

In light of chapter 10, it then became necessary to determine the nature of sin (chapter 11). We discovered that some of our old definitions and simplistic explanations are incomplete. With examples from the Gospels, Acts and some Pauline letters, we saw that all sin can be defined as a failure of love. What keeps us from experiencing and expressing love? It is the presence of the flesh, polluted and forever tainted by the old nature (chapter 12).

Here is the point of chapters 11 and 12. If sin is a failure to love, and the source of sin is the flesh, only by overcoming the flesh can a person truly begin to experience and express biblical love. There is, therefore, only one way to overcome the flesh, and that is through a personal relationship with Jesus Christ. Once a person receives Jesus Christ as his or her personal Savior, he sends into that person the Holy Spirit. With the Holy Spirit comes a new nature; the old nature dies and the new nature is present to re-program the flesh. Only then can biblical love begin to manifest itself in the life of the believer. Theologians call this process sanctification. Sanctification, therefore, must always begin with truth, for it is truth—not love—that sets us free. Nevertheless, the truth is all about love. Therefore, to love biblically, one must have biblical truth. However, there is no such thing as biblical truth without biblical love. To pretend to have the truth and not have love as a result, is to deceive ourselves.

Will believers ever love completely? Biblical love as a natural state will not occur until the millennium. We have speculated that the reason there will be peace on earth during the millennium is because Christ has come and healed whatever it is in us that keeps us from experiencing and expressing biblical love. Whereas the Old Testament was the age of Law, and the New Testament and church period is the age of grace, the millennial reign of Jesus Christ will be the age of love.

That brings us to our final question in Book 1: "How do we then love?"

## Steps to Love

Although Books 2 and 3 go into more detail on this subject, here are some preliminary actions you can take to begin experiencing and expressing biblical love.

First and foremost, it is impossible even to experience biblical love without having a personal relationship with Jesus Christ. Jesus clearly stated, *"I am the way, and the truth, and the life; no one comes to the Father but through Me"* (John 14:6). In other words, it is impossible to know God without first knowing Christ. Our knowledge of Jesus Christ comes through the Bible and the Bible alone. Therein lies the truth. Although you may consider yourself a very good person or a good "Christian" person, if you have not personally invited Jesus to be the Lord and Savior of your life, you do not really know him. If you do not really know him, you can never truly experience the love he has to offer you. You may consider yourself a very loving person, but the love you are claiming you have is incomplete short of a personal relationship with Jesus Christ. Why? Because one cannot love biblically until he or she has experienced God's love through Jesus Christ. God's love through Christ is perfect, unconditional love full of grace and truth.

You may be thinking, "I look at the way some so-called Christians behave and I love better than they do!" I'm ashamed to admit it, but you may be quite right about that. Unfortunately, because of the flesh, because of outright disobedience, and because of just plain ignorance, Christians can be just as unloving as anyone else. Regardless of that observation, however, the truth remains: the truth about love comes only from God's word, and the personification of love comes only through the person of Jesus Christ.

Therefore, if you have never made a personal commitment to Jesus Christ, I would invite you to do so. The Bible tells us clearly that inviting Jesus as Savior involves a simple act of faith. You simply choose in your heart to do so. You do not need to earn God's love because his love is neither earned nor deserved. The truth of the matter is, you cannot be good enough to earn God's love. Furthermore, you probably already realize that you don't deserve his love. God's love is always there waiting for you to experience it. Is there any good reason not to?

If you would like to begin the process of experiencing and expressing biblical love, I encourage you to invite the living Christ into your life. You can do so right now. All it takes is a step of faith. To help you, say with all your heart a prayer like this:

> *Dear Jesus, I need you. I confess that I am a sinner and that I have sinned. I have sinned by failing to love others in a biblical manner. I am sorry for my sins and my failure to love, and I repent.*
>
> *I want to experience and express biblical love. I now invite you into my life, to be my Lord and Savior. I accept your forgiveness of my failure to love, and I accept the gift of eternal life. Through the Holy Spirit who is now given to me, I choose from here out to live in a manner that reflects your truth and your love.*
>
> *Lord, teach me how to live as you want me to live, and show me how to love as you yourself love. In your name I pray. Amen.*

The Bible states that when you invite Jesus to be your Lord and Savior, he sends the Holy Spirit into your life. Through God's word and with the help of the Holy Spirit, your flesh can be gradually re-programmed to both experience and express his love. That is the wonderful thing about being a Christian: God has a wondrous love for you.

If you are already a Christian, however, there are issues perhaps that need to be dealt with. Our tolerance of sin in our lives keeps the Holy Spirit from re-programming our flesh. The Holy Spirit cannot minister to us or through us if we choose to live in unloving ways. If we choose to continue to live in unloving ways, we choose to live in the flesh. As long as we are willfully living in the flesh, we will never love biblically. You may have been a Christian all your life, but if unloving ways are being allowed to run loose in your life, or tolerated in any form, the experience of God's love will be fleeting and the expression of God's love will be impossible. Why? Because living in the flesh is tantamount to living selfishly, the very opposite of selfless, biblical love. Therefore, the step that needs to be taken in your situation is confession of sin and repentance.

If you realize you have been tolerating sin in your life—that is, selfish, unloving ways—and wish to begin living in a manner that is pleasing to God, you need to make a change...soon. If you really wish to experience God's perfect love and begin to learn to express his love to others—to live according to the royal law—then you must confess your unloving ways and choose a life of repentance.

If this situation fits you, I would encourage you to say a prayer like this:

> *Dear Jesus, I have sinned against you by living selfishly.*
> *I have sinned against you and I have sinned against others by living in unloving ways.*
>
> *I have failed to love you as you deserve, and I have failed to love others as you have commanded. I have lived selfishly, and I have been living according to the flesh. I choose this day to repent of my selfish living and unloving ways.*
>
> *(At this point, it would be a good thing to confess every known sin, particularly those involving broken relationships and sins against others.)*
>
> *Lord, thank you for forgiving me of my sins, and I forgive myself as well. May the Holy Spirit begin teaching me how to live selflessly.*
>
> *May the Holy Spirit show me how to love others as you love them. I want to share your truth and your love with others, and I choose to obey your command to love my neighbor as myself, to love one another, and to love others as you have loved me. In your name I pray. Amen.*

Perhaps, however, you are living in a right relationship with God. You know Jesus personally as your Savior, and you routinely face sin issues in your life. As some would say, you have a "clean slate." But there may be a problem keeping you from truly experiencing God's love, and worse, consistently expressing biblical love. You may be living according to the Law. Inadvertently, you may be measuring your righteousness by whether or not you are keeping the Ten Commandments. Or, quite possibly, you may be using as your standard of righteousness various decrees from the church or pulpit, such as "Thou shalt keep the Sabbath," "Thou shalt not dance," "Thou shalt not use another translation," or, "Thou shalt believe such-and-such about the end times." Any number of substitutions could be made. Because they are devised by men, they can be as numerous as the U.S. tax code. Unfortunately, you may not even realize what they are.

I would challenge you to reassess your measures of righteousness. Why is this important? Because the apostle Paul has clearly stated that those who choose to live under the Law are under a curse (Gal. 1:8, 9). Those who live under the Law, even well-intentioned, can never fully experience God's grace, and therefore, never fully appreciate his love. Living under the Law is living like a child. Laws are for children, but love is for mature adults. Adults should not have to live according to a set of rules; they should live according to the laws of love.

If you find yourself in this situation, I encourage you to grow up! Begin loving your neighbor as yourself. Put aside the Law and live according to love! That's the purpose of the Holy Spirit—to teach you to live a life of biblical love.

A prayer like this might be helpful:

*Dear Jesus, forgive me for my ignorance. Forgive me for trying to live a life according to the Law. I need law in my life, but I need the royal law. I commit myself to living a life of love. I will follow your command to "love one another."*

*I will obey your command to love others as you have loved me. I choose to love my neighbor as myself. I choose to believe that to love others is to love the Father, and to love the Father is to love others.*

*Teach me, Holy Spirit, how to love. Teach me, Lord, how to overcome the selfishness of my flesh. Teach me from your word, Lord Jesus, the truths I need to know to love perfectly.*

*This day I commit myself to your love. In your name I pray. Amen.*

Finally, we are reminded that there is no other source for our knowledge of love apart from the word of God. A close encounter with the word of God on a daily basis is the key to knowing God and his love. All spiritual truth comes from God's word. How can we then live without it?

As we close this book, I wish to remind the reader that learning to love is not easy. To begin that process, we must have the knowledge of truth, and the truth is this: biblical love requires dying to self. It will not be an easy journey, but it will be the most worthwhile journey ever taken.

**"Beloved, let us love one another, for love is from God; and everyone who loves is born of God and knows God"** (1 John 4:7).

The End

Dr. Bill Walthall is available for speaking engagements and personal appearances. For more information write:

**Dr. Bill Walthall**
**C/O Advantage Books**
**P.O. Box 160847**
**Altamonte Springs, Florida   32716**

For more information about *The Love Revelation* and the author, visit:
www.theloverevelation.com

To purchase additional copies of this book or other books published by Advantage Books call our toll free order number at:
1-888-383-3110 (Book Orders Only)

or visit our bookstore website at:
www.advbookstore.com

Longwood, Florida, USA
*"we bring dreams to life"*™
www.advbooks.com

Printed in the United States
144048LV00003B/73/P

9 781597 551250